WIN£££sWIN

GIVE YOURSELF 5?
INSTAN

Now you've bought a copy of *Lottery Winners*,
why not enter our *Lottery Winners* competition and
give yourself the chance of becoming one yourself?

Fill in the form below, return it to us, and you will
automatically be enetered in a prize draw where 8 lucky
readers will have the chance of *winning a lottery ticket
every week for a year!!*

Please enter my name in the *Lottery Winners* lucky
draw

Name: _____

Address: _____

_____

_____

_____

Phone: _____

Return to:
Lottery Winners Competition, 38 Soho Square, London W1V 5DF
Competition closes 31 March 1997. No entries will be accepted after
this date. Eight winners will be chosen at random from entries
received.

☐ Tick for more information
on future *Lottery Winners* titles

LOTTERY WINNERS 2
FORTUNE AND FRIENDS

David Monnery

Jackpot

First published in Great Britain 1996
Jackpot Books, Invicta House, Sir Thomas Longley Road,
Rochester, Kent

Copyright © 1996 by Jackpot Books

The moral right of the author has been asserted

A CIP catalogue record for this book
is available from the British Library

ISBN 1 900969 01 7

10 9 8 7 6 5 4 3 2 1

Typeset by Hewer Text Composition Services, Edinburgh
Printed in Great Britain by Cox & Wyman Limited, Reading

1

Becky put the book to one side, took two strides across the kitchen and picked up the ringing phone.

"Hello," a woman said hesitantly. "Is that Mrs Lockwood?"

"Yes," Becky said, the first chill of recognition inching up her spine.

"This is Sheila Browning. At least that's my name now. I don't know if you remember . . ."

"Of course I do." Sixteen years might have passed, but she would have found it hard to forget the voice of Richard's biological mother. The thought flashed across her mind that Sheila had been sixteen herself, and still in school, when she'd got pregnant.

"I . . . I'd like to meet you. For a talk."

"Oh."

"Just with you. A talk."

"We're going away for the weekend, so it can't be till next week."

"Monday?"

"No, we won't be back till Monday night. Tuesday should be . . ." It suddenly occurred to Becky that she should be asking why the woman wanted to see her after all this time. "What is it you want to talk about?" she asked bluntly.

"I'd rather not say on the phone," the woman said. "And I can't make Tuesday. How about Wednesday?"

"OK," Becky agreed. Even if she'd wanted to she could hardly refuse to meet the woman. For Richard's sake, if no one else's.

"Can we meet at the outdoor café in Russell Square? You know the one I mean?"

"Yes. When?"

"My lunch break's from one to two, so at quarter past one?"

"OK, Wednesday at one-fifteen."

"I know this is . . . It's very kind of you."

"No, but . . ."

Maybe there was something in Becky's voice, but the woman quickly added: "Don't worry – I don't want the boy back or anything like that."

"Oh."

"I'll see you on Tuesday."

"All right," Becky said, but the other woman had already hung up. She carefully replaced her own receiver, and as she did so she heard, or imagined she heard, a noise on the stairs. She walked out into the hall but there was no one there. "Richard?" she said tentatively, but there was only the sound of his music. It was either Oasis or Blur – she could never remember which was which.

Had he overheard her end of the conversation and slipped away? She went back over what she'd actually said, and realized with relief that there'd been nothing to indicate with whom she'd been talking.

She went back to the seat by the kitchen table where she'd been working. Sixteen years, she thought, still hearing the woman's voice in her head. It wasn't one she'd ever expected to hear again. Her son's mother.

That would make a good novel title, she thought.

Fifteen years ago, even ten, in those days when she'd still been haunted by the fear that his real mother would try to reclaim him – after all, it happened often enough on TV – such a phone call would have turned her inside out, but now she felt reasonably calm. And it wasn't just that the woman had denied any such intention. Becky knew full well that only one person could take Richard away from her now, and that was Richard himself. She'd been his mother in every way that mattered, and soon he'd be leaving the nest in any case.

No, the person she should be worrying about was him. This was bound to be upsetting, at the very least. He knew he was adopted, knew his mother's first name, but that was about all. At her request they had been denied all knowledge of her surname, and until ten minutes ago they'd had no idea where she was living, or even whether she was still alive.

At odd times over the past few years Richard had wanted to talk about his own adoptive background, but he had never given any hint of resentment or anger – he had just been naturally curious about parents he had never known and whatever genealogical inheritance they had bequeathed him. Now, of course, that might all change. If his mother wanted to meet him, they could hardly stand in the way. If she didn't, then Becky had no idea what they should do.

She sat there looking out the window, letting her thoughts wander. It had rained that morning and the grass was glistening in the afternoon sun. When they got back from Shropshire she would have to do some weeding . . .

To tell Richard that they'd heard from his mother, but that this woman had no interest in seeing him, seemed little short of cruelty. But then to say nothing would be to lie.

Becky told herself that there wasn't much point in a circular tour of her own brain. She'd be able to talk it all over with Edward that evening.

Eventually she took another novel off the pile she'd brought home from the office, reading through the first few pages like any bookshop browser, seeing whether or not she wanted to read more. In most cases the answer was no, but she probably wasn't in any fit state to be fair to the various authors, and it was with some relief, an hour or so later, that she heard Edward's key in the front door.

Walking out to the hall, she found him holding what looked like a pile of newspapers mounted on a square of hardboard. A knife protruded from the pile, and dollops of dried ketchup surrounded the wound.

"It's one of Raul's," he said with a grin. "It's called *Freedom of the Press*."

"What's it doing here?"

He looked slightly abashed, but only for a second. "Ah. I know I should have talked it over with you first, but I had to make a decision on the spur of the moment, and it was only £800."

"Eight hundred?" she echoed in disbelief.

"It'll be worth twice that once the exhibition is over. And isn't it brilliant?"

No was the answer that came to mind, but in the circumstances she didn't want to deflate his good mood.

"I had lunch with three corporate PR men," he went on, "and by the time it was over they were trying to outbid each other with sponsorship deals. It's been a bloody good day."

She looked at him, feeling the familiar mix of

admiration and maternal condescension welling up inside. It was a feeling she had never got used to. "I need to talk to you about something," she said.

"OK, he said. "Just let me open a bottle."

"No, I meant after dinner. I thought we could go for a walk in the park."

"Fine. By the way, what time do you want to leave tomorrow?"

Anyone else would have been curious about what she wanted to talk about, but on this occasion she was glad that he wasn't. "I told Cath we'd be there mid afternoon," she said. "It shouldn't take more than four hours, so about eleven?"

"Great. We can have a lie-in." He poured them both a glass of the Merlot. "Is Richard looking forward to the weekend?"

"Of course not. A houseful of strangers – that's his idea of a nightmare. But he's not complaining too much."

"Maybe he'll fancy one of Neil and Cath's daughters."

"Don't suggest it. He'll be self-conscious enough as it is."

Edward raised his hands in mock surrender. "OK."

His good mood lasted through dinner, which proved far and away the most convivial the three of them had managed during the holiday week. Listening to her husband and son talking about the upcoming cricket season – as safe a topic as still existed between them – Becky could remember meals in years gone by, before Richard's adolescent moods started sparking echoes of his father's. On many evenings she had wanted to bury both their faces in their food.

Richard even offered to wash up, which gave them the chance to get out while it was still light.

Holland Park was full of strollers enjoying the late-spring sunshine, and Becky, reluctant to break the spell, waited until they were halfway round before broaching the subject of Sheila Browning's call. "I had an unexpected phone call this afternoon," she began.

"Oh?"

"Richard's real mother," she said, and felt him instantly stiffen.

"What did she want?" he asked quietly.

"To meet me. Other than that, she didn't say."

He walked slowly on, staring at the trees ahead.

He was angry, she realized. Funny, she hadn't even thought about how this might affect him. And in terms of his relationship with Richard it could hardly have come at a worse time – with the exception of that evening, icy politeness was the best either of them had managed for several weeks.

Reaching a bench, he flung himself dramatically on to it, and sat, arms extended along its back, legs splayed outwards. "So what do you think she wants?" he asked.

"She did say that she didn't want him back or anything like that."

"Then it must be money."

As often happened in her conversations with Edward, Becky wondered why his explanation hadn't even occurred to her. "She might just have discovered that some rare disease runs in her family and thinks we should know about it," she thought out loud.

Edward looked at her pityingly. "She could have told you that on the phone," he said. The more he thought about it, the more he was convinced it had to be money. Perhaps she had seen the picture of him in the *Standard* the week before – it had been a good one – and realized they must have a bob or two to spare these days. He must remember to take a copy down to show the others this weekend. "It'll be money," he repeated. "You'll just have to tell her we haven't got any. None that isn't tied up, anyway."

Becky considered reminding him that he'd just spent £800 on a dubious work of art, but knew it would be a waste of time. "Will you come with me?" she asked.

"When?"

"I'm meeting her on Wednesday."

"The press show for the exhibition's on Wednesday – I'll be up to my ears. And anyway, you told me she wanted you to come alone."

"Yes, I know."

"All you have to do is say no."

"What about Richard?"

"What about him? Oh, you mean she'll try and get at us through him." He shrugged. "We can't let the woman blackmail us ... and in any case, maybe Richard should meet her."

"I think he should."

Edward looked at her. "Are you really upset by this?"

Yes, she felt like saying, but she didn't. "Not as much as I would have expected. It's just the shock, I think. It's Richard I'm worried about. Dealing with his real mother will be hard enough. Dealing with her not wanting to see him will probably be even harder."

"If she doesn't want to see him, then why tell him?"

"Doesn't he have the right to know?"

"You said it yourself – it'll be easier for him if he doesn't."

"Maybe," she said, but she wasn't convinced.

* * *

Ian Mahoney's eyes caught the clock as he hurried on to the concourse of Manchester Victoria station. He always worried when Tom was making the trip alone, and cursed himself for not getting there on time.

But luck was with him – British Rail was proving as unreliable as he was, and the Scarborough train was only just pulling in. Nor, as it turned out, was Tom travelling alone. Ian could now see his son in the distance, walking towards him, happily talking with his stepfather Josh.

The apparent ease of their relationship provoked feelings of both jealousy and sadness, but Ian knew in his heart that he should be thankful to Ellie for providing Tom with such a reasonable stepfather. And at least Josh was having the decency to lose his hair even faster than Ian.

"Hey, Dad," Tom shouted in greeting. A year ago he would have run up and hugged Ian, but he was eleven now, and seemed to have suddenly grown more conscious of the need to display grown-up restraint.

"How are you doing?" Ian said, taking him in a bear-hug. "Hi, Josh," he said over Tom's shoulder.

"I was coming in anyway, so we kept each other company on the train," Josh explained.

"What about this evening? Is Ellie still meeting the five-forty?"

"Yep. I'll only be here for a couple of hours, then I've got to get back to Hebden." Josh ran a one-man printing press in the Pennine town where Ian and Ellie had lived for most of their ten-year marriage.

"OK. See you sometime."

"Yep. Bye. Bye, Tom. Don't eat too many

hamburgers." He smiled as he said it, but Ian heard the echo of Ellie's last go at him for feeding the boy so badly. The trouble was, Tom enjoyed eating delicious crap once a week.

"What are we going to do, Dad?" he asked, as Josh disappeared from view.

"How about the Science Museum? We haven't been there for ages."

"Great..."

"But first I need some breakfast."

"Dad, it's ten-thirty!"

"I was working late last night."

"On a gig?"

Ian smiled at Tom's use of the word. "No, on an article. There haven't been many gigs lately, I'm afraid." He looked around. "Come on, let's walk up to the Burger King in Piccadilly Square, and then we can get a bus to the museum."

They made their way up past the Arndale Centre, which already seemed besieged by harassed mothers and their school-holidaying kids. The Burger King was full of them too, but Tom held a two-person table while Ian queued for coffee, cola and two cheeseburgers.

"You're putting on weight, Dad," Tom said disapprovingly, as they sat looking out across the sunlit square.

"I know. It's since I stopped playing football."

"That was years ago!"

"My diet may have something to do with it."

"Course it does. You've got to eat better. Mum says you'll have a heart attack if you keep going the way you are."

"That's..." The throwaway joke died on his lips when he realized that his son really was worried for him. He repressed a momentary anger at Ellie for causing the boy such anxiety – after all, she was probably right. "I'm working on it."

Tom stared pointedly at the empty burger wrapper. "I am. Just not very well. Let's talk about you. What have you been doing with your holidays?"

Tom told him, and for a while the eleven-year-old was back, revelling in his various enthusiasms. He'd played a lot of football – Josh had just fixed up a real goal with a net for him in their back garden – watched a lot of TV, been to the pictures in Halifax with his friends. Another few years and he'd be going out with girls, or at least lusting after them in the privacy of his own thoughts.

Ian suddenly found himself wondering whether it was time he gave Tom a facts-of-life talk. But then these days kids seemed to know it all anyway. In fact, it was probably harder to avoid the knowledge than acquire it. Still, he was damned if Josh should be the one to talk to the boy. He'd give Ellie a ring in the week and find out what she thought.

They got to the Science Museum around half-past eleven, and for the next two hours slowly made their way around the various halls and outdoor exhibits. Ian loved the steam locomotives and the recreated railway station – the very *first* passenger station – but Tom was less impressed by the trains than the huge hall full of vintage aircraft. As his son sat happily at the controls of an old bomber, Ian remembered his own dad taking him to see the last BR steam train in 1968. He'd been thirteen – two years old than Tom was now – and he could still see the magical plume of smoke, smell the potent blend of coal and tar. It was one of those memories, like the first kiss and the

10

first lovemaking, like the first time he'd heard Miles or Monk or Dylan.

Ian felt a wave of nostalgia for his own childhood. Since passing forty the previous year he seemed to have done a lot of looking back, and the weekend ahead promised more of the same.

"Who's going to be at your reunion?" Tom asked a few minutes later, as if he'd read his father's mind.

"Well, it's at Neil and Cath's, so they'll probably be there. And they're sorry you won't be, by the way."

"So am I, but it's Mum's birthday."

"I know. I should have thought, but the date was already fixed and it was the only weekend everyone else could make."

"Will Jen be there?"

"Yeah, as far as I know. It's all six of us who shared the house in our final year at university. Becky and Edward are the others. You've never met them. I haven't seen Edward for more than ten years."

Tom looked thoughtful. "I thought you were going to marry Jen when you and Mum broke up," he said.

"Why?" Ian asked, surprised.

"I don't know. I must have heard something wrong, or something."

"She's a good friend."

"I know that *now*," Tom said indignantly.

They reached the museum's café, and Ian queued up for sandwiches and Cokes, thinking that kids always seemed to have more intuitive knowledge of the adults around them than the adults gave them credit for. There had been a time when he'd thought of Jen in terms of a sexual relationship – they'd even shared one drunken night some eighteen years earlier, when both

11

had been involved with other people – but that was all a long time ago. As you got older, Ian thought, a lot of things got worse, but some actually improved. These days he could fancy a woman without losing sight of the fact that a relationship with her would be an unqualified disaster.

He thought about Susan, whom he'd met only three days before, and impulsively asked out for dinner. She'd accepted – equally impulsively, he guessed – and in a few days they'd both get the chance to see if there was anything they actually liked about each other. Even if there wasn't, there might be sex, but there wouldn't be the hopeless infatuation or miserable confusion that had marked so many of his relationships before and immediately after Ellie. He had learned something in his forty-one years.

"How's your mum?" he asked Tom, once they'd finished eating.

As always when he mentioned Ellie, Tom gave him an enquiring look, as if to find out if the solicitude was genuine.

In a way it was, in a way it wasn't. There was just no getting away from the fact that two people who had and cared about a kid were bound together whether they liked it or not. And it was all very civilized. It was only in his darker moments that Ian felt his own mental health would have benefited from a cleaner break.

According to Tom, Ellie was fine. Her life sounded busy as ever, and she was probably as neurotic as ever. She was lucky to have Josh, Ian thought. In fact he could do with a Josh himself.

They took a bus back to Piccadilly, and another one south to Chorlton and the house which Ian rented and shared with a Pakistani lecturer at Salford University. Ian had the upstairs rooms, and Tom seemed more impressed by the state they were in than by anything else he'd seen that day.

"Our house is so tidy," he said. "Except for my room, of course," he added proudly.

"This at least I have bequeathed to my son," Ian muttered. "A talent for creating chaos."

For the rest of the afternoon Tom contentedly played games on one of the three computers while Ian tried to complete the assignment which had been due the day before and fielded phone calls from other editors. At four-thirty – a couple of hours earlier than expected – the garage called to say his car was ready, and the two of them went to collect it. Ian then called Ellie to suggest he bring their son back, but there was no answer, and he resigned himself to delivering Tom by train as arranged, since Ellie had a tendency to react badly when he deviated from her script.

It was a rush-hour train at least, so there didn't seem any chance of anything happening to the boy.

"Stop worrying, Dad," he was told in no uncertain terms.

"See you next Saturday," Ian shouted as the doors hissed shut. And there was Tom waving, looking more like seven years old than eleven.

Back at the house Ian surveyed the chaos, seeing it first through Tom's eyes, then Ellie's, then through those of the friends with whom he was going to spend the weekend. Who had rooms like this when they were forty-one?

Neil Thompson switched off the ignition, sighed, and stared morosely out through the windscreen at the brightly lit supermarket. "So how much are we going to spend?" he asked.

"As much as we need to?" Cath suggested. She'd been dreading this shopping expedition all day.

Neil rolled his eyes. "We can't spend what we don't have," he said, as if he was talking to a particularly obtuse child.

"It's called credit," Cath snapped, and instantly raised her hands. "Sorry. Look, Neil. I know we can't afford it, but we have invited them down – it was your idea, remember? – and they're going to want to eat and drink."

"I know," he said, sighing again. "Maybe we could pass a hat round every morning, or charge admission." He turned to smile at her, and the reflected light from the supermarket flickered on his glasses. "I was only saying . . ."

"I know what you're saying," she said, putting a hand on his arm. "We've got a real money problem, and we need to sit down and have a serious talk about what we're going to do about it. But not now, OK? The reunion was a great idea, and let's enjoy it. Catering for ten one weekend every twenty years is not going to make much difference."

"Yeah, you're right," he said. And she was, but it was still hard to stop worrying, with five mouths to feed and only her unreliable income to do it with. Maybe he could persuade the recycling centre's management committee to give him something next month, he thought, as they walked across the car park, grabbed a trolley and started spending what they hadn't got. But it wasn't very likely. Since the council had pulled the plug on their contract the centre had been limping from grant to grant, relying on the voluntary labour of well-wishers to sustain it. As the person in charge, and the only full-time worker, Neil had been paid for as long as there was money in the bank, but for over a month now he had been a full-time volunteer. It wasn't something he could do for ever, but it was hard to just walk away after five years of hanging on. And not just for selfish reasons. If there was no commercial future for recycling, then what price the damn planet?

And there always seemed to be hope. Just before each new application for a grant was refused they'd hear of another possibility. Or receive intelligence of hopeful new machinations on the council.

"None of them are vegetarians, are they?" Cath asked, breaking the spell.

"Ian isn't, but I don't know about the others."

"They all used to eat meat."

"They all used to smoke."

"I should have asked," Cath muttered to herself.

"They'd have said," Neil decided.

"Yeah, but I'd better make sure we have plenty of vegetables. They'll all get used anyway," she added.

"Did I say anything?"

"Not out loud."

He was less subtle when Cath claimed two shampoos off the shelf, their usual and one which cost almost three times as much. "What do we need that for?" he asked, picking it back out of the trolley and examining it for miraculous properties.

"Josey asked for it . . ."

"Is she paying for it?"

"No, she's not. She's really down at the moment, Neil." She gave him an appealing look. He'd always been careful with money, but lately he'd been verging on mean, with both himself and everyone else. There was always a good reason, of course, and there was no doubt they had to do some economizing, but it was the way he did it. Cath suddenly realized that she was ready for a row.

Sensing as much, Neil took a deep breath and replaced the shampoo in the trolley. "What's she got to be so depressed about?" he asked.

She looked at him with disbelief. "Where've you been the last week?"

"Mostly in Telford."

"Wayne Newsome told her he didn't want to go out with her any more."

"I knew that much."

"And the reason he gave was that he needed a girlfriend who he could do things with."

"Like go away for the weekend with him?"

"Exactly. So she's blaming us. If we'd let her go with him, he wouldn't have broken up with her."

"Oh Christ. She's not sixteen yet – what does she expect?"

"She says that she expects to be trusted. Yesterday she told me that if she wanted to go all the way with him she could do it in Crockett Wood during the school lunch hour, and that we should be able to draw appropriate conclusions from the fact."

"Are you still certain she hasn't?"

"Pretty certain, but she's right, you know."

"He's almost five years older than she is. Not to mention being thick as a plank."

"Oh, I'm not saying we should change our mind..."

"But some expensive shampoo will soften the blow?"

"It's a gesture."

Neil smiled at her. "Yeah, OK." She was right again. If only the banks were so generous.

They drove the heavily loaded car back home down

the narrow Shropshire roads, the headlights picking out an occasional representative of endangered wildlife. Every light seemed to be on in the cottage when they got back, but all three children were downstairs: twelve-year-old Angie and ten-year-old Daniel watching a Mr Bean video on the TV, Josey at the kitchen table, Walkman clamped round her dark-brown hair, morosely working on a school project.

It already seemed crowded, Neil thought, and tomorrow the house population would be doubling.

The DLR train pulled into Stratford and discharged its rush-hour load of Docklands workers. Jennifer Hendrie walked slowly down the platform, letting the scrum thin, and took the steps down to the North London line. The number of people waiting for the westbound train suggested a recent cancellation, and promised that the next train would be packed.

If it ever came. She stood with her back against the wall, watching as the clouds above were turned pink by the hidden sunset, thinking about Dennis Symington. If she'd never slept with the bastard he wouldn't be half as angry, she thought. But she had, just the once, and then refused to do so again. That was what had got him – the implication that he was no good in bed.

Maybe he was, maybe he wasn't. Her memories of that night were sketchy at best, and certainly didn't extend to the sex act itself. She did know that she didn't like him, that he had all the integrity of a spokesperson for the Bosnian Serbs and the morals of an unreconstructed eighties yuppie. He was good-looking in a square-jawed sort of way, but then so were any number of male bimbos.

The clouds were losing their pink hue now, the

waiting passengers – or customers, as BR insisted on calling them these days – growing restless.

Of course, the bastard would always have trouble accepting any rejection, but he would have had a much easier time rationalizing hers if she hadn't been given the job he wanted. He was ten years younger, half as bright as she was, and much less experienced, but somehow he'd managed to convince himself that the Indian project was his, and now he'd be out for revenge. She could expect a lack of support verging on sabotage from this day forward, and she wasn't at all sure whether the job was worth the hassle. The project was important to the company but uninteresting in itself; it would involve at least three trips to Bombay, during which she'd be able to soak up all the local colour you could find inside an air-conditioned Western-style hotel.

But she was damned if she was going to give the miserable rat the satisfaction of feeling he'd got one over on her.

The train came at last, packed as she'd predicted, and she spent the journey to Highbury & Islington in a press too tight even for the habitual gropers. After a fifteen-minute immersion in a fog of stale sweat she appreciated the walk up through Highbury Fields towards home even more than usual.

She let herself into the house in Highbury Park and climbed wearily to her second floor flat. Mac was waiting for behind the door, miaowing piteously, as if she'd left him alone for days without food or water. Both bowls were still half full – he'd just been lonely.

Our pets become us, Jennifer remembered from somewhere. It wasn't a happy thought.

After hugging and stroking the cat into some sort

of well-being she examined the fridge for supper. It contained a bar of chocolate, the remains of a Chinese take-away, half a Marks & Spencer salad, a carton of old mashed potatoes, three eggs and two bottles of white wine – one Portuguese, the other Italian.

It looked like Chinese omelette, salad and mash, with chocolate for dessert.

Fifteen minutes later she was sitting with the meal in front of *Coronation Street*, feeling at peace for the first time that day, and Mac was purring contentedly on the sofa beside her.

The programme over, she let herself listen to the messages on the answer-machine. Stuart hadn't called, and she found herself getting irritated again. There was no urgent reason for them to talk – he knew she was going away for the weekend – but he had said he would.

She called Paddington and got the times of the trains to Craven Arms in Shropshire. It would probably be easier to go via Euston and Shrewsbury, but she remembered enjoying the journey up through the Welsh Marches from Newport, and the timing was much the same. She thought about ringing Neil and Cath to tell them when she'd be arriving at Craven Arms, but decided she'd leave it till Newport. There'd be less chance of them meeting a cancelled service.

She poured herself a second glass of the Portuguese and decided to phone Stuart.

"Oh, hi," he said. "Can I call you back in a few minutes? I'm in the middle of a crisis here."

"Of course. I'll be here." She put the phone down, wondering what the crisis could be. Something to do with another woman, she thought instinctively. But what did it matter if it was? They'd already decided to stop seeing each other like that.

She started watching an episode of *Murder, She Wrote* which she'd recorded earlier in the week, but the phone rang while the credits were still running. She had expected to hear his voice, but it was her mother, wanting to know if she was coming up to Middlesbrough for her aunt's birthday the following weekend.

"I don't know yet," Jennifer lied. "But I doubt it – I've just been put in charge of a new programme we're running, and I don't think I'll be able to spare the time."

It would have worked with her father, who had always valued his daughter's academic and business successes, but her mother was another matter. "It's her seventy-second," she said plaintively, as if the number had some magical significance. "And both her children will be there."

Well, yours won't, Jennifer thought. "I'll try," she said, "but . . ."

Her mother moved on, into the usual litany of medical complaints. The truth of it was, she was just lonely, and while the rest of the world was not duty-bound to assuage this feeling, her daughter surely was.

Jennifer supposed she agreed deep down – otherwise she wouldn't feel so damn guilty.

Her mother was interested in the reunion though. "I always liked that Edward," she said. "You should have married him instead of Martin."

Her father, Jennifer remembered, had disliked Edward on sight. He'd hated Martin too, though for different reasons.

Off the phone, she poured herself a third glass, and this time didn't bother to put the bottle back in the fridge. She sat on the sofa, watching the mute tape play, thinking again about the situation at work. Fifteen minutes passed, then thirty, and she went to open the other bottle. On the way past the phone she took it off the hook. She wasn't going to spend the rest of the night waiting for him to ring back.

She'd quit, she decided. There were any number of places she could get another job, and in the meantime she'd have a real holiday, get away from everyone. She could afford a couple of weeks somewhere exotic – the Seychelles, maybe, or Bali. Even if she didn't resign she could take a trip – she was owed enough time and the Indian job wouldn't start for at least a couple of weeks. She could leave on Tuesday. If her passport was still valid. She rummaged around in the desk drawer where she kept such things, and found it still had another year to run.

She was just closing the drawer when she caught sight of Deysi's picture, and felt the familiar pang of guilt. She had never been late in sending the quarterly cheque for her sponsored child in Bolivia, but she hadn't written now for over a year, and the thought of doing so still touched some chord inside her which she couldn't or wouldn't recognize.

She had never told any of her workmates about Deysi, knowing she'd just get a load of smart remarks about how politically correct she was, but she'd never told any of her friends either, and she didn't know why.

This weekend she'd have the chance to tell her oldest friends. And for some reason that thought started her crying.

2

Ian pulled the Renault into the short lane and parked it alongside Neil and Cath's mud-spattered Escort. The top half of their end cottage was visible above the hedgerow, and once the engine was off he could hear Wilson Pickett's "Land of a Thousand Dances" doing battle with a vacuum cleaner.

He grabbed his holdall and walked towards the noise. Once inside the garden he stopped for a moment to admire the view out across the sunlit hills to the east, where the Long Mynd was starkly outlined on the horizon. It looked as though they'd been lucky with the weather.

"It's Ian," a girl's voice shouted out, and red-headed Angie appeared in the doorway smiling at him.

"Hi," he said, struck as always by how much she resembled her mother.

Cath and Josey were preparing sandwiches at the long wooden table which separated the kitchen section from the rest of the huge room. They both smiled a welcome, Josey only briefly, as if she'd suddenly remembered he was a friend of her parental oppressors.

In the smaller room which led off the living room, and which housed the TV, sound system and open fire, eleven-year-old Daniel was watching his dad wield the vacuum cleaner. The boy saw Ian first, and tugged at his father's sleeve.

Neil turned off the machine and turned down Wilson. "Looks good enough for the person who's sleeping in here," he told Daniel, who looked at Ian with a mischievous grin.

It was funny – the boy was almost a year older than Tom, but he always seemed younger. Having two older sisters was liable to slow a boy down, Ian thought. "I take it this is my home from home for the next two days," he said.

"Right."

"I'm sleeping in the caravan," Daniel said. "With the girls," he added disgustedly.

"Lunch," Cath called from the other room.

They went back through. "One day," Ian murmured to Neil, "he'll realize that sharing a caravan with two girls is just an impossible dream."

They sat round the long table eating ham sandwiches and drinking tea. "What time are the others getting here?" Ian asked.

"Jen was planning to get to Craven Arms about one. She'll need picking up. Becky and Edward could arrive any time this afternoon."

"Why didn't Jen get a lift with them?"

"We were wondering that," Neil said. "You've seen her more recently than we have. She hasn't fallen out with them, has she?"

"Not as far as I know," Ian said. "She probably just felt like a train ride." And these days she seemed to prefer solitude, he thought.

Daniel was tugging at Neil's sleeve. "Dad, it's time for *Football Focus*."

"Well spotted. Go and turn it on. I'll be in when I've washed up."

He joined Ian and Daniel in front of the TV in time to catch half the action.

"We should go to Maine Road next weekend," Ian said, and saw Daniel's eyes light up. "The four of us."

"Maybe," Neil said, as an all-too-brief flash of enthusiasm gave way to consideration of the cost. "Football's so bloody expensive these days."

"I might be able to borrow a couple of season tickets," Ian offered.

"That'd be great."

"Or maybe we could hold Edward to ransom."

"I like it," Neil said, his eyes lighting up. His face dropped. "But who'd pay to get him back?"

"Behave, you two," Cath said from the doorway. "He's probably mellowed, you know. Like both of you."

"Mellowed? Us?" Ian asked

Mellowed into what? Neil wondered.

Jennifer stood in the swaying toilet, doing restoration work on the morning's eye make-up. The last time they'd all been together she probably hadn't been wearing any at all, except perhaps for a little lipstick. And her chestnut hair had still been tumbling over her shoulders, not cut short like it was now.

In those days she'd got most of her clothing from theatrical and charity shops, not chain stores and boutiques. Cath and Neil probably still did, and Ian was not what you'd call fashion-conscious. She looked at the smart skirt and blouse she was wearing, and decided she might be overdressed. But what the hell? There was no point in pretending they were all still in their early twenties, and no use her pretending she was anyone other than who she was.

She walked back to her seat, feeling a surge of optimism about the next forty-eight hours. It might prove a rough ride, but that was probably just what she needed. Maybe it would jolt her out of the rut she was in.

As the train pulled into Craven Arms she remembered the only other time she'd been to the cottage. It had been almost ten years ago – Neil and Cath had only finished the restoration work the year before – and she'd still been with Martin 2, whom the others had treated with infuriating condescension. They might have been right about him, but that was still no excuse.

Ian had still been with Ellie then, and the weekend had seemed full of babies.

Now he was on the platform waiting for her with a big smile on his face, and she suddenly felt really glad that she'd come.

"You're looking great," he told her once they'd hugged, and she did. But he knew that the last couple of years hadn't been happy ones for her, and there was no mistaking the strain in her eyes.

They walked across the footbridge to the car and set off on the twenty-minute drive to the cottage. For the first few miles they exchanged news – of Tom, Ian's music, her work, their love lives. "I told Stuart I didn't want to see him any more," she said, and sitting there in the car with Ian it felt real. As long as she had good friends around her she could cope with being alone.

"It's going to be a strange weekend," Ian said, as if he felt some of what she was thinking. "Seeing people after a long time is like looking in a mirror."

"We see each other," she said.

"I know. But it's the six of us being together again. It's twenty years. I can hardly believe it."

"I know what you mean." It was like someone coming up to you and saying: OK, now justify what you've done with your adult life. The problem was, she didn't think she could.

As they sped along a straight section of road Becky stole a glance at Richard in the rear-view mirror. He'd hardly said a word since leaving London, preferring to stare gloomily out of the window, first at motorway verges and now at the rather more interesting Shropshire countryside.

"We're nearly at Bishop's Castle," Edward said beside her. "The local metropolis," he added sarcastically.

A few minutes later they were driving down the steep main street of the old market town.

"There was a piece in the *Sunday Times* magazine about places like this," Edward said conversationally. "There are about six of them spread around the country. Lots of ex-hippies and assorted hangers-on moved out to them in the late seventies, once the remnants of the sixties had turned sour in the cities. The men all ended up as part-time builders, the women as herbalists and fortune-tellers. And their children have all gone native and become small-town hooligans."

They had reached the bottom of the High Street. "Which way?" Becky asked.

Edward consulted Neil's map. "I never could understand his writing," he muttered. "Straight ahead," I think. "Up that hill."

The BMW purred up the narrow road.

26

"In that same article," Becky said, "it also said that these places have more sense of community than anywhere else in the country."

"That depends on whether you consider Morris dancing a community activity or a mental illness."

Becky shook her head. "Cath's a herbalist now, you know."

"I know. Don't worry, I'll be nice. As long as Neil doesn't get carried away with being holier than everyone else."

"Which way now?" Becky asked, stopping at another junction.

"Right," Edward said, wrinkling his nose at the prevalent smell of cow dung. "I can understand wanting a place in the country, but not living in it. In the evenings it must be like living in a Dickens novel, but with a TV instead of books."

"This is a beautiful area, though," Becky said, as a large vista of hills opened up to the east.

"It must be that row over there," Edward said, indicating a terrace of four cottages on the other side of the field. They seemed to be standing sentry above the deep valley beyond.

"It's gorgeous," Becky murmured, and even Richard couldn't resist a murmured "wow!"

As she pulled the car up behind the other two, Cath appeared on the path, her red hair billowing in the breeze. And behind her there was a rounder Ian, a shorter-haired Jennifer, and a Neil who still looked a little like Trotsky. Behind them a bevy of children hovered in the doorway.

The six adults embraced, and then stood around looking at each other, as if they could hardly believe they were all together again.

* * *

"So what's been happening to you two?" Cath asked, once they were all inside.

"You first," Becky told Edward.

He told them about his becoming a director the previous year, his long and successful struggle to attract enough sponsorship to keep the gallery going, the exhibition he was currently organizing. He never boasted – in fact he went out of his way to credit other people – but he left no reason for anyone to doubt that he took pleasure in his own success. But then why should he? It was exactly the sort of success he had always wanted – public, artistic and lucrative, all at the same time.

"How about you, Becky?" Neil asked.

"Oh, I'm still buying books for Dillerman's. No real complaints."

"She's more interested in her street-theatre group," Edward interjected with a smile.

"What?" Ian and Neil asked in unison.

She shook her head. "I've only just joined," Becky protested, glancing across at Edward. His previous comments on the matter had all been either patronizing or merely dismissive, so what had persuaded him to bring it up the moment they arrived? And then she realized – it was a rare chance for him to demonstrate what a bold and independent wife he had. "It's just a small group of people," she told the others. "They put on short plays for street parties and carnivals, things like that. Usually for children, but not always. A bit like the old agitprop groups in the seventies, only not so heavily ideological. In fact most of the plays are comedies."

"More like the Marx Brothers than Marx?" Ian suggested.

"Not really," she said with a grin.

"How are you doing, Richard?" Cath asked. It was hard to believe this tall, angular young man had grown out of the seven-year-old she remembered.

"Fine," he said awkwardly.

"School not too bad?"

He smiled shyly. "It could be worse."

"How are you two doing?" Edward broke in, looking first at Neil and then at Cath, who found herself wondering whether the interruption was intended to protect the boy or upstage him.

"We're doing OK," Neil began. "Unfortunately..."

"He'll regale you all with the saga of Telford Council later," Cath cut in. "Why don't I show you two to your room?"

"We should all have come with an essay," Ian suggested. *"My last twenty years."*

"No thank you," Jennifer muttered.

"Richard," Cath said, "we've put you in the TV room with Ian..."

"Or you can pull the camp-bed out here if he snores too loud," Neil interjected.

"I thought you'd prefer it to sleeping in the caravan with our three."

"Er, yes," Richard agreed apologetically, and caught the look of disappointment on Daniel's face.

"Right." Cath led Edward and Becky upstairs to the girls' room, where the two beds had been pushed together to make a double.

Becky looked out of the window at the valley stretching below. "This is a lovely place," she said, almost to herself.

"I thought everyone who wanted to could go for a walk this afternoon," Cath said. "Down to the village, maybe. It's about a mile and a half each way."

* * *

The breeze had dropped and the sun was still shining brightly in the afternoon sky as the raggedy column began its descent into the valley, first skirting a large cornfield and then tunnelling through a path between hedges before reaching the upper edge of a wood.

Daniel and Richard were in the lead, the eleven-year-old having obviously taken the sixteen-year-old under his wing. Neil and Edward were next, having apparently decided, either consciously or not, to tackle their most difficult partner of the weekend first. They were talking about the history of the area, or Neil was, with Edward asking the occasional question.

Ten yards behind them, Jennifer and Josey were getting to know each other, having been brought together by a shared size in Wellington boots. Angie was trailing along just behind them.

"You don't seem like one of my mum and dad's friends," Josey said after a while, with the bluntness of youth. "And neither do Edward or Becky," she added.

Jennifer smiled. "We're all different," she said. Maybe too different by this time, she thought. "We always were," she added.

"How did you all meet?" Angie asked, appearing suddenly at her side.

"Your dad and Ian and Becky were the original friends, and I became Becky's friend a little later. Edward was my boyfriend for a while – I introduced him to Becky. And your dad met your mum around the same time. And somehow we all ended up sharing a house for our final year."

"Edward was your boyfriend first," Josey echoed in disbelief.

Jennifer smiled. "It's a long time ago," she said, her

eyes on Edward, twenty yards ahead. It was hard to believe they'd once been lovers.

Some thirty yards behind these two, Cath was telling Ian and Becky about Josey's ex-boyfriend, Wayne. "He's everything you'd dread to see your daughter come home with – a lot older, unemployed, unintelligent, utterly devoid of any social graces, and very good-looking. According to Josey he's a great kisser, but I don't know how many others she has to compare him with. Not too many, I hope." She sighed. "Anyway, he wants to take her to the coast for the weekend, and we say no. He tells her he has to have a grown-up girlfriend – code for one he can sleep with – and dumps her. She's hardly talked to me or Neil since."

"I can't see what else you could have done," Becky said sympathetically.

"I know. But . . . you know, we were always so close, her and I, and it feels like something really irreversible has happened – that we can't ever be so close again."

"They grow up," Ian murmured.

"That's what Neil says. Being a parent means eventually being abandoned. Which may be true, but it's not very comforting. She's only fifteen."

"How old were you when you first found someone completely unacceptable to bring home?" Ian asked.

"About nineteen. It was Neil. And despite what my parents thought he was intelligent and polite. He had hair down to his waist, of course, and he was the first person in twenty years to tell Dad he was wrong about anything, but he didn't have a ring through his tongue."

Ian laughed. "Sorry," he said. "I know it's not

funny. I can't wait for Tom to bring home a woman who's ten years older than he is and already has three kids."

"I almost wish Richard would bring anyone home," Becky said. "At the moment I have next to no idea what's going on in that boy's head."

"Does he like the school?" Cath asked carefully. A hatred of private education in all its manifestations was probably the only one of Neil's ideological fixations which she fully shared, but this was no time for ideology.

"He says he does. He gets good marks – they don't think he'll have any trouble getting to university – and he seems happy enough when he comes home for the weekend. He and Edward rub each other up the wrong way a lot – considering how little they see each other, that is – but that's normal for an adolescent boy, isn't it? What worries me is that he keeps himself so much to himself. He has a couple of friends, but they seem more like acquaintances, and some weekends he hardly leaves his room. He just watches TV and plays his music all day. I sometimes doubt whether he'd bother to eat if I didn't remind him."

"You've tried talking to him?"

"Of course. He just says everything's fine."

"Maybe it is," Ian suggested.

Becky shook her head. She had already decided she wanted to talk to Cath about the phone call from Richard's biological mother, and she had no objections to Ian being present, but the subject would keep. For one thing they seemed to be nearing the village; for another it seemed too early in the weekend.

The village shop supplied the ice-creams, and they sat on the step outside to consume them before starting back up the long hill. Daniel and Richard again took the lead, but otherwise the social pack was shuffled, with Cath explaining the different types of herbalism to Edward, Jennifer and Becky talking to the two girls, Ian and Neil anticipating the summer's European Championship in the rear.

It was growing dark when they got back to the cottage, and there was a distinct chill in the air. Daniel manfully accepted that the promised game of football would have to be postponed until the following day, and while Cath checked on the roast turkey – there were apparently no vegetarians in the group – Neil oversaw the cracking open of a six-pack of Coke and two bottles of wine. Once Edward had found and put on Neil's copy of *Al Green's Greatest Hits*, it was possible to imagine that they were back in the house on Tisbury Road.

By seven the turkey was cooked, the candles lit, and they were ready to eat. All ten of them were squashed around the table, and as Edward topped up everyone's drink Cath cast her eye round the candlelit faces. Even Josey looked happy this evening – she'd obviously taken to Jen in a big way. And Richard was smiling at one of Ian and Neil's ludicrous comedy routines.

Her eyes met Neil's and they both smiled, as if to say: "This was a good idea."

"A toast," Edward demanded, raising his glass.

"To present friends," Ian proposed. Everything from wine glasses to Pocahontas mugs made contact across the table, and a water jug was upset in the process.

"Remember the time when Edward flooded the whole house by going out and leaving the bath on?" Neil said, setting in motion a long stream of anecdotes.

For the next few hours, as they ate, drank and drank some more, there was a lot of laughter, and on the one occasion when old disputes threatened to break surface Cath and Becky stood over their respective husbands with wine glasses poised. "Tonight we're celebrating," Cath warned them both. "Hey, don't waste the wine," Ian said. "Get some water."

The four children had been excused once the meal was over, and spent the rest of the evening popping in and out of the TV room. Richard went with the others, but to Becky's surprise he seemed initially reluctant to leave the table, as if he was actually enjoying the company. Neil and Cath's three kids were banished to the caravan at eleven, by which time Daniel and Angie were having trouble keeping their eyes open, and not long after that the adults rather shamefacedly admitted to each other that they were exhausted too.

In the small living room Ian and Richard arranged themselves in sleeping bags on the two camp-beds.

"Now all we need is a gun to shoot out the light," Ian observed.

Richard giggled. "I'll do it," he said.

Darkness filled the room, and the boy struggled back into the sleeping bag without overturning the bed. "Good night," he said, but doubtfully, as if he wasn't sure he wanted the evening to end.

"How did you find it?" Ian asked.

There was silence for several seconds, and Ian was beginning to think the boy had actually fallen asleep when the reply eventually came. "It was interesting," Richard said softly.

"In what way?" Ian asked, once it became apparent that another cue was necessary.

There was another longish pause. "I don't often see Mum and Dad with other people. I mean, they have dinner parties all the time, but I don't sit with them, and in any case the ones at home feel more like plays, you know, like everyone's just playing a part. This is different."

Ian spent a few seconds formulating his next question: "Do your mum and dad seem like different people?"

"Yes, they do. Mum more than Dad, but he . . . he really cares what you others think of him. Most people don't think he cares at all. And Mum," he went on hurriedly, "she seems really different. Younger. Not so careful. I'm not sure how to describe it."

"You've described it pretty well. I suppose we're bound to bring out the younger selves in each other."

"Maybe that's it," Richard said, but from his tone he sounded disappointed with the explanation. "I guess we should get some sleep now," he said a few moments later.

"Yeah, we probably should," Ian agreed. "Sleep well." He wondered what the boy would have made of his truthful answer: that in marrying Edward Becky had sacrificed her spirit on the altar of emotional security. Most of her friends had thought this a bad deal in 1976, and Ian could see no reason to change his opinion twenty years later.

Today had indeed been interesting, he thought, but tomorrow would be more so. Today they had remembered what they liked about each, but tomorrow they would start to remember the reasons why they hadn't all been under the same roof in twenty years.

3

It was shortly after eight when the aroma of coffee percolated up to Becky. She pulled jeans and sweater on over her pyjamas and made her way downstairs, where a similarly attired Cath was standing bleary-eyed over the coffee pot.

They first took their cups out to the sun room cum porch which Neil had built, but the weather was so warm they walked out into the garden, feeling the dew on their bare feet. In the valley below a swathe of mist was still hovering, but away to the east the contours of the south-facing slopes were drawn with stunning clarity. The two women stood in silence for several minutes, the one enjoying a familiar but still deeply satisfying experience, the other enthralled by the rare serenity of it all. London seemed a long way away.

"Do you ever regret moving out here?" Becky asked.

"Sometimes. I don't miss the city the way Neil does, but the social life out here sometimes seems like a bad soap opera. You know: who's sleeping with who this month?"

"You and Neil are OK, aren't you?"

"Oh yes. I don't think either of us could find the energy to have an affair. We use it all up fighting.

No," she added, seeing Becky's face, "it's not that bad. But we have been going through a rough patch. Mostly because of money." She smiled sardonically. "Ironic, isn't it – we spend half our lives not bothering about the stuff, and we end up thinking about it all the time."

"How bad is it?" Becky asked, feeling a wash of guilt. She couldn't remember the last time she'd had a money worry.

"Pretty bad. Neil hasn't earned anything for over a month, and I never know how much I'm going to make with the herbs. So there are debts piling up. We're a month behind on the mortgage – that sort of thing."

"I thought you owned the cottage outright," Becky said, surprised.

"We did, once. We took out a second mortgage a few years ago."

"Oh. Look . . ." Becky began awkwardly. "If things get desperate . . ."

"Thanks," Cath said, squeezing Becky's hand, "but I don't think it'll come to that. Neil will find another job sooner or later."

"He's looking then?"

"Oh yes. I just hope it won't be so far away that we have to move. I love this place."

"I can see why."

"How much do you see of Jen these days?" Cath asked, changing the subject.

"Hardly anything. I met her for lunch just before Christmas, but that was only because Ian was in London. And before that I hadn't seen her for at least six months. It's funny – we were really close once, but these days . . . She's not happy – that's obvious enough."

"I remember feeling really intimidated by you two

in the beginning. Neil gave you such a build-up – these two amazing northern girls who he and Ian thought so much of."

"Well, I suppose that's what brought us together – two northern girls at a southern university. Not much of a bond to sustain a friendship."

"You're still friends."

"Yes, but you know what I mean."

"I suppose so."

There was the sound of a door opening behind them, and Ian emerged, also carrying a cup of coffee. He waved but made no effort to join them.

"That means Richard'll be up," Becky said.

There must have been something in the way she said it. "He seems to have both his feet on the ground," Cath said.

"He probably does." Becky took a deep breath and told Cath about the phone call from Richard's real mother, throwing in Edward's expectations and her own anxieties for good measure.

"You'll have to tell him," Cath decided after a few moments of silence.

"I know. But if she doesn't want to see him it'll seem like he's been rejected all over again."

"Maybe. But I think you're selling yourself short. He'll be really curious about her, but you're his mother. You're where he gets his love from."

Edward lay in bed, waiting for whoever was in the bathroom to get out. The soft mattress had done his back no favours, but overall he felt pretty good. So far at least, the weekend was going better than he'd expected. It had been good to see the others again – even Neil, who seemed less dogmatic than in the old days.

One thing had surprised him: the reunion had brought up a lot of old memories, and he still felt a pang of hurt when he remembered that Becky had turned to him only after Neil had rejected her. He didn't know why he felt it – after all, he'd still been with Jen when Becky had gone after Neil – but he did. A tiny wound perhaps, but one that would never heal.

Jen was still remarkably attractive. There were a few lines around the eyes, but her body – clothed at least – seemed remarkably unchanged by twenty years. Not having any children must have helped, of course. He cast his mind back to visualize her naked, and felt himself stirring under the duvet.

There was a faint rap on the door.

"Yes?"

It opened cautiously, and Neil's son put his head round the corner. "We're playing football soon, and Dad says you're the goalkeeper," he said.

Edward's first thought was that he had no desire to dive around in a cow-pat-infested field, his second that he'd been a good goalie. Neil and Ian had been the stars of their five-a-side team, but they'd all done their bit. "I'd better get dressed then," he told Daniel.

A few minutes later he found Jen sitting alone with a cup of coffee, in a dressing gown short enough to display most of her thighs. There was a rainbow shining in her hair, courtesy of one of the many prisms hanging in the window. She smiled up at him, bringing back more memories.

He grabbed an apple from the bowl and went out to play football.

After the football match – in which Neil, Daniel, Angie and Richard soundly thrashed Ian, Edward and Cath – they retired to the cottage for breakfast; in some cases a second breakfast – and shared out the *Observer* and *News of the World* which Neil had brought back from the village shop. Around noon they all piled into the Escort and BMW and drove a few miles to the bottom of a path which led up to an ancient hilltop fort.

Neil and Becky found themselves bringing up the rear.

"Is the recycling centre definitely doomed?" she asked him.

"Depends what you mean. Universal entropy gets us all in the end."

She showed him a fist. "You know what I mean."

"Yeah, but it does depend. It'll stay afloat as long as there are people willing to do the work for nothing. But then it becomes like charity, you know? The society as a whole relying on the consciences of a few. And as long as those few keep giving – or working for nothing, which is much the same thing – then there's no incentive for government to fund anything. As long as it looks like someone's doing the recycling for nothing, why should they pay to have it done? So yes, we could stay afloat, but it'd probably be better if we sunk, preferably in full view and with a loud bang playing."

"I see what you mean," Becky said thoughtfully.

"And then there's the personal side of it. We can't afford me working for nothing." He laughed. "This is too depressing. Tell me about your street-theatre group – it sounds great."

"I've already told you about it."

"You told us hardly anything, and then you sounded like you were apologizing for it. Doesn't Edward approve?"

She laughed. "Not much. He likes the idea but . . ."

"He thinks it's a throw-back," Neil guessed. "Or a sideshow."

"Both of those. I think he sees it as my hobby, but it's more than that."

"What do you do?"

"A bit of everything. I do some of the writing. We all perform. They're little morality plays really, heavy on laughs and low on ideology. But they're about the usual things – racism, unemployment, homelessness . . ." She looked at Neil. "But I feel such a hypocrite sometimes. "We have three homes . . ."

"Three? You only had two last time I heard."

"We've had three for about ten years. You know about the cottage in Cornwall we inherited from Edward's uncle?"

"Yes."

"Well, Edward sold it, bought a small cottage in the same area for half the money and spent the rest on a small place in the Virgin Islands."

"The Virgin Islands?"

"It was ten years ago. It cost us hardly anything."

I can see why you feel a hypocrite, Neil thought, but he didn't say so. "How often do you go there?" he asked.

"At least once a year, usually twice. Always in January, sometimes in the summer. The rest of the time we rent it out – it pays for itself most years."

Neil was silent for a few moments, not knowing what to say. "I'm really glad you're enjoying your group," he said at last, and saw the grateful look in her eyes.

"I am," she said. "And I'm enjoying having someone to share my enthusiasm with," she added, taking his arm. She supposed saying so was a betrayal of Edward, but if it was she didn't feel any guilt.

Twenty yards ahead of them Ian and Jennifer were having their first private conversation since the car journey from Craven Arms.

"So how are you doing?" Ian asked her. She hadn't exactly kept her distance the previous evening, but there had still been a reserve about her, a holding back, which perhaps only he had noticed.

"Fine," she said. "It's such a beautiful day. Who'd live in London?"

Ian grunted. "I would, if it wasn't so far from Tom. But yes, it is beautiful around here."

"How often do you come down?"

"Every couple of months. Something like that. And Neil comes to Manchester. They all do sometimes."

She grimaced. "I never seem to see anybody these days. Except for people I don't want to see."

"Trouble't'mill?" Ian asked.

"Work's not my favourite place at the moment. I won't bore you with the details."

"Go on, bore me."

"No, I don't want to bore myself either. It's just the usual clichés – rejected male co-worker seeks revenge on ball-breaker boss."

Ian grinned. "It's hard to think of you as a ball-breaker."

"I don't want to think about it."

"OK. You said you'd finished with Stuart."

"I think so."

"Really?" Ian said, struggling to keep the doubt out of his voice.

"Really," she said, turning to look back at the view unfolding behind them. Out here it was easier to believe that it was over.

"Well, I've met someone," he said.

"Yeah? When? Where? Who is she?"

"Her name's Susan. She's the same age as us."

"That makes a change. What does she do?"

"No idea. She came up and talked to me at our last gig."

"A groupie," Jennifer said delightedly.

"A fan. She just came up and introduced herself. And she didn't ask if she could make a plaster mould of my private parts. We just had a nice talk about the music, and I asked her if she wanted to have dinner with me, and she said yes. And that's all I know. She may be married with six kids, or be an escapee from a mental home. She liked my playing, so at least she has great taste in music."

"Physical description? It's me you're talking to, remember? You don't have to pretend you didn't notice."

"She's almost as lovely as you are, Jen. What more can I say?"

At the top of the hill they strode round the overgrown earthworks, enjoyed the panoramic views and beat off an attack by imaginary Welsh hordes. Appetites and thirsts suitably encouraged, they marched back down the hill, piled into the two cars, and set off for Neil and Cath's regular pub in Bishop's Castle, where they filled two of the outside tables and demolished fifteen packets of crisps.

Back at the cottage everyone tried to help in the preparation of the evening meal – a vast vat of vegetarian chilli with three loaves of garlic bread – and more bottles of wine were opened. Around dusk the weather finally broke, and the rain strumming on the windows soon proved something of a portent.

The argument finally erupted just before dinner, when Edward, quoting one of the Sunday-paper columnists with barely concealed glee, announced that "even the left wing of the Labour Party seems to have accepted that the market knows best when it comes to the allocation of investment".

"Yeah?" Neil asked rhetorically. "If there's a real need then the market will always recognize it, right?"

"I don't think Edward would go that far," Becky said hopefully.

Her husband smiled. "I might," he said. "How else do you find out whose needs are real? By asking people? Everyone thinks their cause is deserving. Every little town thinks it needs a hospital."

"Most towns do."

"No, they don't, but that's not the point. Remember what Winston Churchill said about democracy – that it was the worst possible form of government, except for all the others. Well, I think the market's the worst allocator of resources, except for all the others."

"Glib," Ian said.

"Which doesn't mean it isn't true," Jennifer told him.

"It isn't though," Neil said. "Look at the state of the country – look at the world, come to that. Every time some right-wing government decides to let market forces off the leash the gap between rich and poor widens, the environment gets done over, crime shoots up, homelessness increases – you name it."

"And the GNP rises."

"Even if it does, it's only a few that benefit. And they spend their extra wealth on more security guards. It's not only evil, it's crazy."

Edward shook his head. "You must be the last

person in the world who still thinks there's an alternative."

Neil shrugged. "There has to be."

"Socialism?" Edward asked sarcastically.

"Who said anything about that? I'm not stupid enough to think there's an easy fix, though shooting the rich might be a start."

"Not a very humanitarian one," Jennifer murmured.

"And how would you define the rich?" Edward asked. He still had a smile on his face, but there was a deepening hue to his cheeks which Becky recognized.

"The usual way – by their assets. You'd probably qualify."

"I'm sure I would. But I worked bloody hard for what I've got, and so has Becky."

"Aw, come on, Edward," Ian said. "It's one thing to argue that there's nothing wrong with being rich, but don't give us that line. We were all there, remember, on your twenty-first, when your Dad handed over a cheque for ten thousand quid."

"So? Ten thousand quid wouldn't buy a room in this cottage."

"It would have bought the whole row in 1977," Neil said drily. The point is, you got a start most people don't. I'm sure you have worked hard, but so have the rest of us. So do most people. And they . . .' he started, but managed to stop himself from adding that they didn't have holiday homes in both the West Country and the Caribbean.

"Life isn't fair," Jennifer said.

"Dead right," Edward agreed, giving her a grateful look.

"Who's arguing?" Neil came back. "The point is: what we do about the unfairness? Isn't it a bit hypocritical to bemoan the fact with one breath and then take maximum advantage of it with the next."

"There seems to be a touch of hypocrisy in what you're saying, Neil," Jennifer said. "Either Edward really believes that this is the best of all possible worlds, or he's just using the argument as a means of justifying his own selfishness. If you think it's the second, then what's the point of arguing the first with him?"

Neil did think it was the second, but saying so would risk souring the whole weekend. "Oh, I'm sure he's dumb enough to believe his own propaganda," he said.

"You have to be gullible to be a goalkeeper," Ian agreed flippantly, and everyone laughed. The yawning crack was allowed to draw together, and for the rest of the evening no one mentioned politics.

Jennifer lay in bed, her hands behind her head. She could hear the vague murmur of conversations through both the wall and floor, but nothing of what was being said. A thin wash of moonlight shone through the gap, illuminating the poster of a footballer with the improbable name of Ryan Giggs.

She remembered her own room in the Middlesbrough house. She'd had posters on the wall too, but she couldn't remember who they were of.

Had everything seemed simpler back then or was she imagining it? She'd enjoyed her talks with Joscy, partly because the girl so obviously enjoyed talking to her, partly because in a fifteen-year-old's world everything seemed so wonderfully black and white. You were either allowed to do what you wanted or you weren't. You either had a boyfriend or you didn't.

And then you grew out of your teens and set out to conquer the world. Not literally of course – not unless you were Napoleon – but you set out down some road with some notion of success in mind. Or some notions. Success in love, success in work, success as a rearer of children, as a maker of money, a collector of beautiful things. If you were Neil you wanted to leave something changed for the better, if you were Edward you wanted to be admired for doing what you did well. If you were Cath, you wanted lovable children who loved you back, if you were Ian you wanted time to work out what you really wanted to do. If you were Becky . . . Jennifer had no real notion of what Becky wanted. She seemed to have everything, but it wasn't enough.

She remembered something a character on TV had said: some people make a lot out of a little in life, others make a little out of a lot. Becky seemed to be realizing that she'd done the latter and sold herself short. Street theatre didn't seem a great choice of remedies but Jennifer was ready to believe it was better than nothing.

Edward wouldn't understand, of course, but then for him, unlike the rest of them, life was still a pretty simple business. With money and Becky to protect him, he'd never really had to grow up. Which was what gave him his obtuseness, but also his charm and likeability.

Neil had been right that evening, but she'd felt compelled to support Edward. She'd felt sorry for him. In the middle of the argument she'd suddenly remembered a story from the Scottish camping trip which several of them had gone on during one of the summer holidays. There'd been four men, and two tents for them, but no one had wanted to share with Edward, and he'd slept alone while the other three fought for space in the other tent. He had never mentioned it, but it must have hurt him.

She suspected that there was a strong undercurrent of envy in Neil's attitude towards Edward, but if so, it was misplaced. No one had ever left Neil out in the cold, but that evening, behind Edward's infuriatingly smug smile, she'd been certain she could see the wounded little boy.

In the next room Edward snuggled up against his wife and reached out a hand to cup her right breast.

She let him caress her for a moment, but after a while she took his hand and held it between her own. She felt distant from him, and wasn't sure why. Perhaps it was the argument between him and Neil, but that seemed ridiculous. She had always disagreed with her husband's politics – increasingly so in recent years – but there was no emotional charge attached. Unlike Neil she felt no overpowering need to be agreed with.

Then again, perhaps it was the way he had looked at Jennifer all day.

"Have you got a headache?" he asked wryly.

"No. But I want to talk about Richard."

"What about him?" Edward asked, sounding bored.

"We have to tell him about his mother making contact. I can't decide whether we should do it before or after I meet her."

There was a silence. "I think it's a bad idea," he said eventually.

"Why?"

"He's got important exams coming up in a few weeks. It's not a good time to upset him."

"You mean tell him after the exams?"

"Maybe. If it still seems like a good idea. He's spent

the last ten years getting used to the idea that we're his parents in all the ways that count, and I can't see any point in getting all his emotional wires crossed without a damned good reason."

It sounded sensible. It felt wrong. "Do you still find Jen attractive?" she asked, suddenly switching tack.

"Yes, I suppose so," he said guardedly. "She looks pretty much the same as she always did. Apart from the hair, that is."

"It looks good short," she agreed.

He reached out an arm. She allowed herself to be drawn in, and found herself wondering how many women he'd slept with since their marriage twenty years before. Ten, fifty, five hundred? She had no real idea, and had never really cared. She'd known he would always come back to her, and that, on a more practical level, his own well-developed instinct for survival would ensure a disease-free return.

His hand was wandering again.

"Sorry, I'm just not in the mood," she said, gently rolling out from under it.

"OK," he said equably.

Downstairs Ian and Richard were on their respective camp-beds. "So did you find today as interesting as yesterday?" Ian asked mischievously.

"It was amazing," Richard said. "I thought Dad and Neil were going to have a fight."

"I'm glad they didn't," Ian said. "I'd have been expected to separate them."

Richard laughed, but only for a moment. "I don't know how Dad can talk such rubbish," he said. "I think it's obscene that we have three houses."

Neil would be proud of him, Ian thought. "What's the one in the Virgin Islands like?" he asked.

"Oh, the island's beautiful, you know. Jade-coloured sea and huge palms and white sand. There are reefs a couple of hundred metres out where we go snorkelling. It's incredible. The house isn't much, but that doesn't matter. I usually sleep outside, in a hammock on the veranda."

"Sounds idyllic," Ian murmured.

"It is." Richard sighed. "Now I'm sounding like a hypocrite, aren't I?"

"Nope. Who wouldn't enjoy somewhere like that?"

"Neil?"

"Don't you believe it. Neil enjoys good things – you didn't see him refuse that bottle of wine your Dad brought. He just thinks they could be shared round a bit more equitably."

"What do you think?"

"Christ. Twenty years ago I would have been loading Neil's gun for him, but these days . . ." He grunted. "I heard this thing on the radio the other day. It was someone talking about the difference between the Americans and the Irish. An American tramp looks up from the gutter, sees the rich guy in his rich mansion on the hill, and he thinks: one day I'm going to live like that. The Irish tramp sees the same rich guy, same mansion on a hill, and he thinks: one day I'm going to get that bastard down here in the gutter with me."

Richard laughed.

"These days," Ian went on, "my gut instincts are with the Irishman, but I don't really believe that shooting the rich would do much good. When it comes down to it, I don't really think that having a lot of money is one of the key ingredients to a happy life. Not having it is a bummer, and it certainly solves some problems – like the ones Neil and Cath are having right now, for example. But for some people" – he thought of Jennifer but didn't name her – "and I don't just mean rich people, more money would be an irrelevance. Nice, but irrelevant. There's nothing wrong with it – it's just not what really matters."

"What is?"

"Your guess is as good as mine."

4

It rained through most of the night, but by breakfast on the Bank Holiday Monday a fresh breeze was rattling the windows and the sun was playing hide-and-seek with fast-moving clouds. Edward and Becky wanted to set off for London early in the afternoon, so the plan was to have an early lunch at the Fort Hotel in Church Stretton, which Neil and Cath had long wanted to try. By half-past eleven they were on their way, driving through countryside still glistening with the night's rain.

The early departure proved a good idea, for the hotel's restaurant was almost full when they arrived, leaving the adults' and children's tables separated by a family of Japanese tourists. The mood at the former started off subdued, a reflection of the fact that no one but Edward was particularly eager to resume normal life. Cath, though, was pleased to see that Richard and Josey seemed to be enjoying each other's company for the first time, and drew Becky's attention to the fact.

"I don't think you've anything to worry about with him," Ian told Becky. "He seems together enough to me."

"Why, what's he been saying?" she asked.

"Nothing in particular."

"I told you," Edward said complacently, without raising his eyes from the menu. "All sixteen-year-old boys are secretive. It doesn't mean anything."

"I sometimes wish all fifteen-year-old girls were the same," Neil said.

"No you don't," Cath contradicted.

"No I don't," Neil agreed.

The mood began to lighten with the wine, and soon they were mining their collective past for reminiscences once more, as if they all knew that the weekend needed to end on the same nostalgic note on which it had begun. In the meantime their waiter, who looked like a Chippendale and spoke with a lisp, was busy creating a new chapter for their collective history. He not only brought the wrong bottle of wine, slopped his first attempt at pouring a glass and forgot their request for more bread, but contrived to turn each failure into a barely repressed tantrum.

"Maybe it's a test," Ian suggested. "Someone's doing market research on how much people will take. He'll probably pour coffee in somebody's lap next."

In fact he brought the bill without even offering them coffee.

"There's probably people waiting for tables," Becky said,

"They can wait," Edward said, gazing at the bill. He signalled the waiter, who took their order as if he'd been slapped in the face, and then added the coffees to the bill, sighing loudly as he did so.

"Well, at least it was a great meal," Ian said, taking and examining the amended bill. "Given that Neil and Cath have fed us twice, I think we should split this four ways," he said.

"Of course," Becky said.

"Of course," Jennifer echoed, reaching for her purse.

The four of them had enough cash to cover it.

"Are we going to tip the bastard?" Ian asked.

"Only if he doesn't spill anyone's coffee," Jennifer suggested.

"Sounds fair."

The waiter returned with a tray of coffees, which he disdainfully placed in front of them. He then scooped up the pile of notes and walked off, all without a word.

"Ten per cent," Ian said, "and not a penny more."

He gathered contributions from the others and counted it all up. "There's a pound too much," he said.

"Keep it," Edward said.

"Let's buy a lottery ticket with it," Cath suggested. "For all of us."

"You're joking," Neil said, but there was a smile on his face.

"I might have known you'd disagree with it," Edward said.

"It's a circus for the masses. A profitable one, of course. You know what I heard the other day? One of the owners or whatever they are – someone was accusing him, with justification, of being neck-deep in the gravy trough, and his answer – get this – was that it couldn't be true: he earned less than the head of a privatized industry!"

"On the other hand," Ian said, "it's hard to really hate anything which hurts pools promoters and bookmakers."

"It's hurt the charities too," Becky reminded him.

"The charities get just as much from the lottery as they used to get from individuals," Edward claimed.

"So the only thing that's changed is that people can no longer choose which charity they want to give to?" Neil asked.

"I thought you were arguing . . ." Edward began.

"Anyway, *we* can't buy a ticket," Jennifer interrupted.

Ian turned to her. "It sounds like we have an expert with us. If not a player."

"I buy a ticket sometimes," she said.

"OK," Ian said, "time to come clean. Who else has bought one?"

"I have," Becky admitted.

"And me," Cath said, and waited for Neil to explode.

He sighed instead. "So have I," he said. "But only once," he added quickly, as if in search of mitigation.

"Your chance of winning is the same each week," Jennifer told him tartly.

"That's what stopped me," Neil said.

"OK," Ian said, "so we have experience on the team. Now why" – he turned to Jennifer – "can't *we* buy a ticket?"

"We can if we form a syndicate."

"Why can't one of us buy the ticket and dole the winnings out in equal shares?" Neil wanted to know.

"He or she could, but the other five portions would be considered gifts, and the recipients would have to pay a huge chunk of the winnings in gift tax," Jennifer told him.

"Sounds fair enough," Neil said.

"Depends," Ian said. "Personally, if I had half

a million to give away, I'd rather let someone like Amnesty distribute it than our beloved Government."

"You have a point," Neil conceded.

"So how do we form a syndicate?" Becky asked, picking up the pound coin in question.

"We would all need to sign a statement saying we agree to share the proceeds, and then get it witnessed by someone professional. Which doesn't seem . . ."

"No problem," Cath said. "The solicitor we used for the cottage is sitting over there."

"He'll probably charge," Edward said.

"No, he won't," she said. "He and I are on the local film-club committee. Who's got a piece of paper?"

Jennifer had. She wrote what seemed appropriate, and Cath walked across to ask the solicitor if he'd witness their signatures. He came over, obviously amused, and appended his own signature to the document.

"So who's going to keep it?" Cath asked.

"You can," several voices said.

"Who's going to buy the ticket?" Becky asked, holding out the coin.

"We all can," Cath said. "There's a newsagent near where we parked. It'll still be open."

"So now we have the important business to do," Jennifer said. "Choosing the numbers."

"You choose your own numbers?" Edward exclaimed. "I thought you just bought a ticket."

"Some people are so unsophisticated," Ian told Becky.

"Six numbers," Jennifer said. "One each, between 1 and 49."

They looked at each other.

"17," Ian said. "That's the year Thelonious Monk was born."

Jennifer wrote it down.

"15," Cath decided. "Our wedding anniversary," she explained.

"8," Jennifer said. Deysi had just had her eighth birthday.

"Why?" Ian asked.

"It's just my lucky number. We've got all low numbers so far," she added.

"Does that matter?"

"No, I suppose not."

"36," Neil said. "That's for our old house in Tisbury Road."

"44," Edward announced, and explained that that was the number of exhibits on display at the gallery.

"20," Becky said finally. "Because this is our twentieth anniversary. And it's been great."

She was picking up the pound coin just as Daniel appeared at their table.

"Can we go now?" he asked plaintively, and then saw the list of numbers. "What's this?" he asked, only half interested.

"It's your ticket to wealth beyond your wildest dreams," Ian said. "This time next week you'll probably be able to buy Manchester City and put us all in the team."

"Last week on TV I heard someone call the National Lottery a tax on stupidity," Neil said drily.

"So let's go and pay ours," Cath said.

They walked down the High Street to the newsagents, where the Patels were doing a roaring Bank Holiday trade in ice-creams, and the others waited on the pavement while Neil and Becky went in to buy the ticket.

"Thanks for cheering Josey up," Cath told Jennifer.

"I enjoyed her company."

"She enjoyed yours. Come back and see us again, OK?"

"Thanks," Jennifer said, turning away as the tears began to form.

Neil emerged, holding the ticket aloft like a captured trophy.

"The idiot'll probably lose it," Ian said. "And then we'll find out we've won."

As they walked across to the cars Becky drew Cath aside. "Remember what I said. If you're desperate for money, just ask."

"Thanks," Cath said, "but I'm not sure Edward would feel so good about subsidizing Neil."

"I'm not so sure Neil would take a loan from Edward," Becky said. "So we'll both have to be convincing."

"I hope it won't come to that," Cath said.

"So do I."

The six adults hugged each other and shuffled their feet on the pavement, unwilling to let the moment go.

"It's been great," Becky told Neil and Cath.

"It has," Edward agreed, and he meant it.

"Come again," Cath said, as they climbed into the BMW. Jennifer was sitting in the front with Edward, Becky in the back with Richard.

"Come down to London," Becky said through the open window. "And if you ever want to use the house on Virgin Gorda . . ."

"Let's have the next reunion there," Ian said.

"Why not?" Becky said, and the BMW drew away, taking her parting smile with it.

"Are you going back straight away?" Cath asked Ian

as they arrived back at the cottage. "Can you stay for a cup of tea?"

"Probably for two. There's nothing but work waiting for me at home."

Josey and the two younger kids disappeared, upstairs and into the TV room respectively, leaving the three adults sitting round the table.

"Let the post-mortem begin," Ian said.

"We can't start that until you're gone," Neil told him.

Cath placed the pot on its stand. "You know," she said. "I was telling Becky how intimidated I was in the beginning by her and Jen, but this weekend I just kept feeling sorry for both of them."

"Why?" Neil asked, surprised.

"Well, even you must have noticed that Jen's not happy. She's alone – or in the sort of relationship makes you feel that way, which is probably worse – she's having trouble at work and she doesn't seem to have any friends. The first evening here she drank twice as much as anybody else and it hardly seemed to affect her."

"She's been drinking too much for a few years now," Ian said. "And you're right – she's not happy. But I'm damned if I know what any of us could do about it. Every time I see her we go through the same litany of woes. I sometimes think that having me and a couple of others to do that with is what saves her from actually having to do anything about her life."

"Or saves her from going under," Cath said.

"Maybe," Ian said.

"And you think Becky's in the same state?" Neil asked Cath.

"No, it's not the same."

59

"It's twenty years now, and I still don't understand why she married him," Neil said.

"Well, it was partly your fault," Cath said. "Yours and Ian's."

"What did I do?" Ian wanted to know.

"In those days you both treated her like one of the boys."

"No," Ian objected. "Like a sister maybe, but not like one of the boys."

Cath smiled sadly at him. "You didn't understand her the way you would have understood a sister. It was all mind, all ideas and schemes. And she loved it, still does, but it wasn't what she needed. What she needed was a home for her heart."

"OK, but why Edward?" Neil asked.

"He was available. And he wanted someone to hang on to, preferably someone who needed him just as much, if not more, than he needed her. Being Edward, she had to be decorative too, and Becky was certainly that. She still is."

"The perfect accessory."

"That's a bit cruel, Neil. Edward has his points, you know. Didn't you notice how good he was with Daniel?"

"I noticed how bad he was with his own son."

"Ah, well, Richard's the wrong age. He's a challenge, and Edward doesn't like any sort of questioning."

"You can say that again," Neil murmured. "But you still haven't told us why you think Becky's so unhappy. She seems really excited about this street-theatre stuff."

"And it was pretty plain what Edward thought of it all. He has to believe – or at least pretend he believes – that it's just a whim, or it becomes another challenge. And she has to either keep on repressing her enthusiasm or separate it off from the rest of her life, neither of which she wants to do." Cath paused, wondering whether to tell them both about the real mother's phone call, and was saved from making a decision by the sudden sound of crying coming from upstairs. The phone had pinged about a minute earlier, she remembered. Josey had got some bad news. "I'd better go up and see what's happened," she said.

"I'll be off," Ian said, getting up at the same time. The two of them embraced. "I'll see you soon," he said.

"Bring Tom down for a weekend," she shouted over her shoulder.

"Good idea," Neil agreed.

Ian collected his bag from the TV room and said goodbye to the kids, then the two men walked out to the car.

"How's your work going?" Neil asked.

"The usual. Running to stand still. I've got about three pieces that were due in last week, another three tomorrow. And I seem to spend more time chasing money that I'm owed than actually working."

"Money tight?"

"Pretty tight. But once I give Ellie the money for Tom each month I've only got myself to worry about." He turned to Neil. "Have you decided what you're going to do?" he asked.

"Give it one more week. There's a council meeting coming up, and who knows? – we might get lucky."

"I hope so."

"Hope you get lucky with Susan."

"That won't be luck. That's called charisma."

"Sorry, I forgot." He laughed.

Ian grinned back, and engaged the clutch. "Say

goodbye to Josey for me. I'll call you about the football."

Cath found Josey face down on the bed, her body racked with sobs. She sat down beside her daughter and stroked her hair, saying nothing until the crying began to abate. "What is it, love?" she asked then.

"You know it's Wayne," a muffled voice said.

"It seemed a good bet."

There was a silence, then the words came out in a rush. "He says he never loved me, but I know he did."

Cath carried on stroking, feeling sorry for her daughter, but pleased that Wayne had, no doubt unwittingly, chosen to let them off the hook. He could hardly blame never loving Josey on her parents' unwillingness to let her stay out all night.

Josey rolled over, displaying a tear-stained face.

"Why did you call him?" Cath asked.

"I don't know. I just felt good, and I wanted to hear his voice."

It was hard for Cath to imagine anyone wanting to hear Wayne Newsome's petulant whine, but she managed not to show as much in her face. "What do your friends think of him?" she asked.

Josey made a face. "The same as you. But none of them really know him," she insisted vehemently.

Cath found herself remembering a line from a Shangri-Las record: *"Big bulky sweaters to match his eyes; dirty fingernails – oh boy, what a prize!"* "You're right," she said, "I don't know him. But I do know that he hasn't been very kind to you."

"I know," Josey almost wailed, and started crying again. "I'm sorry," she said between the sobs.

"You've got nothing to be sorry for," Cath said, holding on to her.

"You know why I like Jen?" Josey asked.

"No, why?"

"Because both of us always fall for the wrong men."

As the BMW sped down the M40, Edward gave Jennifer a verbal tour of the exhibition he was organizing, describing each of Raul's various pieces with relish. "There's a sort of tree-like object made of wire – it's actually a replica of the molecular structure of the HIV virus. And there are water-filled condoms hanging from the various branches, and each one contains a goldfish. It's called *Safe Sex*."

Jennifer laughed. "He sounds interesting," she said.

"Come to the opening on Wednesday. I'll put your name on the door."

"Oh, yes, maybe. If I can get away from work in time."

"It doesn't start until six-thirty."

"Right." It would be good to get out somewhere different, she thought. It would be good to go down to the cottage again. That morning she'd woken with a strange feeling of stiffness in her face, and it had taken her some time to realize what had caused it – she'd been laughing so much the day before.

In the back seat Becky was staring out of the window at the Oxfordshire countryside. She had listened to Edward's spiel – he would have made a great travelling salesman, she had thought irreverently – and it had sounded so familiar, so comforting. She had heard him use the same phrases, the same intonations, so many times.

She could tell he was in a good mood – his sense of well-being seemed to fill the car. He hadn't exactly paraded his success in front of the others, but had just let it speak for itself. And now he would parade the weekend before his friends at the gallery – a reunion of his oldest friends, all of whom would become more interesting in his reportage than he'd found them at the time. Ian would be the avant-garde musician, Neil an ecological seer, Cath an avatar of alternative medicine.

Becky felt bitterness welling up inside her, and knew where it was coming from. The others had managed to share her enthusiasm for the theatre group, so why couldn't he?

For the same reason he was so determined not to worry about Richard. Because it suited his sense of who he was.

She looked at the back of his head, the thickening neck beneath the wavy hair. So be it, she told herself. She'd manage without his support. She would deal with Richard's mother herself. She would decide when and what to tell him.

She turned to look at her son. His eyes were closed, and he looked about thirteen again. She remembered what Ian had said and hoped he'd been right.

Neil watched Ian's car disappear down the lane, turned back towards the cottage, and then changed his mind. Cath didn't need him to help with Josey, and the other two could look after themselves for half an hour. He felt like some time alone.

He walked down the path which skirted the cornfield, thinking about the previous forty-eight hours. Cath might be right about Becky – she usually was about other women – but it had still been really good to see her again. Jen too. And after all the gloom of the last couple of months it had been good to see Cath enjoying herself so much. He felt really lucky to have her.

But as for Edward . . . Neil had never liked him, even when they'd all lived together, but over the years, despite – or because of – the almost total lack of contact, he had somehow grown to like him even less. Edward had become a symbol of everything that was wrong with the world, and thinking about him produced the same emotional responses as watching the news, variants on anger and gloom. He seemed to sum up everything that was inimical to Neil: privilege, wealth, indifference to others. The bastard had three homes!

There was a touch of envy in his condemnation, and Neil knew it, but that didn't invalidate the way he felt. This was about conscience. This was about how you lived an honourable life.

He sighed and cast his eyes over the valley below. Life had to be so much easier if you didn't care; if nothing mattered but making money.

Twenty years ago he and Ian had both got better degrees than Edward. They were both brighter, but it didn't matter. Edward had had the charm, the public-school background, the breeding.

And, Neil admitted to himself, Edward had possessed the desire to succeed on the system's terms. That was what had really made the difference. He and Ian had only wanted success on their own terms, and that had been impossible, almost by definition. They had wanted to make a living changing the world, but the people who handed out livings were mostly happy with the world as it was.

He'd have to give up working at the recycling centre,

and at least sign on. If it felt like a major defeat, then that was probably because it was one.

He was forty-one, and sometimes he felt like he'd invested twenty years in a fool's dream.

5

At around five to eleven on Wednesday morning Richard watched his mother emerge from the house and walk off down Abbotsbury Road in the direction of Holland Park Avenue. So far, so good. He'd been afraid that on this particular morning she might change the habit of a lifetime and order a taxi.

The rain had almost stopped, but she had her umbrella up anyway. He set off in pursuit, keeping well behind her and making sure not to stare, having recently read in an SAS novel that a sixth sense often alerted people to the fact that they were being watched. A couple of hundred yards from the main road she crossed to the other pavement, a pretty definite indication that she was heading for the tube station. Breaking into a run, Richard sped off down a detour that would get him there ahead of her.

Once inside, he descended the emergency stairs and walked up to wait just inside one of the cross-passages. A few minutes later his mother emerged on to the eastbound platform, and within seconds they were both boarding a Hainault train, some four coaches apart.

It felt pretty weird following her, but kind of exhilarating too. And there was always the chance that he was being a complete idiot, skiving off school to witness his mother having coffee with one of her new theatre-group friends. But he didn't think so. Nothing specific had been said during the phone call the previous week, but there had been something in her voice which had been completely out of the ordinary, and he could think of only two possible explanations. Either his mother had a secret life of her own, which didn't seem very likely, or it concerned his other mother, his biological mother, his real mother.

As the train approached the West End, he carriage-hopped to within one of hers, and from Marble Arch on he kept a careful watch on her through the end-door windows. She got off at Holborn, and since the exit was nearer his carriage than hers, he had to get off in front of her. The hair on the back of his head seemed to stand up on end, but the platform was crowded, and he was able to manoeuvre himself behind her once more. They rode up the long escalator separated by about ten other passengers, and eventually emerged on to High Holborn. He hung back while she crossed first this road and then Southampton Row, and then started after her again. The trail led north for about a quarter of a mile, and then into Russell Square. His mother headed straight for the cafeteria in the north-east corner, hesitated for an instance and then walked up to where a woman in a beret was sitting with a plastic cup of something.

"Sheila?" Becky asked.

The woman nodded and offered a smile both sad and fleeting. She looked tired, Becky thought. More than tired. This woman was thirty-two or thirty-three, but she looked ten years older. She was wearing some sort of uniform beneath the raincoat.

Sheila noticed the look. "I work in the supermarket

over there," she explained, nodding in the direction of Russell Square tube station. "Aren't you going to get a coffee or anything?"

Becky shook her head. "No."

"Well, thanks for coming." She looked round. "The sun'll be out soon."

Becky followed the other woman's gaze. "I always thought Russell Square was the nicest in London," she found herself saying. She could remember many mornings on which she'd had coffee in this cafeteria before starting a day's research in the British Library near by. Fifteen, sixteen years ago.

"Do you work?" Sheila asked.

"Oh yes. I'm a buyer for a bookshop chain. I recommend which books they should stock," she explained. "And how many, of course."

"A lot of reading."

"Too much sometimes."

"It must be interesting though. And your husband?"

"He's in charge of an art gallery – buying and selling, organizing exhibitions."

The woman managed another of her fleeting sad smiles. "And how's . . .? I don't know his name."

"Richard. He's fine. Still at school. He's doing his GCSEs in a few weeks."

"That's wonderful," she said, and sounded like she meant it.

There was a silence.

"Is that what you wanted to ask me?" Becky said.

Sheila sighed and then looked up. "It's good to know," she said, "but that's not what I wanted to talk about." She paused again, and this time Becky restrained herself from further prompting. "I've got AIDS," Sheila said abruptly, almost defiantly.

"I'm sorry," Becky said. She hadn't expected this.

"You understand? I'm not just HIV-positive – it's AIDS."

"I understand."

Sheila gave a wry smile. "A lot of people don't. Anyway, I've just spent several weeks in hospital with pneumocystis. I feel OK now – more or less, anyway – and I'm working again. But it's not going to go away, and I got the feeling from the doctor that I'm going to be in and out of hospital like a yo-yo for the next couple of years." She looked up at Becky. "Anyway, the other day I saw your husband's picture in the paper, and it seemed like God was trying to tell me something."

So it was money, Becky thought, though what good . . .

"I have a daughter," Sheila said. "She's six years old, and I have to make arrangements for her. Her name's Carmen. She's not HIV-positive."

Richard's sister, Becky thought. A pang seemed to shoot across her chest. "What about her father?" she asked, much more calmly than she felt.

"Long gone. And in any case, he's HIV-positive too. He caught it from a needle and gave it to me. Several years after Carmen was born."

"You're asking us to take her? To adopt her?"

"I'm offering. I can't think of anything better for her. She'd have a real brother – a real half-brother anyway – and a good home. It's either you or hoping she's lucky with foster parents – there's nobody else. The neighbour who looked after her this last time won't have her for good."

Becky listened, her mind trying to absorb the reality of it, what it would mean. For her, for Richard, for Edward. Only a few days ago he'd been basking in the belief that his active parenting days were almost over.

"I'm sorry," Sheila said. "This must be a bit of a shock. I don't expect you to say yes just like that. I'm not really expecting anything. I just thought I owed it to Carmen to tell you what the situation was."

"Of course," Becky agreed. "Look, I'll have to talk to my husband," she said. And to Richard, she thought. Just what the boy needed, to hear that his mother was dying of AIDS. "And then we can meet again."

"And maybe you can meet Carmen."

"I'd love to." And she would, but already she was bracing herself for what she knew Edward would say. But maybe he wouldn't. Maybe he'd surprise her.

"This is my phone number at home," Sheila said, holding out a scrap of paper. "It's a flat in Somers Town – just up the road. I'm always there in the evenings."

Becky put the scrap in the purse.

"I've got to get back," the other woman said, looking at her watch. "Thanks for coming," she said again, offered one last smile and walked away through the tables.

Richard followed her out of the park, down Bernard Street, and into a large concrete apartment and shopping complex. She disappeared into the supermarket at the far end, and five minutes later he saw her taking over one of the checkouts. He found a bag of crisps, stood in her queue, and tried not to stare until it was his turn to pay. Then he briefly examined her face as she changed his pound coin. It couldn't be his mother, he decided. This woman was too old for that.

* * *

Becky walked the four-mile journey home, oblivious to the shoppers thronging Oxford Street and the joggers in Hyde Park, turning over and over in her mind what Sheila had told her. It was half-past three when she reached the house, and Edward had said he would be back to change and collect her around five. She put the kettle on for tea, then changed her mind and poured herself a large gin and tonic.

She was still holding the empty glass, staring out of the kitchen window at the garden, when he came in. "Aren't you dressed yet?" he asked from the doorway, more surprised than worried. "I'm going to take a shower," he added, backing out again.

She couldn't believe he'd forgotten what she was doing that day. "I saw Richard's mother today," she shouted after him.

He came back. "Of course. Christ, my mind's in knots today. What did she want?"

Jettisoning her considered resolve to tell him in easy-to-swallow stages, Becky went straight to the heart of the matter. "She's dying of AIDS and she has a daughter who needs adopting. She's given us first option."

Edward stood there staring at her. "What?" he said at last.

She shrugged.

"And if we don't?"

She looked at him with exasperation. "There was no threat involved. If we don't then she'll look for foster parents."

Edward breathed a sigh of relief. "So you told her no?"

"I didn't tell her anything. I said I had to talk it over with you."

"Well, I don't feel any compunction about refusing. Do you?"

"Yes, I do," she said quietly.

He covered his nose with both hands and sighed loudly. "Why, for Christ's sake? Adopting one of this woman's unwanted children doesn't put us under any obligation to adopt any others she's careless enough to have."

"This one wasn't unwanted. And she's Richard's sister. His half-sister."

"Not in any real sense." He extended his arms, fists clenched. "I mean, if we thought blood was that important we wouldn't think of ourselves as his father and mother, would we?"

"I don't think that's . . ."

"Look," he interrupted, "we can't talk about this now. We're running late already, and you're not even dressed."

"Don't you understand?" she said softly. "This is important."

He looked at her as if she was behaving like an idiot. "Of course it's important, but she doesn't need an answer tonight, does she? So we can talk about it tomorrow." He looked at his watch again. "My doors open in an hour and twenty-one minutes."

"I'm not coming," she said.

"What?"

"I couldn't cope, not this evening. I couldn't . . ." "Deal with all those phonies," she was going to say, but she stopped herself. "It'll be a madhouse," she said. "No one'll notice I'm not there."

"I will. Come on, I don't often ask you to do anything for the gallery."

In the past she wouldn't have been able to resist a plea like that, but this time, for reasons that she knew would take some unravelling, it was different.

"I'm sorry," she said, trying to soften the blow, "but I can't. Not tonight."

"Have it your way," he said mildly, and spun on his heel. She knew he was angry, but she didn't really care how much.

In the Docklands office Jennifer could hear two of her male colleagues enjoying a whispered conversation several cubicles down. She thought she'd caught her own name, but she was probably getting paranoid.

One of the secretaries walked by and gave her an amused look. Even paranoids have enemies, she told herself.

"Jennifer," a voice said in her ear, and she almost jumped out of her skin.

"Sorry", Alan Patterson said, sliding one buttock on to the corner of her desk. He was one of the firm's three working directors and her *de facto* boss. "You worked at home yesterday."

It wasn't really a question. "Yes."

"Well, it would be nice if you'd told someone in advance, and made some arrangement to call in. Dennis was waiting half the morning to check something out with you on the Blake account, and then spent the rest of the day trying to get through to you at home . . ."

"I was logged in. And I told him to page me if anything came up."

"He says he tried that too. There must be something wrong with your pager."

"There isn't."

He exhaled noisily. "Look, just sort it out between you, right? We can't afford to waste time on personal feuds. You're in charge of this one, Jennifer," he said, getting up to go. "Put your emotions on hold and get on with it."

It hadn't been said with unkind intent, but she sat there quietly fuming. Men never got told to put their emotions on hold. Most of them wouldn't know how.

She took a deep breath, got up, and walked down to Dennis Symington's cubicle. He looked up at her, veiled amusement in his eyes.

"Why didn't you page me yesterday?" she asked coldly.

"I tried," he said. "There was no answer."

She knew he was lying, and he knew she knew – the amusement was still there. "How many times did you try?" she asked.

"Just the once. I didn't really think you were there."

"Why the hell not?"

He let the smile out into the open. "You once told me that logging in was the best excuse for a day off that had ever been invented."

There was a laugh from one of the other cubicles.

She looked at his smug face, wishing him nothing but ill. "You bastard," she said softly.

He grinned at her.

She turned on her heel and walked back to her cubicle, conscious of the eyes turned towards her. They all liked Dennis, the office wit with the little-boy smile. And none of them seemed to like her very much these days.

She sat in her cubicle, staring out through the window at the grey skies and dark water, feeling decidedly shaky. Open antagonism always made her feel like this, but missing both breakfast and lunch probably hadn't helped.

It was six-fifteen. She'd been planning to work until at least nine, but she now she wanted out of the building. She'd go to Edward's gallery opening after all.

The address was still in her bag. She'd been there once before, but several years ago, and wouldn't have trusted herself to find it from memory. It was somewhere in the maze of small streets behind Waterloo East, no more than a five-minute walk from the main station. She seemed to remember it was next door to an acupuncture clinic.

The journey by DLR and the Waterloo–City line took less time than she'd expected, and she didn't want to turn up at the exhibition soon after the doors opened, so she walked down to the river. None of the food in the Festival Hall's basement cafeteria looked very appealing, but she picked her way through a salad and drank two glasses of white wine. Soon after seven-thirty, reckoning that the opening should be in full swing, she walked back past the station and soon found the gallery.

From the outside, at least, it seemed full of people, and she felt pleased for Edward. And he'd remembered to leave her name on the door, which was both unexpected and gratifying.

After securing another glass of wine she began circulating, keeping an eye out for Edward and Becky as she examined the various exhibits. The condom tree held pride of place in the foyer, and she was pleased to see that the fishes were small enough to execute turns in their latex bowls.

She found herself giggling at all the exhibits and only slowly began to realize that a good proportion of her fellow-invitees were taking the pieces rather more seriously. A surprising number wore grave expressions on their faces, as if stunned by the profundity displayed before them.

"Jen, you came," Edward said, appearing at her side with a huge smile on his face. "What do you think?"

"They're hilarious," she whispered. "But are they meant to be?"

"They're whatever you want them to be."

"You can say that again," a small man with a moustache said morosely, arriving at Jennifer's other shoulder. Edward introduced him as one of the Sundays' art correspondents. "But at least there's a wit at work somewhere in all of this," the critic admitted. "And nothing's made of tyres."

Edward was exchanging gestures of greeting with a man on the other side of the room. "Look, Jen," he said, "do you want to have a meal afterwards? Or just a drink?"

"When does it end?"

"Nine. Not long now."

"That'd be nice," she said. She was enjoying herself. "Where's Becky?" she asked, but he was gone.

Becky had been sitting in front of the television for over an hour, but if anyone had asked her what she'd been watching she wouldn't have been able to say. The same thoughts kept circling her brain like the lines of an insistent song.

Taking on another child wasn't something to do lightly, and she knew that there was a huge difference between adopting one more or less from birth and inheriting a six-year-old. Particularly a six-year-old with this child's history. She could easily have been damaged emotionally by the circumstances of her upbringing.

But Becky had found herself liking Sheila, and found it hard to believe that Carmen had been deprived of love, the emotional oxygen.

And she was Richard's sister.

But . . .

She knew what Edward would say to that. Richard would be off to some sort of college in a couple of years, and he was hardly home now, so the possibility of a real relationship between him and Carmen was remote.

But, she countered the internal enemy, families didn't expire when the children left home. They changed, certainly, but they didn't close down. And who knew what Richard and Carmen might work out over the next seventy years?

No, the argument was nonsense.

He would then remind her that they'd planned to travel more once their time as actively responsible parents was over, but she didn't really think Edward wanted to go anywhere – he just liked the idea that the job was done. He'd been a father, and now he wanted his freedom back. His childhood back, really.

Was she being fair? Did she want to become a full-time mother again?

But then again, was what she wanted really important?

Becky wasn't in any way religious, but the thought crossed her mind that this was almost like a test of character. She and Edward had been so lucky, and now they were being offered the chance to give something back. To Carmen, to Richard. Even to Sheila.

And she knew what Edward would think of all that. It sounded vaguely hysterical even to her. She needed to talk to someone other than him.

She pulled the phone towards her and called the cottage in Shropshire.

It was Cath that answered. "I was hoping you'd ring," she said brightly. "I've been dying of curiosity."

Her use of the word "dying" reduced Becky to silence for a moment.

"Are you OK?" Cath asked, immediately concerned.

"Yes, I'm all right. But it's been a hell of a day." She told Cath what had transpired at her meeting with Sheila, and Edward's initial reaction to the news.

"It must have been a shock to him," Cath suggested. "And in my experience men don't react very well to shocks. They're a bit like primitive robots – changing direction requires a lot of clanking and hissing."

Becky laughed for the first time since that morning.

"He's got his agenda worked out," Cath went on. "Richard goes to school. Richard goes to college and leaves home. Richard ceases being a problem and becomes someone to have the occasional male conversation with. There's no daughter in the script."

"There is in Somers Town," Becky said, more to herself than Cath.

"Don't push him into a corner," Cath said. "He'll probably come round."

"Maybe," Becky said. She didn't know why, but she had the feeling that this time he would dig his heels in.

They talked for another ten minutes, and by the time she put the receiver down Becky felt more certain that her feelings were not, as Edward had suggested, those of a deranged person.

She stared at the phone for at least a minute before

picking it up again and punching out the number for Richard's school. As the answerer's tone of voice made clear, parents were discouraged from ringing their offspring during the week, but Becky wasn't feeling inclined to justify herself. The school charged enough to put up with a little inconvenience.

She collected her half-finished drink while whoever-it-was went to find Richard.

"Mum?" he asked cautiously several minutes later.

"Hello," she said. "How are things?"

"Fine," he said, but his voice sounded strange. "Why have you rung?"

"Just to see how you are."

"Ah."

He sounded relieved, and she found herself wondering what else he could have expected. Maybe there was a bad report on the way, or something like that. "You haven't got into trouble, have you?" she asked.

"Of course not. I'm fine."

"OK. I just felt like talking to you."

"Yeah," he agreed, and for a moment she thought he knew. But how could he?

"Good night then. I love you."

"Yeah, Mum."

She listened to the click of disconnection, and thought about how one day could transform both the future and the past.

The wine bar seemed full of people that she'd seen at the gallery, and despite the prices the wine was flowing just as freely. Edward had ordered a bottle that even Jennifer found expensive, and was now happily telling the waitress that a taste wasn't necessary, and she should just pour. He was obviously a frequent customer, and Jennifer found herself wondering if he'd slept with this particular girl.

He raised his glass. "Here's to a great evening," he said, his face flushed with the combination of alcohol and success.

She felt pretty far gone herself – she usually managed to strike a better balance between food and booze consumption than she had that evening. But even though she'd hardly eaten anything all day the plate of nachos which had come with the wine looked singularly unappealing.

"Why didn't Becky come?" she heard herself ask, and for a moment Edward's countenance clouded over.

He didn't bother to answer though, but just shrugged as if it was as much a mystery to him as it was to her.

She felt a pang of sympathy for him. "It went really well, didn't it?"

The clouds dispersed. "Oh God, yes," he said, setting off on a rambling journey of self-congratulation. The trustees hadn't wanted a show like this – they distrusted anything post-Hockney – but he had pushed and pushed, and after this evening it seemed certain that the sale commissions and admission fees would make this the most lucrative exhibition the gallery had ever mounted. Next time he discovered an artist like Raul he wouldn't need to plead his case for six months before getting a grudging green light.

Though of course what he really wanted was a gallery of his own.

"To the future," Jennifer murmured, raising her glass.

"And past lovers," he rejoined with a smile.

Neither of them was particularly steady on their feet

as they walked back to the gallery, where Edward's BMW was still parked. He looked at it solemnly. "I'm in no state to drive," he announced. "We can call taxis from my office."

They mounted the stairs with difficulty, giggling as they went.

She knew what was coming before he placed his hands on either side of her head and pulled her towards him. "For old times' sake," he said, before their lips met.

She felt vaguely dizzy as he pulled her towards the leather sofa, and in her mind's eye she saw first herself, and then a succession of other women, lowering themselves in freeze-frame slow-motion on to it. She realized she was laughing, saw the surprise spring into his eyes and then fade once more as his fingers grappled with the buttons of her blouse.

An hour later, as her taxi sped up an empty Farringdon Road, Jennifer gazed bleakly out at the litter-strewn pavements, the chained and shuttered shop fronts. It had been pleasurable in a detached sort of way, like a nice meal or a good walk in the country. She felt physically replete, mentally untouched.

One voice inside her head was upset with her for betraying Becky, but another kept insisting that she'd really betrayed herself.

6

Ian combed his hair back from the receding hairline with a defiant flourish, stepped back from the mirror and sighed. His trousers looked even more crumpled than usual, and he wasn't at all sure they looked right with the purple sweater. Come to that, he wasn't at all sure whether to wear a sweater – it was a warm evening and he didn't want to sit there sweating.

He was already feeling awkward and he hadn't even left the house. He still didn't know where he'd found the nerve to ask her out, and now that he had it seemed odds-on she'd be a disaster, either someone who couldn't move without consulting an astrological chart or a born-again Christian with a mission to convert. Or even a closet fascist. At the very best she'd turn out to be a Man United fan with four children and a husband in prison for attempted murder.

The husband had probably been released that day, and was at this moment shadowing Susan to her evening rendezvous, one hand on the wheel, the other on his knife.

Then again, maybe she was just the woman he was looking for. Anyone looking for a relationship at her age – or his – was going to come with baggage attached.

All he had to do was take a good look at her personal impedimenta and decide whether or not he felt like taking some of the weight. And what could be more straightforward than that?

The only problem was the moment, *the* moment. He could still remembering trying to summon up the nerve to kiss his first date – by the time he'd been ready she was going out with someone else. That sort of thing was supposed to get easier with time, but in Ian's experience the opposite was true. While the fear of rejection seemed just as potent, age and feminism had added an embarrassing sense of absurdity to the whole business.

Take it as it comes, he told himself. Don't get too drunk, but do get drunk enough. Step that fine line like a dancer. Let her talk. Blow her away with your willingness to listen. And don't be late.

He took one last look round the room, imagined it through her eyes, and briefly closed his own.

The traffic on Chorlton Road was bad, and he was almost fifteen minutes late arriving at the Queen's Horse. Susan was sitting at the bar with half a pint of Guinness, reading a paperback. Her hair had been tied back at their first meeting but now it was hanging loose, hiding her face as she read. She was wearing a shortish black skirt, a dark-green blouse, black stockings and low-heeled shoes. She had nice legs, he thought, and the swell of her breasts seemed larger than he remembered.

It's her mind you're interested in, he told himself sternly.

"Sorry I'm late," he said, taking off his raincoat and holding his stomach in.

"That's OK," Susan said with a smile. "I was enjoying my book."

The bar lighting wasn't exactly bright, but she looked no older than she had in the dimly lit jazz club. There didn't seem much doubt that she was wearing a lot better than he was. "What's the book?" he asked, perching himself on the adjacent stool.

"It's a Marcia Muller. Do you know her?"

He didn't.

"She writes private-eye mysteries about a woman private-eye in San Francisco. She's good."

"I'll have to try one," he said. "Do you want another drink?" he asked as the barman appeared in front of them.

"I'm fine."

Ian ordered a half of bitter, which felt decidedly light in his hand. "What would you like to eat?" he asked. "There's a good Chinese round the corner, and good Turkish and Indian about five minutes' walk away."

"Have you tried the new Thai in Montell Street?" she asked.

"Nope." He had only ever eaten Thai once, in London with Jen.

"Neither have I, but a friend told me it was good."

"OK then." He smiled at her. "So now I need your life story. Background, school, first love, first husband, etcetera, etcetera."

She wiped her lip. "Middle-class, Blackburn Comprehensive, Brian, John. First and last husband – we separated about eight years ago. The etceteras are Denise and Andrew, and they've both left home for college. I married young." She took a sip of Guinness and gave him a quizzical look. "And I'm about to be an aunt – my sister's due in three weeks. Your turn."

He grinned. "Aspiring middle-class in Wembley,

London. A comprehensive which couldn't quite believe it was no longer a grammar school. Brenda Tarpley, but her parents banned me from her playhouse for taking my trousers off. And Ellie – also a first and last, but with only one etcetera. Tom lives with his mother in Hebden Bridge. I have him for the day every Saturday, usually more in the school holidays."

"Children of the sixties," Susan murmured.

"And sort of proud of it, despite everything," Ian said wryly. "So shall we leave politics and music till we get to the restaurant?"

She smiled at that, and there was something in her eyes which made him suddenly realize that she was as nervous as he was. As they started off on foot she casually put her arm through his, and he felt a sharp, sudden and completely unexpected pang of emotion. Christ, he thought, it must have been a long time.

The new restaurant wasn't too full, and the waiters were still receiving new customers with gushing gratitude. They ordered a bottle of wine and pored over the menu, finally settling on the easy option of satay chicken with vegetable curry and rice.

"When did you start playing?" she asked, once the wine had arrived and been poured.

"When I was about six. My mother was determined that all of us – I've got a younger brother and sister – should learn to play, mostly because she regretted that she hadn't. I hated it, of course, but it never seemed that hard, and then when it came to forming groups at school it was nice to be in demand. I played in a rock band at university, but I guess I lost interest in rock – as music anyway – when punk came along. And one day someone played me a Thelonious Monk album, and I fell in love with jazz piano. I've been a part-time player ever since."

"You never wanted to do it full time?"

"I don't know if I ever really wanted to – it was never really an option. First off, it's not the sort of life which goes with having a family – you're either earning a living at a gig hundreds of miles away from them or you're sitting round at home with no money, wishing you had a gig like that. Second, you have to be pretty damn special, and I know I'm not. I'm competent and I think I've written a few nice songs, but as a pianist I'm not in the least bit special." He looked up at her. "Took me a long time to realize it, though," he added. "And third, I have this feeling that the moment you turn something you love into your main means of support something gets lost."

She was really easy to talk to, he thought, which probably meant he was talking too much. He was about to ask her what she did when the food arrived, and for the next fifteen minutes they concentrated on eating.

Susan finished first. "So what do you do to earn a living?" she asked.

"Computer journalism. I do newsletters for various firms in the business and freelance stuff for the commercial magazines."

"Interesting?"

"Sometimes. I'm usually too far behind to notice. What do you do?"

"I'm an aerobics instructor."

"Yeah?" he asked, smiling.

"I used to be teacher until about five years ago, but I just couldn't take it any more."

"A PE teacher?"

"No, maths. The aerobics just started out as a means of keeping fit – and keeping in shape as well, since I was back in the cattle market after John and I split up. Anyway, I got interested in the theory, took the course. I'm training as a yoga teacher now."

Ian repressed memories of Ellie doing her morning yoga.

"But I'm not a fitness fanatic," Susan insisted. "Just in case you were worrying."

"There's a definite chance that I'm not as fit as I could be," Ian admitted. "But then computers and pianos aren't exactly fitness-friendly."

"You could lose some weight," she said, eyeing him professionally.

"Why don't we talk about music?" Ian suggested, nudging his almost empty plate away from him.

And they did, swapping favourite records and performances for an hour and more as the restaurant slowly emptied.

On the way back to the Queen's Horse and their cars he asked if she wanted another drink.

"No, I'm tired," she said.

His heart sank. "And we never got round to politics," he said wryly.

"Who needs politics now we have Tony Blair?" she asked, stopping beside a blue Uno. "This is mine," she said, and leant forward to kiss him lightly on the lips. "I enjoyed the evening," she said. "A lot," she added.

"So shall we do it again?"

"I'd like that. How about Wednesday?"

"Wednesday's good."

Their lips touched again; she smiled and turned to the car. He closed the door for her and watched the Uno accelerate up the street, turn right into Deansgate and disappear from sight.

"*Yes*," he said out loud, shaking two fists in front of him like a Cup Final goal-scorer.

* * *

Saturday morning, Neil and Cath were clearing away the breakfast things when the post arrived. There was a begging letter from Greenpeace and final demand bills for the electricity and water.

Neil tossed them on the table and stood staring into space for several moments. "We can't pay them," he said eventually.

Cath walked over and put her hands on his shoulders. "We'll work something out," she said. Even if it meant borrowing from Edward and Becky, she thought, but she didn't say anything. Neil might as well enjoy his day with Daniel before they had that argument.

"We shouldn't be going," he said, as if he'd read her mind.

"I thought Ian had borrowed season tickets."

"Yeah, but it costs money to get there, and we'll be eating out . . ."

"Don't be daft. A few gallons of petrol and a couple of hamburgers isn't going to make any difference."

"I suppose not. Where would I be without you?" he asked with a smile.

"You said we were leaving at twelve o'clock," Daniel said accusingly from the doorway.

"Two minutes," Neil told him. "What are you doing today?" he asked.

"Gardening this afternoon, and I said I'd see Marcie for a drink this evening – Josey said she was staying in. In fact she said she wasn't ever going out again. When will you two be back?"

"Don't know," he said, checking his pockets for keys and cash. "I won't drive straight back after the match – the traffic's always terrible. So we'll probably go over to Ian's for a couple of hours, unless he's got other plans."

"He had a date last night."

Neil looked up. "Who with? And how do you know?"

"He told Jen, and she told me. Her name's Susan."

"Dad!" Daniel pleaded.

"I'm coming." He gave Cath a kiss, and started for the door.

"Enjoy yourselves," she shouted after them.

Which would be some trick, Neil thought to himself as he guided the car towards the main road. He had vague memories of being unable to pay bills in his student days, but it had never happened since, and he was unable to shake off the feeling that somehow this was his fault, that he had failed his family. Cath had never said anything, and he himself didn't really think it, but the feeling lurked regardless in the nether regions of his consciousness.

"Who are you supporting today?" Daniel asked him.

"Who are *you*?"

"Middlesbrough, I suppose. I can't really support City, can I?"

"I don't see why not. They're not going to catch United, are they?"

"If you support Middlesbrough, don't get too carried away. Tom is a real City fan, and this is an important game for them. Imagine how you'd feel if Liverpool played United and he was shouting for them."

"I'd hit him."

"No, you wouldn't. You'd just be upset."

"Maybe," Daniel agreed reluctantly. "But what I

don't understand is why anyone would support City when they could support United."

"Who knows?" Neil agreed, though he rather admired Tom for picking City. There was no family tradition involved – Ian had been a Chelsea supporter in his youth – so it seemed as if the boy just had a natural affinity for the underdog. Which couldn't be bad.

As a boy Neil had supported West Ham, but as he'd grown older he'd lost most of his enthusiasm for the sport, only to have it rekindled by his son's passion. In the seat beside him the boy wasn't showing much, but Neil could feel his excitement. Though they took the short trip to see Shrewsbury about once a month, this was only his fourth or fifth Premier League match.

Soon after two Neil found a parking spot in their usual street, and they walked up to the Maine Road ground, arriving at the specified gate some five minutes early. Ian and Tom turned up only five minutes later, which had to be some sort of record. As usual the boys went through about a minute of mutual shyness before remembering they were the best of friends. A deal was struck whereby Daniel would support City in exchange for Tom's support of United on their next trip to Old Trafford.

They bought drinks and climbed to their seats, which were above and behind one of the goals. The two teams were already on the pitch and it only seemed a few minutes before the game itself was underway. The long-suffering City fans received the first intimation of a possible disaster after about twenty minutes, when Boro's waif-like Brazilian star danced through about four club-footed tackles and laid it on a plate for a team-mate. For the rest of the half Tom watched white-faced, his mouth grimly pursed, as City did their best to concede another. Daniel's face loyally reflected his partner's gloom.

Half-time hamburgers did something to cheer them up, and the dark clouds dispersed in a moment when Tom's hero, the little Georgian Kinkladze, equalized with a wonderfully deft flick. City forged forward after that, creating chances for both themselves and their opponents in the process, but it seemed as if both victory and defeat had eluded them until the final minute, when a berserk scramble in the Boro goal-mouth ended with the ball and about four men in the back of the net.

Tom and Daniel went into ecstatic overdrive, and after the final whistle, as they sat waiting for the crowd to thin, Ian and Neil found it hard to remember ever seeing two happier faces.

On the way to the cars they debated supper. The boys voted for McDonald's, but were overruled in the names of their absent mothers. "Let's get a Chinese take-away." Ian suggested. "It's on me," he added quickly, seeing Neil's hesitation.

"No way," Neil protested.

"Look, I just got paid for a job. And next time I'm broke I'll have no compunction about letting you buy me a meal."

"OK," Neil agreed reluctantly.

They drove in convoy to Ian's house in Chorlton, and while Tom showed Daniel his latest computer game Neil and Ian walked slowly round to the Chinese take-out.

"You've been in a good mood today," Neil observed. "Does this mean last night went well?"

Ian stopped in his tracks. "How did you know about last night?"

"Didn't you know we have you under round-the-clock surveillance?"

"Then you should know how it went."

"Jen told Cath," Neil explained. "She was happy for you."

Ian shook his head and smiled. "It went well, I think. No, I'm sure it did. Pretty sure."

"Did you . . .?"

"I never do on the first date."

"I'm glad to hear it. I wouldn't want one of my friends getting a reputation for being easy."

"Or loose."

"Or, God forbid, promiscuous."

"Chance would be a fine thing," Ian said drily. They had reached the Chinese take-out. "So what does Daniel like?" he asked.

"Anything with lots of meat and not much in the way of vegetables."

"So, chicken dishes," Ian decided. "I think we'd better stay clear of the beef – I doubt if the Happy Dragon gets its supplies from the far reaches of the earth."

An hour or so later, with all of them feeling suitably replete, Neil reckoned it was time to head home.

"Can't we just watch the lottery programme, Dad?" Daniel asked. "We've got a ticket, remember?"

Ian and Tom also looked at Neil expectantly.

"OK," he agreed, bowing to the will of the majority.

"The jackpot's eighteen million this week," Tom said.

"That should just about cover our water bill," Neil said sourly.

"What are our numbers?" Daniel asked him.

"I can't remember. Not all of them anyway."

"If we watch it with them," Ian suggested, "we'll recognize each of our numbers as they come up."

Neil laughed. "Right."

They arranged themselves in front of Ian's small TV. There was a shot of a spot-lit machine glowing behind a perforated screen. "It looks like a spin-drier," Ian said.

"From the fifties," Neil added.

"That's Lancelot," Daniel told them. "There's three machines – Lancelot, Arthur and Guinevere – and a different one gets picked each week."

"That's what I call a blow for family values," Ian observed. "Naming the nation's arbiters of destiny after the most famous love triangle in our history. And speaking of the fifties . . ."

A man in a blue blazer and white gloves had emerged, index finger extended.

"Love the gloves," Neil murmured, as the finger pushed home and the balls in the spin-drier started agitating.

"It looks more like a washing-machine now," Ian said.

The first ball was coughed up. It was 15.

"Hey, we got one," Neil said. "Cathy chose that for our wedding anniversary."

"You old softies," Ian joked, just as the next ball emerged – 17. "That's mine," he said, surprised.

"Mum got two once," Tom told him, "but she didn't win anything."

"Your mum bought a lottery ticket?" Ian asked, amazed.

"She buys one every week."

The next ball out was 44, and the two boys turned questioning faces to their fathers.

"No idea," Ian said. "I wasn't really paying attention when we picked them."

"It looks familiar," Neil murmured. "I think Edward picked one of the forties. Something to do with the number of exhibits in his wretched exhibition."

Then 20 emerged.

"I remember that," Ian said, his voice rising for the first time. "Becky picked it for our twentieth-anniversary reunion."

"You've got three out of four," Tom said, amazed.

They were watching the balls now with bated breath.

He wasn't imagining the fifth number – it was his own, 36.

And then everything went quiet for a moment as the sixth ball dropped down. It was 8. There was another silence and the bonus ball emerged. Number 22.

And there they all were: the winning numbers were now in a line at the bottom of the screen, and again Neil had the distinct feeling he'd seen that combination somewhere before. He and Ian looked at each other and laughed.

It was a nervous sort of laugh.

"So how many are you certain of?" Tom asked impatiently. He was scribbling them down on a piece of paper.

"Let's see: 15 was Cath's, 17 was Ian's, 20 was Becky's, 36 was mine," Neil said. "And I'd swear Edward's was 44."

"And Jen had a low number," Ian said. "She said it was her lucky number. I thought it was 8, but perhaps my imagination's playing tricks on me. Maybe it was 6 . . ."

"Where's the ticket, Dad?" Daniel asked. He looked almost frightened by what was happening.

"God knows." Neil brought his palms together over his nose and tried to remember. "Last time I saw it, it was on one of the speakers," he decided.

"Call home," Ian suggested, handing him the phone.

Neil punched out the numbers, but it was engaged. "Josey'll probably be talking to her friends all evening," he said.

"I'll try Jen," Ian said, but her number was engaged too. Edward and Becky's phone rang, but only for the answer-machine. "Christ, this is frustrating," he said, half angry, half amused. "I tell you, if we win it's nothing but the softest toilet paper from now on. And we'll buy City; he told Tom, "and put you straight in the team. Another year and you'll be tall as Nigel Clough . . ."

"Josey!" Neil exclaimed, as he finally got through. "We need to know what the numbers are on our lottery ticket. Can you go and get it – it's on one of the speakers."

She was gone about fifteen seconds. "It's not," she said flatly.

Neil felt a cold sweat break out on his forehead. He still couldn't believe they'd won, but the mere thought that they might have lost a winning ticket was too terrifying to contemplate. "Can you go and have a good look?" he asked, much more calmly than he felt.

"Dad!" she whined. "I'm in the middle of watching something."

"Just do it, please."

"I suppose we've won millions," she muttered sarcastically, and put the phone down again.

The next minute was undoubtedly the longest Neil had ever experienced. He could hear their TV playing in the background, Angie's voice and then Josey's, and finally there were footsteps.

"I've got it," she said, not exactly fighting to keep the boredom out of her voice. "It was down the back."

"Read the numbers," Neil said.

She did so.

"Read them again," Neil said.

She did.

Neil took a deep breath. "We got them all," he said simply, both to her and to the others.

The stunned silence was broken by Josey. "How much did we win?" Josey asked, as excited now as she'd been bored before.

"I don't know. Don't get too excited," he said, as much to himself as to her. "You know what it's like when there are eighteen score-draws – the winners only get about 25p each. We've don't know how many others got the same numbers."

"You have to call them up," she told him. "The lottery people."

"Right, I'll do that."

"Call back when you find out," she implored.

"OK. You look after the ticket." Neil put down the phone. "Josey says we should phone the lottery people, whoever they are."

"Camelot," Tom said. "That's why they have Lancelot and Arthur and all that."

"Makes sense," Neil agreed, but the organization wasn't listed in Ian's out-of-date directory.

"Ring Directory Enquiries," Ian said.

"That costs money these days," Neil objected.

Ian looked at him. "If we've won I'll probably be able to pay for the call," he said mildly.

Neil laughed. "This is ridiculous," he said, and it both was and wasn't. While his head carried on telling him that this sort of thing always happened to other people, the hairs on his forearm seemed to be standing up on end. And as he picked up the phone the thought flashed through his brain that things would never be the same again.

He got the number from Directory Enquiries, and a minute later was talking to the lottery company. He was asked for his name and address and where he'd bought the ticket, and told to ring again in forty minutes, at nine-thirty, when they'd have an unconfirmed number of winners. This would be confirmed at nine the next morning. "Congratulations," the man said, as if he'd said it a hundred times before, and hung up.

The forty minutes ticked slowly by. They thought about trying to reach the others again, but decided to wait until they had something definite to say.

"Even if eighteen thousand people got the same numbers we'd still get a thousand pounds," Daniel said hopefully.

"It's usually more like ten people," Tom said. "Or even less."

Ian and Neil looked at each other. "Whose idea was it to buy this ticket?" Ian asked.

"Jen's, I think. I'm not sure."

Ian went to the fridge for more beers and Cokes. "If I had anything to be extravagant with, then I would be," he said. "But Sainsbury's were right out of my usual champagne and truffles this week. So if you feel like some conspicuous consumption," he told Neil, "just leave a quarter of an inch in the bottom of the bottle."

Nine-thirty finally arrived, and the same man

answered Neil's call. "Well, Mr Thompson," he said, "we can't confirm it until tomorrow but it looks very much as if you are the only winner."

Neil swallowed. "There's six of us. In a syndicate. So, if we are the only winners, how much will we have won?"

"The jackpot was eighteen million. So three million pounds each, I should say. But we'll know for certain tomorrow morning." He sounded as if giving away such sums was a way of life. Which presumably it was.

"So tomorrow morning . . ."

"Call us any time after nine. Someone will take your details and one of our advisers will ring you back to arrange payment."

"We really have won," Neil thought out loud. For a moment he felt subdued by the fact.

"Yes, you have."

Neil put down the phone and repeated what the man had told him. Both Daniel and Tom leapt into the air, punching fists.

"This is going to take some getting used to," Ian said, a huge smile on his face.

"You're not kidding," Neil said, sitting down.

They both sat there, shaking their heads in wonderment.

"I suppose I'd better get back," Neil said, but he didn't move. "I'd better ring Josey first. Have you got to get Tom back to Hebden?"

"No, he's staying over. Ellie and Josh wanted to go out." And how would Ellie react to this? Ian wondered.

Tom's mind was obviously running on the same lines. "Can I ring up Mum and tell her?" he asked.

"She won't be there," Ian said, "and no, I don't

want you leaving a message. I want to be sure of everything before I tell her, OK?"

"But even if it's only two million – or only one – you'll still be a millionaire."

"Yeah, right, but we'll wait anyway," Ian said. Tom's answer had occasioned the same realization in his father that Neil had experienced an hour earlier – that this changed everything. The thought was as frightening as it was liberating, and for a few moments he felt himself almost resenting the fortune which was going to turn his whole life upside down.

On the other side of the room Neil was telling Josey that they'd won a lot of money, but that they wouldn't know how much until the next morning.

It was only a few minutes past eleven when Edward and Becky said goodbye to their dinner-party hosts, and Becky's smile disappeared the moment the door of the Pimlico house closed behind them. She was still furious with Edward from their argument that morning.

"Can you believe that Roy actually spent real money on that fake porcelain?" he chortled as Becky, the designated driver, turned on the BMW's ignition.

"I could believe anything of that moron," she said coldly, pulling the car out into the late-night traffic.

"You're still in ice-bucket mode, are you?" he said wearily. "Just wake me when when we get home, will you?"

Becky drove on, wishing his was an ejector seat. The promised conversation about Carmen, which since Wednesday had been put off more times than a royal divorce, had finally taken place after breakfast that day, and proved about as useful as a Trident submarine. Edward had not been interested in a discussion, only in drawing lines in the sand.

"We're forty-one," he'd started off, "and if we took on a six-year-old now we'd be well into our fifties before we had our lives to ourselves again. I won't do it. I won't offer up another ten years of my life to parenthood just because that woman can't learn the basics of contraception."

There were so many things wrong with this statement that Becky hadn't really known where to begin. "What if I want to?" she'd asked.

"Then you'll raise her alone," had been his answer. There'd been bluster in his voice, and more than a hint of bluster's usual companion – fear. She'd wondered if he even knew whether or not he was bluffing, and wondered whether she cared.

"What about Richard?" she'd asked.

"That phrase is getting worn out," he'd retorted angrily. "Richard is a sixteen-year-old boy. What does he want with a six-year-old sister?"

That must have sounded ludicrous even to him, because he quickly sought to cover his tracks. "I'm not saying they shouldn't get to know each other, but there's no reason why we can't fix that up with her new foster parents."

"And what if they're in Newcastle? Or Cornwall?"

He'd shrugged. "Look, you never came to me and said you wanted to adopt another child. And you've been making more of a life for yourself since Richard got older – your theatre stuff, all that. And now, just because someone's offered you a child on a plate . . ."

"This isn't just any child."

"I know that. It's the second one she's decided is surplus to requirements. That we know about. How many other brothers and sisters do you think Richard has out there?"

"She's dying, Edward."

"I know, and I'm sorry, but it's not my problem."

And that was where the argument had ended. His whole attitude had appalled Becky then, and it still appalled her now.

She turned the car into their street and cruised slowly up towards their house. It was mostly in darkness. Richard had rung the previous day to tell them that he had decided not to come home that weekend, because it would be easier to revise for his GCSEs at school. Ordinarily, Becky would have been pleased by such a sign of diligence, but she had also detected a hint of evasiveness in his voice, which worried her. She'd probably just imagined it, she told herself as she worked the garage-door remote. It was her own guilt speaking – she knew she was keeping secrets from him, and so she assumed he must be keeping secrets from her.

They let themselves into the silent house, and found the light on their answer-machine blinking. Of the four messages, two were blank and one was from their evening's hosts, checking that they'd already set out. The fourth was from Neil, and he wanted them to ring Ian's number in Manchester, regardless of what time they got in.

Becky picked out the number.

"He probably wants to borrow some money," Edward said dismissively, sinking heavily into one of the sofas.

He was probably right, Becky realized, but the phone was already ringing and it was too late to make the call from another room.

Ian picked up.

"It's Becky," she said. "Neil left a message."

"Are you sitting down?" Ian asked.

"No, why? Has there been an accident?"

"No, no, nothing like that. We've just won the lottery, that's all."

"What?"

"Remember the ticket we bought. We got six numbers. That's the jackpot."

"You're joking," she said, but she knew he wasn't. "The people who organize the thing think we're the only winners, but we won't find out for certain until tomorrow morning. At the moment it looks like we'll be sharing eighteen million."

She just stood there. "Tell this to Edward," she said at last, carrying the phone over to him.

He listened, and she watched the smile suffuse her husband's face as the reality of it sunk in. "Is there no way we can find out now?" he asked, presumably referring to the amount they had won. Apparently there wasn't.

Several conflicting emotions were already jostling in her head. It was thrilling, unbelievable, but from that very first moment she had the sense that for her it was also almost irrelevant. She and Edward already had more money than they needed, and the problems they were having with each other would not be solved by more. Becky herself was just feeling her way back into a world beyond work and family. Would this help her in that? It seemed more likely to hinder her, to cut her off again.

She told herself she was being stupid. Money always provided opportunities. It was just up to her, up to them, to use them wisely. Get a grip, she told herself. Who ever complained about having too much money?

Ian put down the phone and, more in hope than expectation, tried Jennifer's number again. This time she answered.

"Oh, hi," she said, in a tone that suggested disappointment.

"We've been trying to get you all evening", Ian told her.

"We?"

"Neil and I."

"I had the phone off the hook." She sighed loudly. "I only just ..." The sentence trailed away into nothing.

She was drunk, Ian realized. "Have you been drowning your sorrows?" he asked.

She half laughed. "Something like that."

"Well, I've got some news for you ..."

"I thought you sounded happy," she said, almost accusingly.

Ian paused, wondering whether it would be better to ring back in the morning. He'd have to anyway, knowing from past experience that there was every chance of her not remembering a word of the conversation. Or even the fact that it had taken place.

"How did your date go?" Jen asked.

"Great," Ian said automatically, thinking that the evening with Susan seemed a thousand years ago. "Remember the lottery ticket you persuaded us to buy?" he asked.

"Yeah, I lost again," she said.

"No, the one we bought together."

"Ah," she said noncommittally.

"It won."

There was a gulping sound, followed by a fit of coughing. Whatever she was drinking had apparently slipped down the wrong way. "What?" she eventually croaked.

"We won. We don't know how much yet, but it looks like a lot." The understatement of the century, he told himself.

"We won?" she repeated disbelievingly. "The jackpot?"

"Yep. I've already thrown away every sock with a hole in it."

"You means millions?"

"Looks like it."

She started laughing, and couldn't stop. There was more than an edge of hysteria in her voice, and Ian started worrying. "Jen," he murmured, trying to get her back, and then: "Jen!", aiming at the aural equivalent of a slap in the face.

"It's OK," she finally managed to say. "Sorry, Ian, but it's just too silly."

Neil and Daniel got home just after midnight. Despite his excitement, Daniel had managed to sleep through most of the two-hour journey, and Neil's mind had been left to spin in a vacuum. He had tried, with limited success, not to think about the win and its consequences. He wanted to start exploring the possibilities with Cath, and for some reason it seemed important not to get out too far ahead of her.

Every light was blazing in the cottage – so much for the bloody electricity bill, Neil thought – and, not surprisingly, everyone was still up. Neil walked into the kitchen feeling like a conquistador arriving home with the news that he'd found El Dorado.

"I rang Ian," Cath told him. "And I can't believe it."

He looked at her, a huge smile on his face. "Maybe it's just a dream," he said.

"Then we're all having it together."

He suddenly remembered. "Where's the ticket?"

"On the table," Cath said. "With the thing we all signed."

Neil picked up the ticket and stared at it.

"If it is eighteen million," Josey said, "then we'll get six. "I'll be an heiress," she added, her eyes shining.

Neil and Cath both burst out laughing.

"Well, I will."

"So will I," Angie said.

Neil sat down and looked at his watch. "In nine hours and fifteen minutes we'll find out how much."

Cath was putting on the kettle. "I've been thinking about that," she said. "I suppose it's natural to want it all, but it feels a bit strange, hoping no one else has been as lucky as us."

"I suppose we could make do with just a million," Neil agreed, smiling.

"I want my own computer," Daniel suddenly decided.

"I want my own room," Josey demanded.

"So do I," Angie put in.

"Then we'll have to buy somewhere bigger," Josey decided.

7

At exactly nine o'clock on the Sunday morning Neil dialled the increasingly familiar number of the lottery organizers. Cath and the three children were all gathered round the breakfast table in their dressing-gowns.

The details were taken down once more, and, as promised, a Camelot adviser rang back within a couple of minutes. "I'm happy to tell you that you hold the only winning ticket," Mr Thompson, the man told Neil, who gave the rest of the family a thumbs up.

Daniel started dancing around, arms aloft.

"I understand you represent a syndicate?" the man went on.

"Six of us. We're old friends." He explained about the agreement they'd had witnessed in the hotel restaurant.

"It sounds in order," the adviser told him, "though of course we'll have to scrutinize it. If you could fax us copies of that and your ticket this morning?"

"Yes, I suppose so," Neil said. The couple in the end cottage had just bought a fax machine.

"Well, provided everything is on order, there's no reason you shouldn't get your cheque – your cheques,

I should say – tomorrow. Now, where would you like the presentation to take place?"

"Birmingham?" Neil suggested. They could all get there without too much trouble.

"Fine, there's a hotel in the centre we've used before – the Minerva. Do you know it?"

"No, but I don't suppose we'll have any trouble finding it." It all sounded so matter-of-fact to Neil, who felt like shouting out: "Don't you realize? We've won millions!"

"Good," the man said. "Some of our advisers will be on hand to answer any questions you might have. About the tax implications of your win – things like that. And there's one last thing we need to know, and that's how you feel about publicity. We won't release your names unless you authorize us to do so, although of course we can't give you any cast-iron guarantee of anonymity. The press are very persistent and pretty much a law unto themselves when it comes to this sort of thing. Alternatively, we can arrange for them to be there, and even keep them in some sort of order for you, if that's what you'd prefer."

Neil instinctively recoiled from the idea of publicity, but he decided that he should talk to the others first. "Can I call you back on that one?" he said. "I'll have to ask the other members of the syndicate."

"Of course." The man gave his name and an extension number.

"They want to know whether we want publicity," Neil told Cath.

"We have a choice? That man who tried to keep his win quiet was outed by the *Sun*."

"He *was* the first winner," Neil argued. "It won't be like that any more. After all, there's a new winner each week. Why should they go to the trouble of digging us up?"

"So why are there so many stories about winners in the papers? I can't believe anyone would actually want that sort of publicity."

Neil shrugged. "Maybe they're too stupid to say no. Maybe they're in shock. Maybe they want to see their pictures in the papers."

"Well, I don't."

"Right. Now I'd better ring the others. Tell them what they've won, and make sure none of them are hungry for fame."

First he rang Ian, who took the news that they had indeed won eighteen million pounds with what seemed breathtaking sang-froid. "I must still be in shock," he decided. He was dubious about the possibility of their keeping the win under wraps. "Have you told your parents yet?" he asked Neil.

"No. I suppose I'll ring them this morning."

"Well, by the time we've all told our parents and families and friends, and our children have told their friends, and everyone we've told has told all their friends that they know someone who won the lottery . . . well, you work it out. But, having said all that, I don't suppose there's any good reason to accelerate the process."

Neil rang the house in Holland Park next. Edward answered, and managed to surprise Neil twice. For someone who was already a rich man, his happiness at the size of their win seemed close to delirium. And when Neil raised the question of publicity, Edward thought he was joking. Who in their right mind would deliberately let themselves in for a mountain of begging letters? Neil, who had vaguely expected Edward to want the publicity – for the gallery if nothing else

– was suitably nonplussed. Becky, according to her husband, shared his opinion in the matter.

Neil put the phone down less sure of his own feelings. If Edward was strongly in favour of something, there was usually something wrong with it. And now he thought about it, there did seem to be something almost dishonest about accepting such a sum of money in secret, as if they were ashamed to have won it, or frightened that others would ask for a share.

He tried explaining this to Cath, who just smiled at him.

Ian rang back. "It's OK with Jen," he said. "I had to tell her everything again," he added. "Her memory of our conversation last night was somewhat vague."

Neil told Ian about his misgivings.

"Maybe you're right," was Ian's answer. "But I think we could all do with some time to let this sink in. There'll be nothing to stop us giving it all away in a blaze of publicity a month from now."

"I guess . . ."

"Assuming there's any left," Ian added.

Once Edward had finished explaining the facts of life to Neil, Becky had picked up the phone and called Jennifer.

"Oh, hi," Jen said.

There was an awkwardness in her voice, but then lately everybody Becky talked to sounded as if they were hiding something, and they couldn't all be nursing guilty secrets. "Can you believe it?" she asked.

Jen laughed. "No, not really. I've been buying tickets every week since it started, but I never expected . . . I mean, I didn't even really *want* to win a huge sum of money." She laughed again. "That sounds crazy, doesn't it?"

"No. Look, why don't you come over and have lunch with us? We should be together on a day like this."

"We'll all be together tomorrow, won't we?"

There was the evasiveness again. "Are you OK?" Becky asked.

"Fine. Hung-over, but fine. I've got to ring my mother and . . . I've got lots of things to do."

"OK. We'll see you tomorrow, then." She felt like suggesting they meet at Euston, but had the distinct feeling Jennifer would say no to that as well. She put down the phone and stood there, listening to Edward's bath running upstairs.

She should tell Richard, she thought, and called the school.

He didn't sound as excited by the news as she'd expected, although perhaps he was taking his cue from her. He sounded more intrigued than anything else, as if life had just given him a new puzzle to work on. "There shouldn't be any publicity," she told him. "But we can't be certain."

She could almost hear his shrug of unconcern. "I've got to get back to work," he said.

"OK."

"I bet Dad's pleased," Richard said.

"Over the moon," Becky told him.

Richard made a noise that seemed half scorn, half affection.

"I'll call you again tonight," she said.

"OK," he agreed, and hung up.

She could hear Edward singing in the bath – it was Abba's "Money, Money, Money" – and suddenly her mind was filled with thoughts of Carmen and Sheila.

Tomorrow she would talk to Cath about it all, while they were collecting their cheques for three million pounds.

Money should have nothing to do with emotional independence, she told herself, but it did. It had only been ten hours since they'd received the news of their win, but already she felt stronger in herself, more determined to follow her own instincts.

In the bathroom upstairs her happy husband was trilling: "*Money, money, money, nothing's funny, in a rich man's world . . .*"

Ian drove Tom home by the scenic route, partly because its greater length would give him more time to decide on what he was going to tell Ellie. The Renault seemed to find the climb through the Pennines harder going than usual, and this provided Ian with a few moments of anxiety until he remembered that tomorrow he could go out and buy a new Rolls.

At one time he and Ellie had driven this road quite often, and had often fantasized about owning one of the beautiful old houses which leaned imperiously over the twisting mountain road. Now he could buy any one of them. The thought gave rise to a deep sense of loss, which he knew had as much to do with age as it did with Ellie.

What was he going to tell her? I just thought you should know — I've just won three million pounds?

Obviously he wanted Tom to share the win with him, but how? He could turn their Saturdays together into shopping extravaganzas, and send the boy home each week with a busload of gifts, but that would hardly be fair to Ellie and Josh. Or good for Tom, come to that. So should he give Ellie money regularly, so that she, Josh and Tom could all enjoy a better standing of living? If he was Josh, he wouldn't think much of an arrangement like that.

So what could he do? What was the ruling on ex-wives and mothers of your children? There should be a handbook for lottery winners, he thought. There wouldn't be much of a market, but they could charge a fortune for each copy.

Come to that, what should he do about his own family? Since his father had retired, Ian's parents had lived in Buckinghamshire. They weren't rich, but they didn't have any money worries either. Maybe he'd send them on a cruise. His mum would probably like that.

His sister Cilla lived in Florida with her American husband and their two kids; his brother Dominic in London with his wife and their only son. Both families were better off than he'd ever been before this, but presumably they would expect something. The problem was what. A million each seemed a lot, a £10 WH Smith token rather too niggardly – so something between the two. Fifty thousand each seemed like a nice sum, but would they expect a hundred?

He didn't even like his American brother-in-law, so why should he give him anything? The bastard would only spend it on joining a golf club which didn't accept blacks or Jews.

He sighed and glanced sideways at Tom, who was being unusually quiet. "What are you thinking about?" he asked.

"About the money. It's a lot, isn't it? I mean, really a lot."

"Yes, it is. And before you ask, no, I don't know what I'm going to do with it."

"I wasn't going to ask that."

"Ah."

The boy stared out of the window.

"So what else were you thinking?" Ian prompted.

"You'll stay in Manchester, won't you?"

So that was it. "Why, are you expecting me to move to the South of France?"

"Well, you might. Manchester's not the nicest place in the world. You're always complaining about the rain."

"True. But I'm not going anywhere, not until you're grown up anyway."

Tom gave him a doubtful smile.

"That's a promise," Ian told him.

"You can go on holidays," Tom said.

"And you can come on some of them. Where would you like to go?"

"Mount Everest."

"Hmm. I'll wait for you at the bottom."

They were coming into Hebden Bridge now, and Ian suddenly knew that he wasn't ready to say anything definitive to Ellie. She was working in the front garden when they arrived, wearing jeans and a sweater, her blonde hair tied back with a black ribbon.

"Dad's got something to tell you," Tom told her straight away.

"Hi, Ian," she said. "So what's happening?"

"I've come into money," he told her. "A lot of money. At the reunion last week we bought a lottery ticket between us. And we won. Last night."

She looked at him disbelievingly. "This is a wind-up, right?"

He shook his head. "I know, it's ridiculous. But it's true."

"It is, Mum," Tom assured her. "They won eighteen million pounds."

"Oh my God. You won the jackpot."

"Us and only us. Look, Ellie, it's a lot to take in. I need time to think about it."

"Of course . . ."

"I don't want . . ." he began.

"I know," she said, smiling. "I'm really happy for you," she added.

"Thanks," Ian said. For some reason tears were gathering in his eyes. "I'll give you a call in a couple of days." He gave Tom a hug and walked back to the car.

Jennifer was having rather more trouble conveying the same news.

"You've won a lot of money?" her mother asked for the second time.

Since Maureen Hendrie didn't usually have any trouble understanding simple concepts, Jennifer decided there must be some tangential thought process at work.

"Yes, a lot," she said, hoping her mother wouldn't ask how much.

"Enough to give up work and come back home?"

So that was it. "If I wanted to give up work, I could," Jennifer said patiently, "but I like my work."

"It'll be different if you've won a lot of money," her mother said confidently. "You remember that man at your father's work – his name was Brian Docherty, I think. He won the pools and he was determined to keep working, but in the end he had to leave. He told your father it just wasn't the same if you didn't have to do it. He even stopped drinking for a while because that changed too – it didn't taste the same if you hadn't had to work for it."

Jennifer listened, feeling the usual mixture of guilt and exasperation.

"So when are you coming up?" her mother asked. "You should bring something for your Aunt Evie and Lynn. I don't need anything, but you should bring them something."

"I will, but I don't know when. Not yet."

"Next weekend would be a good time."

"I'll try. I'll ring you when I know, OK?"

"All right," her mother said, in a tone that suggested the opposite.

"Take care then," Jennifer said, and put down the phone before her mother could say anything else.

She reached for the bottle. Brian Docherty might have stopped drinking, but she had no such intention.

The Minerva was a modern hotel in Birmingham's city centre, no more than five minutes' walk from New Street station. Edward, Becky and Jennifer, who had met on the train, waited in the lobby for the others, listening to the fountain recycling water in its twenty square yards of jungle.

For once Ian wasn't the last to arrive; he had also come by train, sparing himself Neil's twenty-minute search for a parking space. Neil and Cath had come with all three children, reckoning that this was one experience they wouldn't get a second chance at.

Announcing themselves at reception, they were shown through to one of the conference suites, where about a dozen Camelot advisers, six cheques and a magnum of champagne were waiting for them. Someone was sent out for something the kids could drink, and returned several minutes later, conspicuously out of breath, with a two-litre bottle of Pepsi.

The cheques were duly handed over, the champagne uncorked, and the smiles of everyone concerned lit up the large room. Several of the advisers turned out to be bank managers. The six winners accepted all the cards that were offered them, but refused to make any spur-of-the-moment commitments. The lottery organizers also offered them a free night in the hotel, which everyone politely declined. There was no sign of the press.

And suddenly it was over. On the pavement outside Cath asked a passer-by to take a group photograph with her camera, and the morning of their elevation to millionaire status was recorded for posterity. It was almost noon, and the pubs were open, but with the children in tow they settled for two opposing benches in a convenient park. They sat and grinned at each other, not really knowing what to say.

"So who's got plans?" Ian asked eventually. "Who's giving up work?"

No one seemed to be. "I was only leaving because no one would pay me," Neil said. "Now I can pay myself."

"You can even give yourself a rise," Ian suggested. He looked round at the others. "This must be the lull before the luxury," he said, but he felt as flat as everyone else looked. Maybe thirty-six hours was the body's limit when it came to pumping adrenalin.

Some two hundred yards away, on the other side of the small park, Brian Scanlon sat down on a convenient bench. He had taken about a dozen photographs with the pocket zoom camera he carried for such eventualities, and was pretty sure that several of the pictures would prove adequate to the task he had just devised for them.

Scanlon worked for one of the leading tabloids, and he had come up to Birmingham on the same train as Edward, Becky and Jennifer. This had not been accidental, but neither had it had anything to do with the group's lottery win. He had been following Edward Lockwood on quite another mission, as part of an exposé he was putting together on the arts world. Stumbling over one of Camelot's private ceremonies had been something of a bonus, to say the least.

For some time now the tabloid editors had been looking for new angles when it came to lottery stories, and this looked to Scanlon like a real possibility. Here were Saturday's mystery winners – winners, moreover, who were already well off by most people's standards – busy concealing their good fortune from the public gaze. People who might well be tied in to sleazy goings-on in the poncy arts world. Guilty people. Undeserving winners.

Looking across the park at the group, Scanlon felt the familiar mixture of anger and contempt. He hated people like this – the privileged middle class, who sent their children to private schools and lived in their half-million-pound houses in Holland Park, who made their fortunes by obscuring the difference between crap and genuine art, and selling the corrupted product as an ideal investment. Admittedly he didn't know much about the other four – not yet anyway – but he was willing to bet that most of them would turn out to be bogus in one way or another.

They were all getting up now, preparing to leave, hugging each other like there was no tomorrow. Scanlon walked slowly across the park, passing through the gate some thirty yards behind the group, and carried on down the hill after them. After a couple of minutes they all stopped beside a rather battered-looking Ford Escort, and after more hugging one couple and all three of the children climbed in. Scanlon memorized the registration number, turned round, and wrote it in his notebook.

The car sped away in a cloud of exhaust, and the other four continued on down the hill towards New Street station. Guessing that the three who had come up from London would be returning there, he got as close as he could to the balding male, and managed to overhear him asking what platform the Manchester train was leaving from. There was always the chance that he was planning to leave the train before he reached Manchester, but Scanlon doubted it. Finding a phone, he called the Manchester office, described the man and his clothes, and asked for him to be tailed to wherever he was going, which would hopefully be his home. Then he got aboard the London train, made sure he was further forward than the other three, and settled down to enjoy the journey. Since he already knew where the Lockwoods lived he would follow the chestnut-haired woman home from Euston.

As the train swished its air-conditioned way through the bleak industrial landscape of the Black Country, Ian thought about what he had noticed that morning. Ludicrous as it seemed, there was obviously something going on between Jen and Edward. And, equally bizarrely, Becky seemed utterly unaware of it.

There had been no clandestine looks, and certainly no clandestine touches, but Ian had no doubts about it. Looking back, he could remember a similar tension between the two principal parties during the reunion weekend. Edward had always been prone to try his luck with whoever seemed available, but what the hell did Jennifer think she was doing?

Ian was worried about her – every time he'd seen her over the last couple of years she'd seemed like more of a loose cannon, increasingly oblivious to the well-being of others and herself. Having an affair with Edward seemed like a sudden escalation of the urge to self-destruct, a course of action which was almost guaranteed to leave her feeling bad about herself.

He supposed he would have to talk to her, but he couldn't say the idea filled him with enthusiasm.

They were leaving Wolverhampton now. Ian got up, made his way back through three coaches to the buffet, and ordered a can of Heineken. As the steward plonked it in front of him, he realized for the first time that he hadn't got a penny on him. He had a cheque for three million quid, but no money. He had driven to the station that morning, and used credit for the train ticket. He had not transferred his wallet from his usual battered leather jacket to the borderline-respectable suit he had chosen to wear in Camelot's honour.

"Sorry, forgot my money," he told the steward, who gave him a sour look and snatched back the can of beer.

Ian walked disconsolately back to his seat and sat staring out of the window, his mouth still dry, thinking about his immediate future. He had two articles to deliver over the next few days – one by Friday at the latest, another by Monday – and he could think of few things he fancied less than writing them. So why should he? Professional pride and courtesy? Maybe, but both the expectant editors would have dumped him long ago if they'd been able to find anyone cheaper. And no one should be expected to get on with work in their first week as a millionaire. He'd call in and say he had the flu. Or the Black Death.

The train was only ten minutes late rolling into Piccadilly. Ian didn't notice the thin young man who followed him down London Road to the cash machine, and then back up to the underground car park, where he recovered the Renault. He drove south to Chorlton, oblivious to the taxi on his heels, and stopped at his own bank to deposit the lottery check. Not quite knowing how to go about this – just paying it in over the counter seemed a bit ostentatious – he asked to see the manager. This entailed a ten-minute wait, but was worth it just to see the shift in the man's expression when he saw the cheque.

At Piccadilly station Ian had noticed a poster advertising the Yorkshire Moors, and as he pulled up outside his house he took the sudden decision to go away for a couple of days. A nice posh hotel, with time and space to walk and think. He needn't come back until Wednesday evening, when he had his date with Susan. Not for the first time, he found himself wondering how she would react to his sudden wealth.

He spent only a couple of minutes in the house, but it was enough. The journalist, having noted down the address, was on his way back to the paper's regional office in the city centre. Ian threw his bag into the back of the Renault and headed for the moors.

To say that Neil, Cath and the children drove back to Shropshire in high spirits would be something of an understatement. Every once in a while someone would demand to see the two cheques again, and they would be passed around for inspection and rapturous stares. It had started off as a need for reassurance that the impossible had actually happened, and it ended up as a standing joke that reduced everyone to near-hysterics.

They stopped for a late lunch at a restaurant in Bridgnorth, and as the three children availed themselves of the facilities, Cath made a decision. "I think we should get back to business as usual tomorrow," she told Neil. "The kids should go to school, and we should go to work. Or we're all going to explode with excitement."

"We should do one thing different," Neil said. "Put something in the bank."

"Yes." Cath shook her head, as if she still couldn't believe it.

The kids were not so thrilled to discover they were going back to school next day. "Surely six million's worth a proper holiday," Josey insisted. "Like America or somewhere."

"We'll do that," Cath assured her, "but in the school holidays."

"What do we tell our friends?" Angie wanted to know.

It was a good question.

"Nothing?" was Neil's instinctive response, but Cath didn't agree.

"They don't want to keep things from their friends." She turned to the kids. "Look, it's up to you – you can tell your friends whatever you want. Maybe it would be best just to say that your Mum and Dad have won some money, without going into how much, because that makes other people jealous. Do you understand?"

"Of course," Josey said indignantly. "I don't mind people knowing. I'm still the same, aren't I?"

Cath offered a silent prayer that her daughter's friends would know that too. Later that evening, after the last of the children had been sent to bed, she and Neil found themselves talking about their own friends.

"Who are we going to tell?" she asked.

Neil took a sip of his hot chocolate. "Well, we've told our families," he said. "Are you going to tell Annie and Lynn?"

"I want to, I think. They are my best friends, after all. I mean, you can't keep a secret like that and still be friends, can you?"

"No, I don't think you can. So by the same token we'll have to tell Jo and Tim and Marcie and Gerry."

"How about Nick and Diane at work?"

"I suppose so." He looked at her. "I know it's crazy, but I'm worried that this is going to change the way everyone sees me."

"It will, at least in the beginning. I think we just have to trust people, and ourselves." She gave him a reassuring smile, and then snuggled up beside him on the sofa. "How about going to bed early?" she asked.

"What for?" he asked wide-eyed.

"I'll refresh your memory upstairs," she said.

Since arriving back from Birmingham early that afternoon Becky had spent the better part of seven hours not knowing what to do with herself. She had tried cleaning – despite the fact that their cleaning woman was due the next day – tried watching TV, tried just sitting and thinking. From Euston Edward had headed straight for their accountants, and had still not come home. She had no idea where he was, but supposed he was out celebrating with someone.

She supposed she should have gone with him, rather than let it appear that she was abdicating responsibility for her half of the money, but she could deal with all that when the time came, once the other issue between them had been resolved, in one way or the other. And in any case she had wanted their next major argument to be in private, not in someone else's office.

Maybe he thought the issue had been resolved – after all, he had not referred to it since their fight on the previous Saturday. Maybe he thought that forcing her to choose between himself and Carmen was hardly a choice at all.

But it was. A tough choice, certainly. She wasn't going to throw away almost twenty years of marriage just like that, but neither was she prepared to simply ignore her own wants and needs just because they conflicted with Edward's. A compromise would have been nice, but in the first place her husband had given no indication that he was willing to be flexible, and in the second it was hard to imagine what the formula could be. In the last resort they would either be taking on the responsibility for Carmen or they wouldn't.

Several times Becky had almost called Cath to talk the whole thing over, but each time she had stopped herself, knowing instinctively that this was one of those decisions she had to make alone.

But how? She wanted to take the child on, but she was afraid – she admitted it to herself – of losing Edward. Did she have the right to deprive Richard of his two parent family for the sake of a daughter? Did she have the right to deprive him of a sister? Would Sheila be willing to hand over the child to just her?

There was only one way to find out. She dialled the number Sheila had given her, and after what seemed a long wait, the familiar voice answered.

"It's Rebecca Lockwood," Becky said.

"Oh. I had almost given up on you."

"I'm sorry it's taken me so long to call back. I've been ..." Becky stopped, suddenly realizing two things – that she didn't want to have this conversation on the phone, and that she wanted to meet Carmen. She wanted to meet her more than she would have thought possible two weeks before. "I'd like to meet your daughter," she said, almost apologetically.

In the Wapping office, Scanlon was placing the blown-up photographs on the editor's already overflowing desk. "Look guilty, don't they?" he said. "I thought 'SHAME OF WINNING' would look good."

Hugh Harrison grunted.

"We just run the picture tomorrow," Scanlon continued. "No names. Turn it into a mystery. Who are these people? The whole country will be looking out for them. Then by Wednesday we've found them. Unlike the competition."

"So who are they?" Harrison asked

Scanlon leant over the desk. "This one with his face turned away is Edward Lockwood. He's the gallery director I've been looking into. He buys up pictures or sculptures, mounts exhibitions which drive up the artist's selling price, and then cashes in."

"Is that illegal?"

"Nope, it's free enterprise. But it sounds sleazy enough. And this Lockwood is a piece of work. Most of the stuff I picked up on him came from women he'd screwed once and tossed over. Real notches on the bedpost stuff. The wine bar near the gallery seems to be full of women with a grievance against him."

"Better and better."

"He's quite well known though, which is why I think we should use this picture. Don't want to give the competition a running start." He moved his finger. "This is his wife, Rebecca. She works for a bookstore chain. The gorgeous one is a business software designer in Docklands. Small, exclusive firm. Probably fifty grand-plus a year. Lives in Islington." Scanlon grinned. "Not your usual lottery winners, are they?"

"They don't look like they bought tickets after cashing the weekly giro. But I'm not sure that's going to make them interesting to our readers."

"Oh, it will," insisted Scanlon. "Don't you get it? These people don't deserve to win. They've already had more luck in life than most people, and they sure as hell aren't entitled to more."

Harrison looked at him for a moment, and then burst out laughing. "OK," he said eventually. "What about the other three?"

Scanlon grimaced. "They don't fit quite so neatly. These two live in Shropshire. He's a volunteer worker at a paper recycling centre and she's some sort of herbalist."

"Ex-hippies."

"Probably. The other man is a freelance computer journalist. Nothing special."

"So what's the connection?"

"Don't know yet. But they're all the same age, so it's probably school or university."

"Maybe a sex angle."

"Maybe."

Harrison leaned back in his chair. "OK," he said. "The picture tomorrow, and then what?"

"We do interviews tomorrow afternoon for Wednesday – the usual stuff, to start with. In the meantime we carry on digging up dirt on Lockwood, and make a start with the others. If nothing good comes up in time, we can still go with what I've already got on Thursday."

Harrison smiled. "Make it work," he said.

Scanlon walked back to his own desk, thinking that the only thing his editor had in common with the captain of the *Enterprise* was a gleaming head.

8

It was another gorgeous day in Shropshire, an armada of fluffy white clouds sailing majestically through a bright-blue sky. Cath, having run the kids to school, had come back for another cup of coffee before she and Neil set out for work, and they sat out in the garden, basking in both the sunshine and their economic salvation. One thing at least was now certain – they wouldn't lose the cottage in which they had invested so much time and effort.

And that was the key, Cath thought. It was not the things they could buy with the money – it was the security it gave them. They would no doubt have their fair share of problems with children and parents and health and the state of the world, but they need never have another money worry. And after the last few months that sounded like heaven.

Not that there weren't things she wanted. A large greenhouse came immediately to mind. And she had always wanted to see the statues on Easter Island.

She turned to Neil. "What are we going to buy?" she asked.

"You mean this week?" he replied with a grin.

"Any week. What have you been itching to own?"

He grunted. "Nothing really, though I'm sure I'll

be able to think of something. A jukebox," he said suddenly. "One of the old ones. I'd love one of those."

"I was thinking about one of those luxury cruises," Cath said, "but then I realized who we'd be surrounded by."

"Other rich people," Neil said drily.

"Exactly."

"I don't know about you," he said soberly, "but I'm going to have a hard time living with this if I don't give a sizeable chunk of it away."

"Agreed," Cath said, "but how sizeable is a sizeable chunk? And who are we going to give it away to?"

"I've no idea," Neil said.

"Half seems like a good chunk to me," Cath murmured. "I think we could make do with just three million, don't you?"

He looked at his wife, thinking that this generosity of spirit was one of the reasons he'd fallen for her in the first place, and one of the reasons he loved her still. "As long as I get my jukebox," he said.

"It's a deal." She looked at her watch. "Oh hell, my first patient'll be here in five minutes," she said, getting up.

"And I've got to get going," Neil said, doing the same.

"Are you going to tell them today?" she asked.

"Don't know," he said, kissing her goodbye. "I'll be back around six," he added over his shoulder, heading for the car.

Once on the road he slipped in a Temptations tape and turned up the volume. The exuberance of the singing, even on the sad songs, suited both the day and his mood. Even some of the lyrics seemed tailor-made:

"The past is behind you, let nothing remind you ... don't look back!"

What was he going to tell Diane and Nick at the centre? In the twenty-fours which had followed their win he'd more or less assumed that the one certain thing he wanted to do with the money – apart from getting the family out of debt – was to put the recycling centre on a sound financial footing. That would involve arranging for one person – which would have been him – to receive a full-time salary, and to sink enough capital into the venture to ride out the inevitable rises and falls in the price of paper.

So far so simple. Telford's paper users would continue to get their waste recycled, fewer trees would be felled and the planet would be marginally better off.

But the whole point, in the beginning at least, had been to weave the notion of recycling into the existing infrastructure. It didn't have to be done by local councils, but it should certainly be funded by them. And for a centre like theirs to operate like a local sugar daddy, able to perform its necessary function because and only because one of those involved had won a lot of money, seemed to miss that point.

And if he wanted to fund an ecological project, there would be no shortage of other options. Options which didn't duplicate work the public sector should already be doing, as it was in America and Scandinavia and God knows how many other places. Options which would be more fulfilling and interesting for him than another five years of sorting paper.

Of course, it wasn't an either/or. There was no reason he couldn't give the centre five years of funding as a goodbye present and then move on.

But move on to what?

* * *

The DLR train was slowing into the curve by the Poplar depot when Jennifer first caught sight of the picture on the newspaper's front page. The man was holding it at an awkward angle, but even so she had no trouble recognizing the six of them or reading the banner headline: "TAKE THE MONEY AND RUN". She herself seemed to be looking straight at the camera.

She instinctively bowed her head and half covered her face with a hand, convinced that half the people in the carriage had already recognized her. The man who had leered at her on the platform at Stratford had probably not been after her body at all.

Another few minutes, and the train reached her stop. She grabbed a newspaper from a stall, gave the woman too much money, and ignored the call to come back for her change. On a bench beside the water she pored over the picture and read the accompanying article.

It was not a particularly clear photograph – only she, Becky and Ian were easy to recognize – but it was an effective one. She couldn't put her finger on why, but there was a definitely furtive quality to the grouping, which tied in brilliantly with the headline's insinuation of stealth and concealment.

The story seemed designed to amplify this effect. The only facts on offer concerned the size of their win and the city in which the photograph had been taken – otherwise it was all allusion and innuendo. The writer didn't actually say that the people in the photograph were well off, but that was certainly the impression he left on the reader. He couldn't therefore conclude that the winners were undeserving, but that impression too was indelibly etched. Being undeserving, they would feel guilty, and feeling guilty they would seek out anonymity. They might not be criminals, but this was clearly a crime, as the huge "wanted poster"-style photograph made only too clear.

"Who are these people?" the caption asked. They need exposing, went the unwritten postscript.

Jennifer realized her hands were shaking. She resisted the impulse to head straight for the station – or, better still, a taxi – and run for home. It felt so unfair, so vicious, and she felt so powerless to do anything about it.

There was only one thing she could do, she realized, and that was to ignore it. If anyone repeated any of this to her face, then she could either try to justify herself or slap their face, but there was no way you could expect the tabloids to be interested in truth.

She stood up, tossed the paper into a convenient bin, and started for the office. The thought of facing her colleagues was hardly a happy one, but as the moment approached she realized with some surprise that at least a part of her was almost looking forward to it.

"Is it you?" the first voice asked when she was only halfway through the door.

"Yes," she said defiantly.

To her surprise this admission produced a flood of people offering their congratulations, and some of them even seemed genuinely pleased for her. Some didn't of course, and some made little attempt to mask the underlying resentment in their voices. "So when are you going to give yourself up?" Dennis Symington asked sarcastically. But even he seemed almost awestruck by the fact and size of her win. Or maybe he was wondering if there was any chance of his getting his hands on any of it.

Five minutes later she was alone in her cubicle, the

initial excitement over. Half of her felt relieved it was out in the open, the other half upset by the realization that things would never be the same again. She had not made any close friends in her four years at the firm, but she had formed good working relationships with several people, which extended to lunch-time and after-work gatherings in the local pubs and restaurants. Now that she was "the woman who won the lottery" all this was bound to change; relationships would become awkward at best, poisoned by envy at worst.

She tried to concentrate on the work at hand, but it was difficult, and made more so by the apparent assumption among her colleagues that she would have other things on her mind. "Still here, then?" Dennis Symington murmured as he passed her cubicle around mid-morning, and a few minutes after that she was summoned to Alan Patterson's office.

He was watering the palms which lined the picture window overlooking the dock. "I guess congratulations are in order," he said, turning to greet her with a smile.

"Thank you," she said.

He resumed watering. "I once read that nearly everyone who wins a lot of money swears that they intend to keep working," he said, "but that most of them quickly change their mind." He glanced round at her. "It's probably an unfair question," he continued, "but have you any idea what you intend to do? The reason I ask . . . well, you know how important the Indian project is to the firm's future, and if there's any doubt in your mind that you'll be here to see it through, then the sooner I know about it the better."

All of which made perfect sense, she thought. He expected her to leave and he'd prefer it if she did so at the time most convenient for him. "It's not an unfair question," she said, though she had a feeling it was. "But I have no intention of leaving. I enjoy my work here." She gave him a wry smile. "And what else would I do?" she asked, at least semi-rhetorically.

"I should think most people would devote at least a fortnight to shopping, and then take off on a very long and luxurious holiday," Patterson said. "Personally, I'd take the Orient Express to Venice, and then eat and drink my way round the Mediterranean. You wouldn't see me near a spreadsheet for years."

"I can always do that once the Indian project's on-line," she said.

"OK," he said. "I don't want to lose you," he added, but she could tell that in some way he'd been disappointed by her response.

Back at her desk, and feeling the need to talk to a fellow-winner, she first tried Ian's number in Manchester and then the cottage in Shropshire. At the former she got the answer-machine, at the latter only ringing, but she didn't really feel like talking to either Becky or Edward.

He wanted to talk to her though, and the phone rang only seconds later.

"Jen?" he began. "Have you seen the papers?"

"I've seen the one with our picture," she said.

"The bastards told us there wouldn't be any press," he said angrily.

"Well, obviously there was. But I doubt if it was Camelot's fault – what reason would they have for lying to us?"

"Christ knows. Publicity for the lottery, I suppose."

"It really needs it," she murmured.

He didn't seem to hear her. "Someone must have

told them, and it wasn't any of us. I feel like suing the bastards."

"Edward, calm down," she said. "They told us there was no guarantee, remember? And there's nothing we can do about it now anyway."

"Christ," he said, but his rage was deflating. "Why didn't you return my call?" he asked calmly.

"Because I didn't know what to say." Which wasn't true – she just hadn't wanted to pretend that Becky was the reason she didn't want to see him again. And she hadn't wanted to tell him the truth either. Which was that the only things she had found to remind her of the young man she had once loved had been things she had tried to ignore even then.

"So let's meet."

"No. It was just once for old times' sake," she told him, with more gentleness than he deserved. "And let's leave it at that." She put the phone down and sat staring out of the window, feeling more isolated than ever.

Ian had spent the morning walking on the moors near Ilkley. He could see the town spread out beneath him, the Metro train looking like a toy in its neat little station. He couldn't make out the hotel where he was staying – it might be expensive but it wasn't large.

The hours of solitude hadn't produced any decisions, and the more he thought about it the less sure he was that there were any to make, always assuming that staying true to himself wasn't something which required a conscious effort. Maybe it would, but if so he hoped there would be enough friends around to tell him so. He was in his forties, after all, and he had that many years of memories to remind him what normal everyday life was all about.

Basically, he was just going to be a richer version of who he'd always been. Money wasn't going to turn him into a better piano player, a better father, a better lover, but it was going to make life a hell of a lot more comfortable. And as for all those things which he'd wanted but had not been able to afford . . .

It was time to shop, he decided. He made his way back down to the road, and aimed the Renault in the direction of Leeds. He was half a mile down the road when he realized, for the first time, that he could buy the piano of his dreams – a Steinway, a Bösendorfer. The sky was the limit. The fact that he rarely played the piano he had at home, preferring to practise down at the club with whoever was on hand, seemed irrelevant.

But he wouldn't buy a piano today. His first stop in Leeds was the city's best record shop, where he purchased long-coveted multi-CD sets of Thelonious Monk and Miles Davis. They cost almost three hundred pounds between them, but the pang of extravagance which accompanied the purchase only lasted a few seconds. As he read through the accompanying booklets in an arcade coffee shop a warm glow of happiness seemed to rise up through his chest and wash across his brain.

Next he found himself outside a travel agent's, emerging a few minutes later with about twenty brochures featuring destinations from Tahiti to the Silk Road. The temptation to buy a holiday in the South Seas for him and Susan was almost irresistible, but the more cautious voice in his head prevailed. He wasn't at all sure how he was going to present the news to her, or how she was going to take it when he did, but the one thing he was sure of was that he couldn't just let the money take over. He couldn't let it look as though he was trying to buy her.

It was almost dark when he got back to the hotel, and after leaving his purchases in his room he went down to the bar for a drink. It was there that he found his own picture staring up at him from a discarded paper. He read through the article, initial anger slowly mingling with bitter amusement. The whole thing was so ludicrously transparent.

Then he started thinking about the others. Edward would no doubt be outraged, Neil and Cath annoyed, at least for the kids' sake.

He walked across to the phone and called Ellie, but the line was busy. Coincidence, he wondered, or had the press tracked his son down? The whole business was getting less amusing by the minute.

And Jen was in pretty bad shape to begin with, he realized. He called her, expecting the same engaged tone, but got the answer-machine. She picked up when he announced himself.

"Where are you?" she asked. Her voice sounded exceptionally bright, almost brittle.

"I'm calling from Peru," he said. "The Yorkshire Moors, actually. I felt like a couple of days in the wilderness. Like Christ. Only he decided not to yield to temptation. How are things in London?"

"Fine, if you like feeling like a wanted criminal. I felt like drawing the curtains the moment I got home, but I managed to hold on until dark."

"And no huge crowd has gathered outside demanding that you shower them with silver?"

"Just one journalist. A very smooth young man in his late twenties, not at all like the stereotype. He asked me the 'usual questions', as he put it. How we picked the numbers – I told him the ones I remembered: Monk's birth, Neil and Cath's wedding anniversary, Becky's twenty years. How we knew each other, what we intended doing with the money. I said I had no idea yet, but that I was carrying on working. That was about it, really. He was only here about ten minutes."

"I don't suppose he apologized for all the insinuations in today's edition."

"He did, sort of. Or at least, he said he'd had nothing to do with it. And he asked why we'd asked for no publicity, so as to give us the chance to set the record straight."

"What did you say?"

"I asked him to tell me what sort of narcissistic moron would actually want publicity. He laughed."

"Nice one," Ian said, managing to keep the doubt out of his voice. To anyone else she would probably have just sounded overtired, overstressed, but he had known her a long time, and it sounded to him as if she was barely holding herself together. He thought about phoning Becky and asking her to look in, and then remembered why that might not be such a good idea. He wondered whether he should ask her about Edward, and decided that would be something better done in person. "I'm coming down to London at the beginning of next week," he decided out loud. "Can you put me up?"

"Of course."

"Great." Something occurred to Ian. "This journalist – did he say how he found you?"

"No, he didn't. I suppose I should have asked."

"Well, I shouldn't worry about it," Ian said, though once he'd put the phone down he found himself doing exactly that. Something smacked of manipulation in all this, and he didn't like it. But at that moment there didn't seem to be much he could do about it.

He turned his thoughts to Susan. He had been reluctant to tell her about their win over the phone, but now, with his face plastered all over the newspapers, it seemed the lesser of two evils. He wanted to make sure she hadn't fallen for the newspaper's barely concealed allegations of moral turpitude.

She sounded OK about it all. "I'm glad we didn't meet this week," she told him, "or you'd have been wondering if I was after you for your money."

But there was an uncertainty in her voice which hadn't been there before, and twice she asked if he still wanted them to meet the following evening.

"Is there any reason why I shouldn't?" he'd asked.

"Well, I imagine you could have gorgeous twenty-year-olds draped over each arm if you felt like it," she replied. It was a joke, but one with a seriousness buried in its core.

Cath was just finishing a consultation with one of her regulars when the woman, without any preamble, bluntly asked her if she intended to continue charging for her services now that she and her husband had won the lottery.

"How did you know?" Cath asked, just as trenchantly.

"You mean you haven't seen it?" the woman riposted.

"Seen what?"

The woman told her, ending up by repeating her previous question: "So are you going to charge or not?"

"I haven't really thought about it yet," Cath told her. She had never liked this woman, and liked her even less at this moment. "I haven't noticed that people stop charging for their services the moment they get rich," she added pointedly, although, almost perversely, she found herself admitting the absurdity of charging people a few pounds for advice and herbs when she and Neil had millions in the bank.

At the very least, she thought, she would stop charging those people who she knew were hard up.

The woman was taking the usual fee from her purse, but there was resentment on her face.

"I'll think about what you said," Cath told her.

The woman, who clearly hadn't believed a word of it, was just backing her car out of the short lane when a second car arrived. Another woman, considerably younger, climbed out, walked up the path and showed Cath her press credentials. Her name was apparently Lysette Bradley.

"I'd like to ask you a few questions," she said brusquely, adding, "if it's a convenient time, of course," with something less than complete conviction.

"It's as good a time as any," Cath said, "but I've only got about five minutes."

"That should be enough," Bradley said, following her into the sun porch and setting up a miniature tape recorder. "It's for your protection as well as my memory," she explained.

"I haven't seen the paper today," Cath volunteered. "But I gather you implied that we were trying to keep our win quiet."

"Not me personally," Bradley said quickly. "I suppose someone could have read that into it," she said disingenuously, "but between you and me, they often get carried away with their own cleverness.

Anything for a catchy front page." She smiled winningly. "But you were trying to avoid publicity, weren't you?"

"There's a difference between not courting publicity and deliberate concealment, isn't there?"

"Yes, I suppose there is. So none of you have anything to hide?"

Cath laughed. "Like what – bodies in the garden?"

"I've no idea."

"We haven't got anything to hide," Cath said dismissively.

Bradley shrugged. "Most winners seem to like getting their pictures in the paper. They like sharing their win with the world."

Cath just looked at her.

"OK, just a few simple questions. How did you choose the numbers?"

"We chose one each. I picked 15 for our wedding anniversary, Neil – my husband – picked 36 for the street where we all lived . . ."

"Which street was that?"

"Tisbury Road in Hove. Someone else" – she felt reluctant to name any of the others – "chose 20 because it was our twentieth-anniversary reunion. I can't remember any of the others," she lied. She felt reluctant to give this woman anything.

"And you all met as students?"

"Yes. Look, I'm sorry, but I have to pick up the children from school."

"No problem. I think I've got all I need. Thank you for your time."

A few minutes later, driving down towards Bishop's Castle, Cath found herself wondering about the questions which had not been asked. In tabloid stories people were always defined by their age and occupations, but Lysette had not bothered to ask about either. It was as if she already knew all that, and the interview itself just a necessary formality, almost an afterthought. But why?

She shook her head and turned her attention to more important things, like whether or not she intended to become Shropshire's first free herbalist, a one-woman alternative NHS.

Becky took a taxi to the Shaw Theatre in Euston Road and then walked north into Somers Town's maze of council flats, following Sheila's directions. The schools had just emptied out and there seemed to be a group of kids on every corner, most of them sharing smokes of one kind or another.

The lobby in Sheila's building smelt of urine and dope, and Becky, deciding she'd rather be stiff than sorry, took the stairs rather than the graffiti-covered lift to the fourth floor. Sheila answered the door and ushered her into the living room of the two-bedroom flat, which Becky, somewhat to her shame, found surprisingly cosy. She wasn't sure what she'd been expecting — something more in tune with the lobby and lift, she supposed — but this living space looked every bit as cared for as her own.

"Mum," a small voice said behind her, and she turned to see a six-year-old girl with curly black hair sidling up beside Sheila and staring at their visitor. Becky thought she could see a hint of Richard in the slight downturn of the girl's mouth, but she was probably imagining it. And in any case what did family resemblances matter?

The child was looking up at her, intense curiosity in her eyes, and Becky wondered what, if anything, her mother had told her. She felt like picking the girl up and hugging her, but it seemed wrong to do so – like jumping the gun – until a final decision had been taken.

"This is Carmen," Sheila was saying. "And this is Mrs Lockwood," she told her daughter.

"Hello, Carmen," Becky said.

"Hello," the girl said, her face breaking out in a smile.

"OK, so why don't you go and watch the TV," Sheila said. "Mrs Lockwood and I have got some things to talk about."

Carmen walked backwards to the door, still smiling, then abruptly turned and ran into the next room. A moment later the unmistakable sound of a cartoon could be heard.

"I put the TV in there just for today," Sheila explained.

She looked even worse than she had the previous week, Becky thought.

"Do you want some tea?"

"Not unless you do."

"It just makes me pee." She grimaced and sat down. "I'm sorry I made that crack about almost giving up on you yesterday. It's just . . . I mean, I'm not talking days or even weeks, but I have to get this settled before . . . you know."

"I know."

"The doctor tells me she's in no danger being around me as long as there's no blood or saliva mixing, but I'm not sure I believe them. Sometimes I think they haven't a clue about what makes this thing tick and they just tell you the first thing that comes into their heads."

"What will you do if we take Carmen?" Becky asked.

"Die a happier woman."

"No, I mean . . ."

"I know what you mean. I'm sorry. I don't know . . ."

"Can you get into a hospice?"

"I think so. The doctor said he thought he could arrange it."

Becky took a deep breath. "Look, Sheila, I have two things to tell you." She clasped her hands together. "First . . . this is silly, but Edward and I and some friends, we've just won the National Lottery. Last weekend."

Sheila only looked surprised for a moment. "That's nice," she said in a neutral voice.

Becky felt like crying. "It's a lot of money," she said, "and I'd like to pay for you to go somewhere nice."

"Go out in style," Sheila said, as if she was thinking out loud.

"I know Richard would want us to help," Becky said. "And I know he'd like to meet you if he knew."

There were tears in both women's eyes now. "No, no, I don't want to put him through that," Sheila said. "He's better off as he is."

"It's up to you."

"I'll think about it. What was the other thing you had to tell me?"

"My husband doesn't want us to take Carmen. So far, that is. But I want to, and at the moment . . . well, it's up in the air. Things are not very good between us and . . . well, what I'm trying to say is that I may be able to offer her a foster-mother but not a foster-father."

"One person who loved her would be enough," Sheila said firmly.

"There'd be Richard too."

She managed another smile. "It would be lovely if they could be together."

When Becky got home Edward had the offending newspaper ready to show her. "Have you seen this?" he asked.

She took a look. "It's us," she said brightly, and then her face darkened as she realized the implication behind the headline. Looking up at Edward, she was surprised to find him smiling.

"One of their journalists has been here," he said. "He almost apologized, but I told him to go screw himself. I'm seeing Lowenstein again tomorrow, and I'll find out if there's anything actionable in what they've printed. I've been with the accountant most of the afternoon. Do you want to know what he advised?"

"Not at this moment, no."

"The Channel Islands," Edward said, as if she hadn't spoken. "But you don't need to worry about it," he added, seeing the look of surprise on her face, "we're still at the data-gathering stage." He grinned boyishly. "I asked Lowenstein's opinion about something else, just out of interest."

"What?" She closed her eyes and saw Carmen's face.

"The share-out. The pound we bought the ticket with came from four of us, remember, not six."

She looked at him with astonishment. It hardly seemed worth pointing out that the four of them had paid for the meal because Neil and Cath had paid for everything else, or that Neil and Cath could have burnt the syndication agreement and kept the lot, had they been so inclined.

"He said we might have a case," he said, and then took in the expression on her face. "What are you looking at me like that for? I only asked out of interest – I'm not planning on doing anything about it."

She just kept looking at him, as if he was a creature from another planet.

"Where have you been, anyway?" he asked.

"I've been to meet Carmen," she said coldly.

"Who?"

"Richard's sister, remember?"

His eyes narrowed. "I told you . . ."

"You told me I had to choose between you and her. It's a choice that seems to be getting easier every day."

9

The best thing that could be said about Wednesday morning's paper was that it was an improvement on Tuesday's. At least they – or the three of them who had been contacted – got to express their feelings, though not surprisingly Cath's common-sense explanation for their dislike of publicity got second billing to Jennifer's, the lead writer wondering out loud how all the other lottery winners would react to being called morons. And Edward's refusal to say anything, this time complete with a picture which did show his face, was afforded more significance than anything the two women had said.

There were fewer of the nasty insinuations which had marked Tuesday's piece, and the reasons for most of the numbers chosen were faithfully recorded. The exceptions were 8, and 17 – which the paper claimed had been chosen in memory of the Russian Revolution.

But maybe the worst was over. After all, how much mileage could they get out of a story like this?

Jennifer went into work, where her colleagues treated her much the same as they had the day before, keeping their emotional distance without actually radiating unfriendliness. Ian went for another long walk on the moor outside Ilkley. Edward drove across to the gallery and lunched with the investment adviser his accountant had recommended. Becky thought about seeking out a new solicitor, but decided against for the time being.

In Shropshire Neil and Cath continued with their "business as usual" policy, or at least tried to. Neil went in to the recycling centre, where Nick and Diane were obviously still trying to work out how they felt about his news of the day before. The usual Wednesday-morning round of wastepaper collections from industrial premises and offices was as exhausting as ever, and the only off-key note was sounded when Neil was slow to say he'd buy the lunch-time round in their local, as he had on the previous day. "I'm still rich," he said, quickly making amends, but it felt like a telling moment nevertheless. Was he supposed to always buy the drinks now? He obviously didn't mind doing so from a cost point of view, but it felt as if some necessary balance in his relationship with the others had been upset.

Cath had only two patients that day, both of them old friends, and both of whom made a point of paying before any awkwardness could develop. She was grateful for their thoughtfulness, but their awareness of the need still made her feel uncomfortable. But, she told herself, there was no use pretending that everything could stay the same – both they themselves and everyone they knew would need time to adjust.

When she picked up the two girls from the bus stop in Bishop's Castle they were full of ideas for a swimming pool down by the caravan. Another girl in Josey's class – "she's an MP's daughter" – had one in her back garden, and it had only cost about £20,000.

"Only," Cath murmured. But why not? They all loved swimming, so why not have a pool?

They reached Daniel's school, but for once there was no sign of him at the gate. They sat waiting in the car for several minutes, attracting the notice of several groups of departing boys, and Cath was about to go in search of her son when he appeared, walking with one of the teachers, a Mrs Turnbull.

He was sporting a huge black eye.

Cath almost leapt from the car. "Daniel, are you all right? How did it happen?" she asked, looking first at him, and then at the teacher.

"He was in a fight," Mrs Turnbull said. "But he won't tell me what it was about."

"Daniel?"

He looked up at her belligerently, but she could see he was on the verge of tears. "It was nothing," he said. "I don't want to talk about it," he added, almost in a whisper.

Cath shrugged at the teacher, who gave her a sympathetic smile. They both knew what it had been about.

Once they were home, and once the girls had been persuaded, without too much difficulty, to go and mark out a possible swimming pool site, Cath wheedled the story out of her eleven-year-old son.

"They just wanted money," he told her. "They said I must be getting much more pocket money now, and I should share it round."

"What did you say?"

"I said I didn't get any more pocket money yet, but even if I did I couldn't share it with everyone. I couldn't, could I?"

"No, of course not. So what did they say?"

"Martin Hull said I'd better buy them something

or else. So I said, 'Or else what?' and he pushed me. I don't think he even meant to really – he just got angry. But I fell down and one of the others kicked me. Not very hard. It looks worse than it feels," he concluded bravely.

She shook her head.

"Can I go and help them with the swimming pool?" he asked.

She nodded, and sat there wondering whether they could or should take the matter any further. Normally her first instinct, given that Neil was on the road somewhere, would have been to call either Lynn or Annie, but this time she hesitated. Cath had told them both about the win on the previous day, and though both had seemed, initially at least, genuinely pleased for her, she had been surprised and disappointed to detect slight hints of envy and resentment in their response. Later, thinking about it, she had admitted to herself that in their position she might have felt the same, at least in the beginning. Such negative feelings would fade, she was almost sure, but it would take time.

But then, perhaps the one thing she had to make clear to her friends was that they were still needed. Cath bit the bullet, called Lynn, and told her what had happened.

Lynn was sympathetic but not surprised. "You're going to have to expect things like this," she said, and Cath had the fleeting realization that one part of her friend – maybe a very small part, but a part nevertheless – was actually seeing what had happened to Daniel as some kind of retributive justice. People who won that much money, went the other's unspoken thought, deserved to pay in some way.

Cath didn't say anything, but once the call was

over she felt shaken by it, and when Neil came in he found her badly in need of a hug.

"It's all getting strange," she told him in the garden, as the kids washed up and they examined the pegged-off space for the swimming pool.

"Maybe we should take out an ad in the local paper telling everyone we're still the same people," Neil said, only half jokingly, and told her about his moment in the pub with Diane and Nick.

"Maybe we should publicize the fact that we're going to give half of it away," Cath suggested.

"You realize half the population will think we're mad and the other half will say we're do-gooders?"

"But isn't that what we always wanted to be – mad do-gooders?"

Neil laughed, but quickly grew serious again. "Maybe. But what are we going to do about the kids?"

Ian drove back to Manchester that afternoon along minor roads, enjoying the scenery and the lack of urgency. It seemed a long time since he hadn't been hurrying to either get somewhere or get something finished. He half expected to find the press corps camped outside the house in Chorlton, but the street was its usual empty self. Javid wasn't home, and he spent almost an hour in the bath, thinking through the events of the previous week, and particularly his conversation with Susan the night before.

He brushed aside the flitting image of himself with a buxom young blonde on either arm, dried himself and dressed to the sound of one of his new Monk CDs. He supposed he should be angry about the paper's creative association of his 17 with the Russian Revolution, but it was so ludicrously blatant that he found the whole business impossible to take seriously.

To take the car or not to take the car? It would be hell to park, but arriving in a taxi would smack of extravagance, and acting like a lottery winner was something he was keen to avoid. He would take the Renault, but fill her up with the best petrol.

After arriving at the pub on time – and checking his watch twice to confirm the fact – he settled down with a pint of bitter to wait for her. She was nearly twenty minutes late, but she looked even lovelier than he remembered. Who would swap someone like her for a vacuous nymphet? he asked himself.

"So what you going to do with it all?" she asked, once they were seated in the relative privacy of a booth.

"God only knows," he said.

"Are you going to make your CD?"

"I hope so. I hoped so before all this happened, but I suppose now I'll have no problem paying for the studio time. And it'll be a lot easier to get the musicians I want."

"That's great."

He smiled wryly. "Yeah, it is."

"But?"

"It's ridiculous, I know it is, but being able to afford it all somehow . . . I don't know, cheapens it, I guess. I don't suppose people who are born with money – or who earn a lot of it – have this problem, but I keep thinking I don't deserve it. I know a lot of musicians who deserve to be heard just as much as I do."

"That's ridiculous. Understandable, but ridiculous. There may be a lot of talented musicians who never get heard, but that doesn't mean that those who do get a break have no talent . . ."

"I know . . ."

"I've thought about this a lot," she said. "We all like to look for reasons why things happens to us, but so much of it just comes down to luck – how bright you are, how good-looking, how healthy, where you're born, who your parents are – it's endless. Winning the lottery is just another piece – a pretty extreme piece, I admit – but that's all it is, just one more twist of fate. Life is about what you do with the luck you get, which means unlucky people can still triumph and really lucky buggers like you get the chance to screw up on a grand scale."

"Thanks," he said ironically, but he meant it just the same.

"Make your CD," she said.

"Yes, ma'am."

They decided on a French bistro they both knew for dinner, and Ian was pleased to discover that this time she hadn't brought her car. They drove the mile across town, and then cruised around in a vain search for a parking space. Ian had the half-serious thought that he should simply park illegally and pay the fine, and foolishly shared it with Susan.

She didn't say anything, but her look was eloquent enough. He kept looking, and was rewarded with a space.

In the restaurant they tried to recoup the ground both sensed they had lost, but on this occasion they didn't have much good luck to work with. About ten minutes after ordering one wine they received another, which Ian politely sent back. After another ten minutes the right wine finally appeared. "Someone die in the kitchen?" Ian asked conversationally.

The waiter scowled at him.

"We're not in a hurry," she told Ian.

"I know." He started telling her about the waiter at the hotel in Church Stretton, and realized halfway through the story that he was sounding like someone who spent his life complaining about and making fun of ordinary working people. The food arrived just in time to save him.

They were eating the main course when a woman abruptly loomed over their table, causing the candles to crazily flicker. She was probably in her thirties, though it was hard to tell through the layers of foundation on her face. "You're the lottery winner, aren't you? The one they can't find." She giggled and offered him pen and napkin. "Could I have your autograph?"

Ian looked at her as if she was mad, then laughed. "Why not?" he said, taking the pen and paper.

The husband or boyfriend was right behind her. "Shake hands?" he asked. "They say the luck rubs off," he explained, leering at Susan's cleavage.

The couple were gone as quickly as they'd appeared, leaving both Ian and Susan glancing round the room and wondering from which direction the next attack would come.

There were lots of looks turned their way, but no one else approached their table.

"Let's talk about you," Ian suggested, and for the next ten minutes they did. He heard about her two children, her ex-husband, her parents in Devon, and money wasn't mentioned once. It was only when she explained – somewhat reluctantly – that her car had suffered a major breakdown the previous weekend that Ian made his next mistake.

"You should get it fixed," he told her.

"I would if I had the money," she said, and the awkwardness was back again. But this time it didn't have time to fester, for only seconds later a journalist was asking Ian for an interview.

"Not now," Ian told him.

"You're refusing to talk to me?" the man asked.

"No, I'm just refusing to talk to you this evening. Come and see me tomorrow morning. I assume you know where I live."

"It's a deal," the man said. He re-pocketed his tape recorder and walked out, ignoring the greetings of the bistro owner, who had no doubt phoned the paper in the hope of getting some publicity for his restaurant.

Ian asked for the check and paid it, leaving the usual ten percent tip. As they got up to leave there was a scattering of applause from the other tables.

"Christ, it's only money," he exclaimed on reaching the pavement outside. He meant that winning the lottery hadn't actually been an achievement, like writing a great piece of music would have been, or succouring the poor of Calcutta, or teaching Alex Ferguson to lose gracefully.

But that wasn't the way Susan took the remark. "The cry of the rich down the ages," she said. "I'm sorry, Ian, but I don't think this is going to work."

"That didn't sound the way I meant it," he said.

"No? Well if it didn't, I'm sorry, but I still don't think it's going to work." She hailed the taxi which an unkind fate had just brought round the corner. "Thanks for the dinner," she said, and before he could say anything else she was gone.

"Hell!" he told the empty street. Driving home to an empty house he found himself wondering where all the vacuous nymphets were when you really needed them.

* * *

Richard approached the supermarket in the Bloomsbury Centre with more than a little trepidation. For one thing he wasn't sure whether he wanted the woman to be his real mother; for another he had no idea what he intended to do about it if she was.

After the supermarket episode on the previous Wednesday he had spent a couple of days arguing himself out of the assumption that a woman that old could not be his mother. She might have been forty when she had him, and in any case poor people couldn't look after themselves as well as people like his adoptive mother. And the more he had thought about it, the more he had doubted whether this woman could be anyone else. Why else the secret meetings, the strange tone in his mother's voice when she spoke on the phone, the terrible seriousness on the two women's faces as they had talked in the café in Russell Square?

In any case he had to find out, and on Saturday evening, knowing his parents were out at a dinner party, he had slipped home and laboriously worked his way through the filing cabinet in his father's study. After almost two hours of searching he had found the paperwork for his own adoption, and contained therein the name of his mother – the name he had always been told they didn't know – Sheila Moyer. Even if the woman in the supermarket wasn't his mother, he could now start looking for her. If he wanted to.

Entering the supermarket, he still didn't know what he wanted. Just the truth, he supposed, but that sounded too simple.

She was sitting at one of the tills again, and he could see she was wearing a name-tag. No doubt she'd been wearing it the previous week as well, but he hadn't noticed it. He joined her queue, grabbed a Snickers from the rack beside the till, and waited his turn.

It said "Sheila". He felt a lump in his throat, and almost dropped the change she gave him.

Outside he threw the unopened chocolate bar into a bin and sat down on a bench from which he could see the supermarket entrance, wondering what came next. Sheila was quite a common name – should he make sure? Maybe he could ask someone if there was a Mrs Moyer who worked there.

And if it was her, then what? Did he go up and introduce himself? What if she didn't want to meet him? And why should she? If she'd wanted him she'd have kept him in the first place.

The minutes went by, but he was no nearer a decision. He couldn't bring himself to go back in, and yet he couldn't bring himself to leave.

At four o'clock she solved the problem for him. He saw her being relieved at the till, and a few minutes later she emerged into the sunlight, a light jacket over her uniform dress, and started walking slowly northward along Marchmont Street towards Euston Road. Richard followed, stopping frequently in order to maintain the fifty-yard distance between them.

At Euston Road she crossed at the lights outside the Shaw Theatre and took the street opposite, which ran alongside the new British Library. A few minutes more and they were entering another world of multi-storey flats and weed-infested concrete spaces. Richard had removed his tie several hours ago, but what remained of his smart school uniform was enough to make him feel suddenly conspicuous.

His mother – his biological mother, he told himself – entered one of the blocks of flats. He hung back, hoping she would emerge on one of the open walkways above, and received his reward when she appeared briefly on the third floor, passing by one door and opening the next with a key.

Should he go up?

No, he thought, not until he knew what he wanted to say. He stood there for no more than a minute before retracing his steps to Euston Road, and there he started walking west. He was going home, he decided. He needed to ask his parents why they had lied to him.

Becky thanked Cath again and put down the phone. It didn't necessarily follow that because Daniel was being bullied then so was Richard, but boys had a habit of being boys, and she was worried. She punched out the school's number and asked to speak to her son.

After ten minutes of hanging on, he still hadn't been found, and Becky was beginning to rerun the bullying scenes from *Tom Brown's Schooldays* in her mind. She demanded to speak to the housemaster, who eventually appeared, made sympathetic noises and then left her hanging on for another ten minutes before picking up the receiver again.

"I can't find him," he said without preamble. "In fact he hasn't been seen since lunchtime. He called in sick for cricket apparently, but he's not in any of the obvious places. And I got the distinct impression from his friends – though none of them would actually say so – that he's playing truant."

"Oh," Becky said. She had been slightly thrown by the mention of Richard's "friends". Why did he never bring any of them home?

"I will inform you the moment he deigns to return," the housemaster said.

"Thank you," Becky said, feeling both stupid and

a little angry. What did Richard think he was doing? What else should she ask?

The housemaster had assumed the conversation was over and hung up. She was still lowering the phone to the table when she heard the sound of a key in the front door. "Edward?" she asked.

"No, it's me," Richard said.

"What are you doing here? I've just been talking to the school . . ."

The expression on his face stopped her – that and his hands, which swept outwards in unison, as if they were trying to clear his path through a cloud of fog. "I've seen my mother," he said abruptly.

Becky wanted to reach out and hug him, but instinctively knew that he couldn't have coped with it. "I saw her yesterday," she said.

"Why did you lie to me?" he asked, an almost pleading look on his face. "Why did you tell me you didn't know her name?"

"That was part of the adoption agreement. She didn't want you to know."

"Why not?"

The appeal in his eyes almost broke Becky's heart. "I'm not sure," she said. "At the time I thought she just didn't want to be bothered with you. Now I think it was more likely the opposite – she didn't want to be a bother."

He took a deep breath, but said nothing.

"Did you speak to her?"

"No, I just followed her home from the supermarket. I followed you there last week," he added. "I heard you on the telephone, and I just knew it was her."

She closed her eyes for a few seconds. "There's something you don't know," she said slowly, "and there's no easy way to tell you. Your mother has AIDS."

He looked at her, a stricken expression on his face.

"I'm sorry, Richard," she said, walking forward. He let her take him in her arms, and for several minutes his body shook with dry sobs. It took all Becky's strength not to wail with him.

"I want to meet her," he managed to say as the sobs subsided.

"You can," she said. "And there's something else. The reason she called last week – we hadn't heard from her since adopting you – was to tell me that she had this illness, and that she had a daughter who would be needing foster-parents. She's your sister. Her name's Carmen and she's six. I went to meet her yesterday."

"Why didn't you tell me about this last week, or at the weekend?"

"Because nothing has been decided. Your father and I . . ."

He stiffened. "Don't tell me. You want to take her and he doesn't."

"It's not as simple as that," she said, though it was. "It's asking a lot of someone to take on someone else's young child, particularly when the someone is over forty."

He looked sceptical. "But you want to?"

"Yes, I do. Richard, I'm sorry we didn't tell you earlier, but . . . well, the reasons always seem good at the time."

"And we have all this money," Richard said suddenly. "Isn't there something . . . ?"

"There's no cure, Richard."

He nodded, as if she'd merely confirmed what he already knew.

10

Contrary to expectation and hope, they were still front-page news on the Thursday morning, or at least Edward was. While the qualities concentrated on either beef and its defecting customers or John Major and his defecting MPs, the tabloids were settling into their new role as the moral inquisitors of lottery jackpot winners.

There was a blow-up of Edward and Jennifer on the front page, which had been cropped from one of the original photographs. It was innocent enough in itself, but when put together with the information that his wife's name was Becky, it could hardly have been more suggestive. In the accompanying article Brian Scanlon castigated modern art in general for being both ludicrous and morally reprehensible, and Edward in particular for being both its lackey and its Arthur Daley. The exhibition of Raul's work was discussed and dismissed as "sixth form philosophy at its mercenary glibbest", and Edward's purchase of one of the pieces before the exhibition opened made to look like insider dealing pure and simple.

The art might be puerile, but there was still money to be made by those who dealt in puerility, as Edward's three properties clearly demonstrated. There were photographs of the house in Holland Park and a huge tropical villa which had doubtless been plucked from the files. The accompanying caption didn't actually claim that this was the Lockwoods' Virgin Gorda house, but there was no mistaking the implication.

Like most rich socialists, the article claimed, Edward Lockwood sent his son – his adopted son – to public school. His wife, the writer added gratuitously, worked for the chain of bookstores which had recently stopped stocking a much-loved fifties children's author on the grounds that her stories were sexist and racist.

Becky laughed when she read that last part, but Edward didn't find anything to amuse him in the article, and she could see his point. He might be a go-getter, he might like money, but she had never thought of him as corrupt, and that was the word – unspoken though it might be – which hung over Scanlon's article. Looking at his face as he stared angrily into space, she knew he'd been hurt by the article, and in that moment she felt a brief resurgence of caring for him.

She had wanted to talk to him about the events of the previous day – about Richard's discovery – but now was obviously not the moment.

"I'm going to phone Lowenstein," he said, his face setting in the familiar mould of determination.

Cath and Neil went through the story together, sitting in the Escort outside the newsagent's in Bishop's Castle. Neil read it with mixed feelings. He knew it was unfair, but he couldn't quite repress the feeling that Edward deserved every word of it.

"I like their cottage on Virgin Gorda," Cath said wryly.

Neil was watching the people going by on the

pavement outside, and noticing that about half of them were casting lingering glances at the car and its occupants. "Maybe we should take a holiday now after all," he said.

Jennifer read the article on her way to work. It was bad, she knew it was, but somehow she found it hard to care. She had slept badly again, mostly on account of the wine, and had spent the hours between two and four watching taped soap operas. Stuart had rung again the previous evening, but for once his timing had been off, as another friend had phoned half an hour earlier to tell Jennifer that he'd been seen with his ex-wife at a party. When challenged with this he hadn't bothered to make excuses – as usual he'd gone on to the attack, accusing her of trying to monopolize his life. She'd put the phone down on him, and he still hadn't called back an hour later when she took it off the hook.

Why did she want him? Why did she want any of them?

Reading the paper, she found herself feeling sympathy for Edward, even though she knew it was misplaced. He'd look all hurt like a little boy for a while, and then he'd fight back and win. There was no stopping people like Edward; they were like rivers – you could divert them, even dam them, but they always found a way through.

And in any case, who would take crap like this seriously? *Neighbours* was better written.

She soon found out. At the office the looks seemed chillier than the day before, and she was settling into her seat when a summons arrived from Alan Patterson. He had the offending paper spread out on the desk in front of him.

"I'm sorry, Jennifer," he said, "but we can't have this sort of publicity."

She felt like telling him where to get off, but that would have made it too easy. "I can't control what the papers print," she said.

"That's not the point," he said. I can't . . ."

"There's a picture of me on the front page," she interjected, "a completely innocent picture. I'm not fondling a married man, I'm not undressed, I'm not holding a bag of stolen goods. I'm not even mentioned in the text, and nor is the firm. Where's the bad publicity?"

"The firm was mentioned yesterday. The whole country knows you work here."

"So what?"

"So I want you to take some leave. Paid leave, though I don't suppose you need the money."

"And what about the Indian project."

"Dennis can deal with that."

"Dennis wears slip-ons because he never learnt how to tie shoelaces. I've spent the best part of a year setting up this project, and you're taking me off it just because of a photograph in the paper? This time tomorrow people will have forgotten they ever saw it."

He pursed his lips.

"This is nothing to do with the picture, is it? It's to do with the money."

"It's not the money," he said. "Not *per se*. We have to work as a team, Jennifer, something you find difficult at the best of times. Now you've won this money . . . it creates tensions and, well, you don't need the job any more, do you?"

She felt her anger turning cold. "And all this crap about paid leave is just window-dressing," she said, standing up. "You can't fire me without a good reason, so you're just hoping that I won't come back."

"That's not true," he said, but without any real conviction.

"Just make sure you keep paying my salary," she said, "and I'll make sure it goes to a good cause."

"Jennifer . . ."

She walked back to her cubicle, grabbed her bag and jacket, and still inwardly shaking with anger, ignoring the questioning looks of colleagues, strode out of the office and the building. Her feet led her along the familiar route to the DLR station, and she was on the train for Stratford before she had any real sense of what she was doing.

Where else was there to go but home?

Her mother was waiting on the answer-machine with one suggestion. When was she coming up north, to her real home? They were all worried about her in Middlesbrough, especially after the newspaper stories. Her mother had never really trusted Edward – he was just a little too charming when you thought about it – but she would never in her wildest dreams have believed he would turn out like this.

As for the money, well, her Auntie Evie was wondering about it, that was all. She knew that Jennifer would be generous – she always had been with money – but perhaps it would be a good idea to buy people some nice presents and bring them up this weekend . . .

Jennifer stared at the answer-machine for several seconds, then reached into her bag for her chequebook, made out a cheque to her mother for £100,000, and stuffed it in an envelope. After a moment's thought she tore the top sheet off the pad by the phone and wrote: "Use this to buy presents for yourself and everybody else, love, Jen."

She found a stamp and walked down the road to the postbox outside the grocery store. The queue for food was too long to bother with, but she bought a bag of cashews with the four bottles of wine at the off-licence next door. Back in the flat she opened one of the bottles, poured herself a long glass and sat down on the sofa facing the TV. Her head was beginning to throb, but doubtless the wine would see to that.

The journalist introduced himself as David Slocumbe. Ian let him into the house, and led him up the stairs and into the room he used for work and relaxation. As usual, all available flat surfaces were topped by mountains of books, magazines, papers and computer discs, and most of these were crowned with an unwashed empty mug.

"You don't mind if I record this?" Slocumbe asked, pulling a mini-recorder from his jacket pocket.

"Not at all," Ian said, flicking a switch on his own audio system. "I'll do the same," he said unnecessarily. "Some of your colleagues have a habit of making things up. And one thing you can say for winning the lottery – I'd have no trouble affording a good lawyer if I wanted to sue someone for libel."

He smiled at Slocumbe, who at least had the decency to smile back.

"So fire away."

"You saw my paper this morning?"

"Yep."

"Have you got any comment on your friend Edward Lockwood's art dealings?"

"I can't think of any."

"You've known him a long time."

"As far as I can tell, your paper has accused him of two things: being in love with modern art and being a believer in free enterprise. Both of which he is, and has been as long as I've known him. But as far as I know neither is a crime."

"Umm. So let's get back to you. How does it feel winning all that money?"

Ian thought for a moment. He wanted to be as honest as he could – it was the only way he could think of to clear the air – but not at the expense of leaving hostages to Slocumbe's journalistic creativity. "Good, I guess," he said. "It's a shock though, winning that much, and there's no textbook to give you pointers." He shrugged. "I won't pretend I know what I'm going to do with it all, not yet anyway. Obviously I want to help out my family and my friends. I want to buy some of those things I've always wanted but could never afford. I want to keep enough in the bank so that I don't have to worry about the future."

"What about charity?"

"I don't know yet. I expect I'll give some of it away, but I haven't decided who to. It's too early. I'm not even sure the cheque's cleared yet."

"Why did you try to keep your identities secret?"

"That's a load of crap," Ian said. "Camelot told us we had a choice – publicity or no publicity. We thought about it, and we couldn't see any advantages in publicity. I mean, given the choice, would anyone prefer being investigated by the great British press to being left alone? It's a non-contest."

"There's a lot of people who don't seem to have minded. Are they all morons?"

"I can't speak for them. My guess is that they didn't get time to think things through – like I said, the whole thing's an enormous shock. We were lucky – there were six of us, and we could help each other keep our feet on the ground."

"Maybe you should write that textbook you were talking about," Slocumbe suggested, switching off his machine.

"Maybe. Is that all?" Ian asked.

"For the moment. I might be interested in doing a follow-up in a month or so – see if I find you knee-deep in vestal virgins."

"No chance," Ian told him. He showed the journalist out, collected his post, which consisted of about a dozen different offers of free hours surfing on the Internet, and walked back upstairs to make a cup of coffee. Looking at the calendar on his fridge door he realized Javid was two days late with his share of the rent. And since the lecturer had never been as much as a minute overdue in the past, Ian found himself reluctantly drawn to the conclusion that he was testing the beneficence of his jackpot-winning housemate.

Edward spent half an hour talking to his solicitor, who reluctantly advised him that there were no grounds for legal action in the morning's paper. "The tabloids employ almost as many lawyers as they do journalists," Lowenstein concluded, with more than a trace of wistfulness.

Edward thanked him curtly, hung up, and sat in his study wondering where the euphoria had all gone to. The reunion had made him feel good, and the exhibition opening had put him on top of the world. Getting Jen on to the office sofa had been the delicious icing on a very good cake. And then there'd been the win.

But now he felt like shit. The fucking newspapers

were making him look like a crook, and Becky was treating him like a moral leper because he refused to spend another twenty percent of his life on another adopted child. Jen had more or less told him to piss off, and the gallery owners had decided it would be a good idea if he lay low for a while.

He told himself most of it would blow over in a week or two. After all, nothing had really changed. The newspapers and gallery owners couldn't take his talent away, and there was always a market for that. In any case, with six million pounds sitting in the bank, he could write his own agenda.

Becky was the only real problem, and here he felt stumped. He'd enjoyed the reunion, and of course it had netted them a fortune, but it had set his wife off on an emotional roller-coaster. True, she'd already been upset by the woman's phone call, but ever since the weekend she'd seemed like a different woman altogether.

She was only forty, so it couldn't be the menopause, not yet. Maybe she was just broody, whatever that meant. Richard was leaving the nest, and she needed someone or something to take his place. For a second Edward regretted being less than enthusiastic about the ludicrous theatre group – it was certainly a less disruptive hobby than adopting children.

He supposed he could understand her feeling at a loose end, but not why she seemed so determined to take it all out on him. The other night he had felt, for the first time since the earliest days of their relationship, that she might really leave him, and it had been a strange feeling. There'd been a vague sense of liberation, but also a sharp sliver of panic.

Why was her behaviour so over the top?

And then it occurred to him. She must have found

out about him and Jen. Maybe Jen had even told her – the bitch. That would explain it, he thought.

He sighed. Didn't she know it had nothing to do with her? None of them ever had. It was her that he loved, her that he needed.

Becky, having spent the day escaping from home at the office, came back soon after five to find Edward still in his study. There was a strange look on his face which she knew she was supposed to notice, but for once she couldn't be bothered. "I need to talk to you," she said, and somehow managed an accompanying smile.

"OK," he said.

She told him what Richard had told her. How he had followed her to the meeting with his real mother in Russell Square, and then followed Sheila back to the supermarket where she worked. How he had searched Edward's desk for the adoption documents and discovered the name of his real mother. How he had gone back to the supermarket, read the same name on her identity tag, and followed her home. How he had come back home the previous night, wanting to know why they had lied to him. How she had told him the whole story, including the fact that his mother was dying and looking for a home for her daughter.

Edward listened without interrupting, an incredulous look on his face. "And I suppose you also told him that I was against adopting her?" he asked when she was finished.

"I didn't have to."

He shook his head. "Why am I getting all the blame here?" he asked. "Not wanting to adopt another child isn't a crime, is it?"

She looked at him coldly.

"And why do I get the feeling that there's something else going on here? This is revenge, isn't it?"

She looked at him. "For what?" she asked, but the words were hardly out of her mouth before she knew. All those looks at the cottage, Jen's reluctance to come over on the Sunday. She tried to ignore the sinking feeling in the pit of her stomach. "This has nothing to do with you and Jennifer," she said.

"I think it has," he said abruptly. His tone changed. "I'm sorry, Becky. It just happened. We were both drunk. It didn't mean anything."

"No," she agreed, "I don't suppose it did." She wanted to run from the room, but she managed to hold herself still for a few moments more. "I'm sorry for what I said the other night," she said. "I didn't mean to issue you with an ultimatum." She took a deep breath. "But I do want to adopt Carmen," she told him, "and I'd like to feel that you've thought the whole thing through, rather than just given me a knee-jerk response."

The phone rang in the middle of *EastEnders*, but Josey seemed to be expecting the call. "I'll get it," she said, leaping up, and for the next few minutes they could hear the excited murmur of her voice in the distant kitchen.

When she came back her face reflected the old tell-tale mix of happiness and anxiety, and Cath knew to expect the worst.

She didn't have long to wait. "That was Wayne," Josey told them, trying hard to keep the excitement out of her voice. "And he's got tickets for Blur in London tomorrow night. Blur," she repeated, just in case they hadn't realized whom she was talking about.

171

"You must be joking," Neil said, causing Cath to give him a "let me handle this" look.

"I thought you and Wayne had broken up," she said reasonably.

Josey shrugged. "People break up and get together again all the time. People in real relationships have rows – you told me that." She pursed her lips. "I really want to go. Mum," she said beseechingly. "I mean, you know I like Wayne, but it's Blur as well. I'll never get another chance to see them."

Cath weighed her words carefully. "I can see why you want to go," she said, "but London? That would mean missing school, wouldn't it?"

"You already let us miss one day this week because you thought it was a good idea. And what's one more day anyway?"

"How would you get there, and where would you stay?" Cath asked, silencing Neil with another look.

"Wayne says we can get the midday bus, and he has friends who have a flat," she added, with rather less certainty. "There'll be lots of us, honest. Nothing will happen."

"Maybe not, but you know we're not going to let you go off to London to stay with people we've never met."

Josey's face fell, then rose again. "Couldn't we stay with Auntie Jen?" she asked. "Just the two of us, I mean."

Cath looked at Neil. "What do you think?"

He knew what she wanted him to say. "I don't like you missing school, but if it's a one-off, and Jen's there and hasn't already got something else arranged . . ."

"Ring her," Cath told Josey. "The number's in the

book by the phone upstairs. If she's there, I want to talk to her too."

Josey took the steps two at a time.

"Are we hoping Jen's in or out?" Neil asked Cath.

"God knows. I'm just glad we didn't have to give her a flat no. And if Jen's willing, then she'll see they don't get up to anything."

"And if she's not?"

"Then we say no. I'm not letting her and Wayne Newsome run loose in London for twenty-four hours."

"Good, you were beginning to worry me for a bit."

She made a face. "I'll say no, but I can't help feeling it'll just make her more likely to throw herself at his feet."

"You'd think she might have noticed the timing," Neil said. "Two days after our win's in the paper he decides he wants her back."

"I'm surprised it took him two days," Cath murmured.

"It took him that long to read the article," Neil said.

Cath smiled. "Yeah, but she loves him. And us standing in the way is just going to make her love him more." She sighed. "I suppose that means I'm hoping Jen says yes."

But Josey's slow descent suggested otherwise. "All I got was the answer-machine," she said dejectedly.

"Did you leave a message?"

"I asked her to call back the moment she came in."

"I hope she doesn't come in at three," Neil said.

Josey scowled at him.

"Well, you'd better ring Wayne," Cath told her. "Tell him you can go if Jen says you can stay there, but not otherwise."

"He'll want to know this evening," Josey thought out loud.

"Then he may be out of luck," Neil said gratuitously.

Becky walked up the service road which ran between the elegant row of Georgian houses and Highbury Park. There was a time when she'd come here quite often, but the last visit had been at least two years ago, and maybe even three.

There was a light on in the first-floor flat's front room. She rang Jen's bell, and asked herself what she was doing there. There didn't seem much point in angry accusations of betrayal, and she certainly didn't intend asking Jen not to see Edward again. So why had she come?

She rang the bell again, and waited by the entryphone, but still there was no answer.

Becky walked back across the service road and stared up at the lit windows. There was a flickering effect behind them, which could only come from a television. Feeling the first stirrings of anxiety, she recrossed the road, determined on ringing bells until such time as someone let her into the building, but luck brought her back to the door just as it opened to let someone out.

She tried to brush past him, but he moved his not inconsiderable bulk to block her path. "Who are you going to see?" he asked.

"Jennifer Hendrie," she said brightly.

"You're a journalist?"

"I'm just a friend," Becky said, realizing the reason

for his obstructiveness, and wondering whether to admit that she was a fellow-lottery winner. "Her light's on," she added, "but she isn't answering the bell."

"Lets try it again," he said, moving past her.

She seized her chance. "It's OK, I'll knock on her door," Becky said, moving quickly towards to the stairs.

He took a couple of steps after her, opened his mouth to say something, then obviously decided not to bother. She heard the front door slam behind him just as she reached the door to Jen's flat.

She rapped on the frosted glass and waited, but there was still no sign of life within. Putting her eyes to the letter-box she could see only an empty hallway and the open doorway to the illuminated front room in the distance. If the TV was on, she couldn't hear it.

Maybe she'd imagined the flickering light. Maybe Jen was just out.

She pushed at the door – it was certainly locked. Then an old memory resurfaced – she and Jen had come back here from a shopping trip, and Jen, unable to find her keys, had reached a hand through the letter-box . . .

Becky reached in, felt for the string, and pulled out the key.

Jen was lying on the front-room sofa, her face buried in the cushions, one leg bent awkwardly behind her, the other hanging over the edge of the chair. "Oh Jesus," Becky murmured.

She turned Jen's face to the light, and, heart in mouth, checked that she was still breathing. She was. Next she placed a hand over the heart. The beat seemed regular but faint.

She sat there for a moment, noticing the empty

wine bottles and the plastic bottle of pills, trying to remember the first aid she'd learnt in the Guides all those years before. Turn her on to her side, a voice from the past told her. Check the lips and ears for blueness, listen at the nose and mouth.

There was no blueness, and the breathing seemed regular enough, but neither words nor pinches would open her eyes. Becky went back down the hall and phoned 999 for the first time in her life. "Ambulance," she said in reply to the woman's first question. "Address?" the woman asked.

Becky told her. "My friend's unconscious," she volunteered. "She may have taken an overdose."

"Ten minutes," the woman told her, and Becky went back to the front room. The plastic bottle was almost empty, but that was surely a good sign – no one attempting to commit suicide would leave a few pills behind.

Jen was still breathing regularly, but her skin seemed cold. Becky went to get the duvet from the bed next door and covered her up with it. Then she sat beside her, holding a hand, thinking about the irony of it all. On the other side of the room the muted TV news was offering its usual glimpses of a world gone mad.

A few minutes later, hearing the siren in the distance, she walked quickly down to the front door and let the ambulance team in. Back upstairs the man took one look at Jennifer and said: "Christ, it's her!"

"Someone famous?" his female partner asked, as if Becky wasn't in the room.

"The woman on the front page this morning. One of the bunch who won the jackpot last week." He grunted. "Funny time to attempt suicide," he muttered to himself.

"How is she?" Becky asked.

"Looks like she'll be all right," the man said without looking up. "Have you any idea how many of those pills she took?" he asked.

"No."

"I don't suppose it matters. Just a few with alcohol and . . ." He shrugged.

They lifted Jen on to the stretcher and carried her downstairs and out to the flashing ambulance. Becky ran alongside, and they were already halfway down the road when she realized she hadn't turned off the TV. But then Jen probably wasn't going to be worrying about her electricity bills for a while.

A few more minutes and they were all rushing through the doors of the Accident and Emergency department. A young Asian girl took the details from her, before suggesting she take a seat while the doctor was examining her friend.

For a long half an hour she watched the stream of urban wounded flow past her, and waited with ever-increasing anxiety for word that Jen really was all right.

"Are you Jennifer Hendrie's friend?" a voice asked, startling her. Its Asian owner didn't look old enough to be a doctor, but the tiredness in his eyes told a different story.

"Yes," she said, getting up.

"Your friend is going to be fine," he said. "I've admitted her for the night, but I think she should be able to go home tomorrow."

Becky breathed a sigh of relief, but still felt she had to ask the crucial question: "Was it the pills?"

"It was the mixture of the pills and the alcohol. And no, there's no way of telling if it was an accident or not." He gave her a sad smile. "Perhaps she will tell you tomorrow. And if it wasn't an accident, then we have psychiatric counselling services available . . ." He was looking over her shoulder. "I'm afraid . . . excuse me."

Two youths had just half fallen through the outer doors, one of them covered in blood.

Becky asked the girl at reception how she could find Jennifer, and was just turning to follow her instructions when a man almost bumped into her.

His face lit up when he saw who it was. "Rebecca Lockwood," he said triumphantly. "Can you tell me why Jennifer Hendrie tried to kill herself?"

Becky's heart sank. "She didn't," she said coldly. "It was just an accident. Now, please . . ."

He was too busy expressing his disbelief to move. "That's not what I've heard from other sources."

"Which other sources?"

"You know I can't divulge . . ."

"Then just get out of my fucking way!" Becky suddenly shouted, causing every face in the waiting room to turn her way. For a second even the journalist looked nonplussed, and she seized the moment to push past him and head down the corridor. It was the first time she could ever remember talking to anyone like that, and she had to admit it felt good.

She found the lift the receptionist had directed her towards and summoned it. Looking back up the corridor she could see no sign of possible pursuit – the bastard had presumably gone of in search of other people to persecute.

On the fourth floor a sign pointed her towards Bevan Ward, which proved to be a series of open spaces rather than the traditional long room lined on either side with beds. A staff nurse was working at a desk, and Becky asked her if she could sit with

Jen. "I think it would be good if a friend was there when she woke up," she said.

The nurse smiled. "As long as you're quiet."

"There's one other thing. The press may try and get in."

"Why, is your friend famous?"

"Not really. She – we – won the lottery last week."

Comprehension dawned on the nurse's face. "I thought I recognized her."

"So is there any way of keeping the press out?" Becky persisted.

"I'm sure we can keep them off the wards," she said. "I'll talk to Security," she added, picking up the phone.

Becky went over to sit beside Jennifer's bed, thinking that getting her home wasn't going to be as easy as getting her here had been. When the story got out the hospital would probably be under siege, and so would Jen's flat. In fact all of them would have the press camping out on their doorsteps.

She should warn the others, she thought, but felt too tired to move.

Somehow it was all turning into a nightmare. Jen doing something as this stupid as this ... It made Becky aware of the thread of hysteria which seemed to be infecting her own behaviour. Was it the reunion or the win? Or both? Probably the latter – they'd given themselves an emotional double-whammy.

And they'd been idiots to think they could just carry on as normal. They needed time to get used to what had happened, time out of the spotlight. They needed, she suddenly realized, somewhere to regroup. And it was hard to imagine anywhere more suitable than their own house on Virgin Gorda.

The staff nurse was walking towards her. "The press won't be allowed up here," she whispered, "but Security would appreciate it if you'd go down and give them a statement. It's always better to give a hungry dog something, isn't it?"

Becky felt like refusing but didn't. "I'd just like to call a couple of people first," she said. "Is there a phone up here that I could use?"

There was one in the corridor outside, and after rummaging through her purse for a suitable coin she dialled Ian's number in Manchester. Much to her relief, he picked up the phone.

"Ring me back, would you?" she asked, and gave him the number. A few seconds later the shrill ring cut through the breathless hush of the sleeping hospital.

"What's up?" he asked anxiously.

She told him.

"Oh Christ," he said when she'd finished.

"She's going to be OK," Becky said.

"This time. Look, I'll be down sometime tomorrow morning. I'll get one of the early trains."

"Great. I feel . . . well, I'm sure she'd want you to be here. I don't feel I know her any more. It's not just this – I felt it at the cottage. There's just something . . ."

"I know what you mean," Ian said. "Are you OK, Becky?"

"I suppose so. Ian, I've just been thinking – the papers are going to go to town with this, so why don't we just accept defeat and hide out on Virgin Gorda for a few days?"

"I don't know . . ."

"We can't just take Jen home and leave her on her own."

"No, you're right." He laughed. "Why not? When are you thinking of?"

"Soon as possible. Tomorrow, even."

"It's my day with Tom tomorrow, but Sunday . . ."

"Sunday's probably better – it'll give us time to . . ." Her voice trailed off as she thought about Richard and his mother. "Can you ring Neil and Cath for me? They ought to know about Jen – and tell them they're invited."

"OK."

"I'll stay with Jen until you get here."

"Right."

She hung up the phone and walked back to the bed. Jen's face seemed more peaceful than it had, but maybe she was just imagining it. She supposed she ought to go and talk to the reporters, but what was there to say other than that her friend had accidentally mixed herself a dangerous cocktail of wine and pills? It didn't really matter what she said because she already knew what the morning papers would say – or rather insinuate. They'd say that one of the undeserving jackpot winners had been suitably punished for her temerity.

Ian had hardly finished punching out Neil and Cath's number when Josey picked up the phone.

"Oh it's you," she said with obvious disappointment. "You don't know where Auntie Jen is, do you?"

"I'm afraid I do. She's in hospital."

"What?"

"She's going to be all right. Now can I talk to your dad?"

11

The sky was just beginning to lighten when Becky, dozing in her chair, was woken by the touch of a hand. She turned to see Jen staring at her, a surprised expression in her eyes.

"I'm in hospital," Jen whispered, as if that was the last place she'd expected to find herself.

"Yes."

"What happened?"

"You mixed alcohol and the wrong pills."

Jen closed her eyes. "That wasn't very clever," she murmured.

"You're going to be OK," Becky said, and found herself wondering why a doctor hadn't put in an appearance during the night. Though maybe one had, and she'd slept through it. "How are you feeling?" she asked.

"A bit woozy, but not too bad. There's a sort of headache, but it's like it's in another head. Sort of far away."

"Do you want anything?"

"A drink of water would be nice."

Becky went to fetch one. Watching Jen sip at it, she decided it was time to ask the question. "Jen," she said tentatively, "it was an accident, wasn't it?"

Jennifer managed a half smile. "I'm not suicidal.

Not quite." She yawned. "But how did I get here? How did you get here, come to that?"

"We came together in an ambulance. I found you in the flat."

"What were you doing . . .? She grimaced and reached out a hand. "I'm sorry, Becky. I know that doesn't mean much, but . . . these days I never seem to think about consequences until it's too late. But I am sorry."

Becky knew what for. "Don't worry about me," she said, squeezing Jen's hand between her own. It still felt cold. The fact that Edward had slept with her somehow didn't seem important any more.

"What happened to us?" Jen murmured after more than a minute had passed.

"The likely lasses," Becky said reminiscently. "I don't really know. I think you began to find me boring. And I expect I was – all I was really interested in was being a mother."

"And you got tired of hearing the same sad stories from me."

Becky smiled. "What's the current problem's name?"

"Stuart. Only he's not the problem – I am. Trouble is, knowing it and doing something about it are different matters." She sighed. "I lost my job yesterday."

"How? Why?"

"I was told that having someone as rich as me in the office wasn't good for morale."

"They fired you for being rich?"

"Worse – they put me on permanent paid leave. I'd have worked for nothing, but they'd rather pay me not to. Ironic, isn't it."

"You'll find another job – if you want one, that is."

"I don't know. It's hard to imagine life without work, don't you think?"

"Yes, but it doesn't have to be paid work. And you don't have to work for anyone else."

"I suppose not."

"Well, you can come on holiday with us. We're all going to Virgin Gorda for a few days."

"All of us?"

"All us lottery winners. At least I hope Neil and Cath will come. Ian said he will. Ah, I forgot to tell you – he's coming down this morning."

"They all know I've been an idiot?"

"I had to warn them. I'm afraid we'll be front-page news again this morning."

Jennifer groaned.

"'Lottery Millionairess in Suicide Bid' ", I should think. I should probably go and find a paper so that we know what we're in for."

"No, don't go."

"OK," Becky said, a little surprised. She wasn't used to seeing Jennifer display any vulnerability.

"It's funny," Jen said, as if she knew what Becky was thinking. "The reunion was really upsetting for me. I mean, I enjoyed it, but the feelings were much more powerful than I expected, and I think I just ran away from them the moment it was over." She stopped, thinking that her unconscious had obviously had other ideas, and that sex with Edward had been its way – a pretty pathetic way admittedly – of keeping those feelings alive. She bit her lip and looked at Becky. "But I guess if winning the lottery gives me the chance of getting my oldest friends back, then it'll be worth it."

They looked at each other for a long moment, and then both burst into giggles.

* * *

Edward hadn't slept particularly well. Becky hadn't come back, and though reason told him she'd gone to friends or a hotel, he found himself suspecting that she'd chosen to pay him back by sleeping with someone else, probably one of her theatrical buddies. And the idea of her with someone else upset him much more than he'd expected it would.

He'd taken to bed with him the fear of losing her, and drifted in and out of an anxious sleep for most of the rest of the night.

Next morning he was eating a solitary breakfast, half oblivious to the accompanying oldies on Capital Gold, when the name Jennifer Hendrie broke into his consciousness. Listening to the rest of the news item he was able to piece together the story: Jen, after taking an overdose in her flat, had been saved by the timely arrival of friend and fellow-lottery winner Rebecca Lockwood.

So that was where she had been. She'd gone round to have it out with Jennifer and ended up saving her. Edward found himself thanking God that the media hadn't got hold of the whole story.

And he was glad that she hadn't slept with anyone else. He really did find it hard to imagine life without her.

Maybe adopting this other kid wouldn't be so bad. He couldn't quite shake off the feeling that he was being taken advantage of, but if the woman really was dying . . .

They could afford two day-nannies, maybe even a live-in – the house was big enough, and in any case they'd probably be moving somewhere bigger. How old was the child? Five? Six? It would only be a couple of years before she was sent off to school.

Edward poured himself another coffee, thinking that Becky was worth at least that much.

And then there was always the PR angle. The offer of a home to the child of an AIDS victim should go a long way towards repairing the damage which had been inflicted on his public reputation over the past few days. And no one could accuse him of mounting a publicity stunt if the child was his adoptive son's sister.

Ian was woken by the doorbell extension ringing on the landing outside his bedroom. The clock said eight-fifteen – he had forgotten to set the alarm.

"Shit," he muttered, grabbing his dressing-gown and half-stumbling down the stairs. As he yanked open the door it occurred to him that his caller might only be another journalist.

But he wasn't. A postman was standing there, a large sack in front of him, a van idling on the other side of the hedge. He picked up the sack and swung it across the threshold. "All yours, mate," he said with a grin. "And don't read 'em all at once."

Ian watched him retreat down the path, and then stared down at his morning post. "Oh Christ," he muttered.

He carried the sack upstairs, parked it in an armchair, and started a bath. Half an hour later – clean, dressed, breakfasted and ready to go – he unravelled the mailbag's fastening and took a look inside. There seemed to be hundreds, maybe even thousands, of letters, and they were all addressed to him. He grabbed a handful off the top and headed out of the house, just in time to find a deputation from the press struggling with the gate latch.

The questions were all about Jennifer.

"I'm going to London to see my friend," he told them all, inserting his key in the Renault's door. "She didn't try and kill herself – it was just an accident. And that's all I've got time to time to tell you." He gave them a smile and took his foot off the clutch.

None of them set off in pursuit, but then why would they? What else could he give them but the ritual denial? It was just a ridiculous game, Ian thought, and maybe by the time all this was over he'd have mastered the basics.

He left the Renault in the car park near Piccadilly and walked briskly to the station. It was little things which made the difference, he thought to himself. Normally he wouldn't have dreamed of paying for a whole day's parking – he'd have come in on the bus to avoid it – but now he didn't need to give it a second thought. He bought a first-class return to London and checked the departures board – the next train didn't leave for twenty minutes. Until Becky's call he'd spent most of the previous evening wondering whether to call Susan, and, if so, what he should say. Now, spotting a row of phones, he decided to make it up as he went along.

Not that improvisation had seemed his strong suit the other evening, he thought, as the phone began ringing.

The wretched answer-machine clicked on, and he manfully resisted the temptation to hang up. "It's Ian, he said after the beep. "I'm at Piccadilly. I'm off to London for the day." He paused. "I may have behaved like a bit of an idiot the other night – to be honest, I'm not sure if I did or I didn't. But if I did, then I'm sorry. I know we've been incredibly lucky, but it takes some getting used to." Another pause. "I'd like to see you again, that's all."

He put the phone down, wondering whether he'd made a fool of himself. What the hell, he thought. He'd been honest.

At the bookstall he picked up yet another newspaper with a familiar face on the front page, and walked down the platform to the first-class carriages. Once ensconced in his seat he took a deep breath and read through the relevant article. It was more or less what he'd expected – only the revelation that Jennifer had "stormed out of her computer glam-job" the day before surprised him. The writer couldn't seem to decide whether Jen was an unstable neurotic who had almost managed to kill herself with incompetence or a guilt-ridden jackpot winner suiciding on excess. The only picture of her was clearly at least a day old – she was standing outside the Highbury Park flat – but there was a smaller one of Becky which could have been used to frighten small children. She actually seemed to be snarling at the camera.

Ian smiled despite himself, and put the paper to one side as the train glided past the Longsight locomotive depot. He took off his jacket, and the ten or so envelopes which he'd hastily stuffed into a side pocket fell out.

He opened and read the one on the top. It was short, at least. The writer merely wanted to suggest that Ian invest some of his money in a scheme for importing BSE-free cattle from Bosnia, where they were apparently wandering the hills, there for the taking.

Ian leaned back in his chair, imagining himself as the boss of a cross-Europe cattle drive. A bit like Billy Crystal in *City Slickers*.

He opened a second letter, hoping they would all be as entertaining as the first.

This one wasn't. A couple in Huddersfield had read his interview in the paper, and, if he really hadn't decided what to do with all his money, then their only daughter Tasha desperately needed one of those operations which were only performed in America. In Pittsburgh, to be precise. The operation and everything that went with it would cost £50,000, which they realized was a lot of money, even for a jackpot winner, but they had only managed to raise £4000 in three months of trying, and time was running out.

The facts alone exercised a pretty hefty pull on Ian's heartstrings, and there was something so dignified about the way they were stated. He carefully folded the letter and put it back in his pocket. He already knew he would check this couple out, and that if they were genuine he would give them the money. After all, £50,000 wasn't a big chunk out of three million. In fact, it was not even two percent.

The other letters stared hopefully up at him.

"Forget it, lads," he murmured. There was no way he could send all the sick children to Pittsburgh.

But it was impossible to just throw the letters away. He opened another, and was glad he had. A man who signed himself Marv "The Incredible" Jackson was offering him a seat on the first interstellar flight to leave earth, which would blast off from a secret site near Blackpool at some time in the following year. The one-way fare was a mere quarter of a million. There was no quote for a return ticket.

Ian kept that letter too, thinking he'd have it framed, and went through the other six, which were less entertaining than Marv's and less harrowing than the one from Tasha's parents. But he was glad the sackful at home was receding with every rattle of the carriage wheels.

He bought himself a coffee and watched the countryside roll by. He'd done this trip so often that he practically knew it by heart, but today the heart of England seemed a deeper green than usual, and the fields almost seemed to glow beneath the pale-grey sky.

The train reached Euston soon after noon, and the journalists he was half-expecting to find at the barricade were nowhere to be seen. He took a taxi to the hospital and, noticing a suspicious-looking scrum of people outside the main entrance, had himself dropped off a couple of hundred yards down the road. From there he worked his way round the back, found an innocent-looking door, and ended up threading his way through the hospital kitchens. A pretty black nurse directed him towards Bevan Ward, and he spotted Becky down the corridor, just hanging up the phone.

She smiled when she saw him. A tired smile.

"How is she?" Ian asked.

"She's OK. She's asleep at the moment, but we've had a long talk. They did decide to keep her in for another twenty-four hours, but the doctor says it's only a precaution."

"I thought the National Health was short of beds."

"She's not on the National Health. I got her a private room – it seemed easier to keep out the press that way."

"Makes sense. Anyway, thank God she's OK. How are you doing?"

"Pretty well, I think. Tired, though." She looked round and her eyes lit on a line of semi-comfortable chairs. "Let's sit down."

"So was it an accident?" he asked, once they were seated.

She gave him a cryptic look. "It's the kind of accident that happens when you don't care," she said quietly. "But she's all right, and maybe something good has come out of it – I feel like I've found a friend again." Becky saw the look of doubt on Ian's face. "She told me about her and Edward," she added.

"I didn't know," he said, "but I guessed."

She shrugged and got up. "Can you remind her that I'm picking her up tomorrow morning? Just in case she's forgotten."

"Sure . . ."

"And I've booked flights for everybody. British Airways to Miami, leaving Heathrow eleven-thirty on Sunday morning. The tickets will be at the British Airways desk, OK? I booked one for Tom too, just in case."

"Wow. OK. I'll have to talk to Ellie about that. Are you going home now?"

"No. I decided on an Edward-free day. I've got to go and feed Jen's cat, and then I'm going to check into a hotel, have a few hours' sleep, and then go out and buy a change of clothes. I want to see Richard, and I've got a theatre-group meeting this evening."

"Have fun," Ian said. He hadn't seen Becky like this in more than twenty years. "And if you want to avoid the reporters at the front door try going out through the kitchens – that's the way I came in."

"No need," Becky said. "I'm beginning to enjoy telling them where to get off."

She disappeared with a cheery wave, and Ian quietly let himself into Jennifer's room. She was still asleep, her mouth slightly open, her hands palm to palm beneath her cheek, like a little child.

* * *

Becky waited in the school's visitors' room, surrounded by the forbidding portraits of previous headmasters. They were all old men, and none of them looked as if they'd had a doubt in their lives. Not for the first time, she wondered why she had ever agreed to Richard coming here. In the past her great consolation had been that he actually seemed to like it, but recent events had started her wondering just how good she was at reading him.

During the taxi ride from central London she had come to terms with leaving the country for a week. It might seem ridiculous, but, at present, there didn't seem much doubt that Sheila was better equipped to take care of herself than Jennifer. In fact, Becky found herself thinking, Sheila had dealt with a hard life rather better than either she or Jen had dealt with an easy one.

She hoped Richard would like her when they met on the following afternoon, would appreciate who she was. But that was probably asking too much – he was only sixteen.

"Hi, Mum," he said, sitting down beside her. "How's Jen?"

"You know about it all?" She supposed she shouldn't be surprised.

"You and your friends are beginning to rival *Coronation Street*," he said matter-of-factly.

"She's fine. I'm sorry about all this," she told him. "Is it making things difficult for you?"

"No, not really. There aren't too many boys with poor parents here, and if anyone says anything I tell them winning the lottery's the only honest way of becoming rich these days."

Becky laughed.

"So what did you come to tell me?" he asked.

The tone was casual, but there was worry in his eyes.

"Two things," she said. "I've arranged for us to meet Sheila – your mother – tomorrow afternoon." She looked at him. "You *are* sure you want to?"

"Of course. Are we going to her flat?"

"It seemed the best idea. I'll pick you up here at midday, OK?"

"Fine. Have you and Dad decided yet – about Carmen, I mean?"

She hesitated, but only for a moment. "I've decided," she said. "If Sheila still wants me to take her then I'm going to."

His instinctive smile turned into a frown. "But what about Dad?"

"He'll have to make his own decision."

He looked at her for several seconds before asking: "Are you sure?"

"Couldn't be surer," she said.

"OK," he said, as if he wanted to think about it some more before saying anything else. "So what's the other thing you have to tell me?"

"I've invited everyone to Virgin Gorda for a few days, maybe a week. It was Jen's accident gave me the idea. We've all been, well, I suppose 'traumatized' is the word, by the last week, and it seemed like a good idea to get away from the newspapers and help each other back to sanity. You can come, of course, but it's up to you – I know your exams are getting close. But it might be nice, revising on the beach."

"What about my . . . what about Sheila?"

"I asked her if she wanted to come, but she said no. I think she just wants to spend time with Carmen while she can, in their own home."

"But what if she . . . gets worse suddenly?"

"Nothing's going to happen in a few days."

"How can you be so sure?"

"That's what she told me. While we're away a solicitor will be drawing up the adoption papers, and when we come back . . ."

"I don't think I'll come," Richard decided. "I need to work," he said. "And, well, I'll be here if anything does happen."

"She has friends," Becky said gently.

"Yeah, but . . . and I do need to work."

"OK. You won't feel deserted if we go?"

He looked surprised. "God, no." He grinned suddenly. "I don't think I could bear to spend a week listening to you lot complaining about how hard it is to be rich."

As she walked back to the waiting taxi Becky decided that maybe she hadn't done such a bad job as a mother after all.

Jennifer lay in the hospital bed, watching the last of the sunlight creep up the opposite wall. Ian had just left, leaving her alone for the first time that day, and though she was grateful for both his and Becky's company, she also felt glad to be on her own once more.

Perhaps that's the trouble, she thought. She had got so used to living most of her life alone that she couldn't cope with other people for more than a few hours.

The thought of spending a week with the others, even in the Virgin Islands, was a scary one, but she knew it would be good for her psyche. Who else did she have to hang on to? She didn't suppose she'd ever see her work colleagues again, which didn't seem such a terrible loss. And as for Stuart . . . he wouldn't even want her for the money. He'd take it willingly enough, and he'd go to bed with her, but he still wouldn't really want her, not as a partner, not as someone to share a life with.

But was that what she really wanted? It was all very well for her to complain that she always ended up with the wrong men, but they weren't arriving by post – she was choosing them.

Was she actually selecting them for their unsuitability? Because she knew she couldn't cope with someone suitable?

And if so, how had she got like this? What was wrong with her?

Becky had rung Middlesbrough for her the night before, and she herself had called that afternoon. Her mother had seemed determined to come down at first, but she had managed to dissuade her. All too easily, the thought now crossed her mind.

Jennifer felt a rush of self-hatred. She hated the idea of her mother turning up, had almost told her so in those very words, and now felt vaguely hurt that she hadn't come anyway. "There's no pleasing you," her father used to say, though always with a laugh.

Her mother had seemed more interested in the cheque than the overdose. She'd been full of plans for distributing her daughter's largesse, but Jennifer thought it most likely that it would spend several days lying in state on the living-room mantelpiece.

Why did so many parents end up more interested in the son or daughter they had wanted than the one they actually had?

When the taxi deposited her outside Ladbroke Grove tube station Becky still had an hour and a half to kill before the theatre group meeting at eight. The sun was still shining, so she found a pub with a garden and sat outside, washing down a microwaved moussaka with two glasses of white wine, before walking up the hill to the house of the couple who were hosting the evening's gathering.

She was feeling more than a little trepidation at the prospect of facing the other members of the group. She didn't really know any of them that well, and she wasn't at all sure how they would react to the fact of the lottery win and her husband's recent monopolization of the nation's front pages.

Some were certainly surprised to see her, and she thought she detected a few envious glances, but nobody was outwardly hostile, and most people offered good-natured congratulations or commiserations, depending on their level of cynicism. Once the meeting was underway Becky found it almost possible to forget how much had changed since the last one.

The group's secretary went through the summer festivals they'd been invited to perform at, and there was an animated discussion of what they were going to perform at which. Talk of the props led to talk about transport, and the lamentable state of the group's van.

Becky was aware of several quick glances in her direction, and felt a momentary surge of resentment. It vanished as quickly as it had come – after all, what was more natural than to look to those with money when something needed buying? "I'd like to buy us a new van," she said.

Later, when they were discussing possible new performance pieces, she put some more money on the table. "There's a film called *It Could Happen To You*," she said. "Has anyone seen it?"

Only one woman had.

"It's about a man who wins the lottery ... but I won't go into the story. There's one scene in which he and the woman who's won it with him buy a sackful of subway tokens – it's set in New York – and hand them out at a station so that lots of people get free rides home that night. Now I don't want to do that, but I would like to offer some money for something like it, something that would help people and make a point at the same time. Not a fortune," she added with a smile. "Maybe a few hundred pounds."

The man on her left remembered one such performance. "You mean, like when they tossed pound notes off the Stock Exchange balcony and the brokers clawed each other's eyes out trying to get to them."

She smiled. "I'd rather work out something in which the money went to people who needed it."

The chairperson nodded. "So let's all think up ways to spend Becky's money by the next meeting . . ."

She walked home from the meeting feeling good, and not even the prospect of confronting Edward could completely vanquish her sense of a day well spent.

He was waiting for her, sipping at his cognac as the Third World burned on *Newsnight*. "How's Jen?" he asked.

"She's all right. Edward, I've asked everyone to Virgin Gorda. I think we all need to get away for a few days."

She expected an explosion, but he simply nodded. "That's a good idea," he said. "I've been doing some thinking," he went on. "I've decided you're right. We should adopt the girl."

She felt a wash of contradictory emotions – relief, affection, disappointment. "Do you mean it?" she asked.

"Yes, of course," he said, managing to repress most of the irritation.

She walked up and kissed him. "Richard'll be so pleased," she said.

The picture quality on their new big-screen TV was wonderful, and the home-theatre sound system which went with it was truly amazing. It was a pity the programmes were still such crap.

Neil looked at his watch again.

"It's only ten to," Cath said. "Another ten minutes," she added hopefully, though in her heart of hearts she found it hard to believe Josey would be home on time. After losing out on the trip to London her elder daughter was not likely to be in a conciliatory mood. Cath's only real hope was that the gold-digging Wayne would have the sense to realize that he needed Josey's parents' approval. But he was probably too cocky to realize he needed anyone's.

Neil turned back to *Newsnight*, and for a moment it seemed as if Jeremy Paxman was in the room with them. "How did Josey like the news of our trip?"

"I don't think it really registered. But she'll love it." She smiled. "Maybe she'll meet someone else."

"Maybe she'll phone Wayne every night, and we won't even be able to say we can't afford the calls."

They both heard a car in the distance, and sat listening until it began to fade again.

"It's hard to believe," Neil said conversationally. "Our fifteen-year-old is out with a twenty-year-old, and the best we can manage is to put limits on the time they spend together. They could be doing anything out there, but we'll be happy as long as they've done it by eleven o'clock. You know, it makes me nostalgic for Victorian times. Or Spanish chaperones."

"Or young Muslim women veiled from head to foot?" Cath asked sweetly.

"Sometimes I wonder."

Cath looked at her husband. "And I bet when you were sixteen you had fantasies about the fifteen-year-old down the street?"

"Fantasies, yeah."

"And if she'd offered you a taste of paradise I suppose you'd have turned her down?"

Neil grinned. "Maybe not. But I was a Scout. I'd've been prepared."

"Let's hope Wayne is."

"Oh God, let's hope he doesn't need to be." He looked at his watch. "It's eleven o'clock," he said, getting up and walking to the window.

"Now don't get angry with her over a few minutes."

"How about a few hours?"

"Ever the optimist." Cath got up. "Do you feel like some hot chocolate?"

"Why not."

She went through to the kitchen to make it, leaving Neil staring out into the dark. When she came back he was still there.

He took the hot chocolate and stared at it. "This world revolves around people between ten and forty, he said, "and this is the drink for people who are either too young or too old to join in the fun. It's about the only thing left which hasn't got caffeine or alcohol in it." He took a sip. "It's good though. You don't think they could have gone to London anyway, do you?" he asked.

"Not to see Blur – they'd never have got there in time. And anyway, I don't think Josey would pull a stunt like that."

They could hear another car approaching, and this one stopped. There were murmuring voices, a man's laugh, and then silence. Neil and Cath looked at each other, remembering teenage kisses.

Josey appeared a few minutes later.

"You're twenty minutes late," Neil said, more mildly than he felt.

"Oh, am I?" She smiled at them both. "But it's OK, Dad."

"Well . . ."

Cath was looking closely at her daughter, and particularly at the glassy film on her eyes. "What have you been smoking?" she asked.

"Nothing."

"Josey!"

"Oh, only a little dope."

"Dope?" Neil echoed disbelievingly.

She gave him a weary look. "Come on, Dad, everyone smokes dope these days. All my friends do. You and Mum used to smoke it – I've heard you talk about it."

"Not when we were fifteen."

"I'm nearly sixteen. And kids grow up faster now – I've heard you say that too." She sighed dramatically. "I'm whacked. I think I'll go to bed."

"Wait a . . ." Neil began, but Cath gave him a warning look.

"We'll talk about this in the morning," she told Josey.

"OK." She smiled at them both again, and looked about twelve. "Good night, then."

"Well, at least she's forgotten about Blur," Cath said, once Josey had disappeared upstairs.

"I should think everything's a blur," Neil retorted. "Maybe we should move to the Virgin Islands while she still qualifies."

"If she does," Cath murmured.

12

Saturday morning brought another sackful of letters to the house in Chorlton. Ian sat and stared at it, wondering how many missives of heartbreak it contained. What self-destructive trait had caused him to publicize his indecision over what to do with the money, and so invite the deluge? If he'd said right out that he intended to spend the money on a stream of bimbos no one would have bothered him.

And Tasha's parents would still be looking for money. The day before he'd called his new solicitor from the hospital, and asked him to have the family checked out. Ian found it hard to believe that the writers of the letter he'd read could be frauds, but it seemed worth making sure. If Tasha was a figment of someone's imagination he didn't think he'd have much trouble finding a kid who wasn't.

He got up, poured himself another cup of coffee, and reluctantly rewound the tape on the answer-machine. There'd been no message from Susan when he got back late the previous evening, but she might have tried to leave one – the tape had been full of people asking him for money. He should have thought of switching to an ex-directory number before he gave the interview.

He wandered across to the piano and idly picked

out the opening notes of one of his own compositions. He hadn't put in any practice time for over a week, and he hadn't spoken to anyone in the band since Tuesday, which wasn't good.

Nor, he suddenly realized, had he got around to informing the two editors that they wouldn't be getting the articles they were expecting. They might have guessed as much – always assuming they'd seen a paper – but he still felt a surge of guilt. Maybe Susan had been right after all.

The two sacks of mail sat in their armchairs, giving him accusing looks.

"Not today, chaps," he said, looking at his watch. He was going to be late for meeting Tom.

He was, but not as late as the train, which was running thirty minutes behind schedule. He bought a paper and took it into the buffet, hoping rather than expecting that Jennifer's crisis would have finally exhausted press and public interest in them. After all, Andy Warhol had said one day everyone would be famous for fifteen minutes – not fifteen days.

They should be so lucky. There was another double-page spread, which Ian read with the now familiar mixture of anger and amusement. The paper had managed to find someone who must have known them all in 1976 – the informant wasn't named – and he or she had volunteered the information that Edward and Jennifer had once been lovers. It wasn't clear from the article whether they had stopped being lovers when Becky and Edward got together, but the description of the house in Tisbury Road as "a sixties-style commune" was suggestive, to say the least. It was also alleged, inaccurately, that Becky and Neil had been an item, and that Cath's interest in herbalism masked a deeper obsession with witchcraft. Ian was somewhat disappointed to discover that the worst they could find to say about him was that he was a jazz musician.

The breathless discovery that Jennifer – and not Becky – had attended the exhibition opening ten days earlier was kept back for the finale. Had betrayal in love, the writer wondered, been at the root of Jennifer Hendrie's suicide attempt?

Ian put down the paper in disgust, finished his coffee, and went back outside. The train was now running forty-five minutes late – not a bad trick for a two-hour journey – and its arrival platform had been changed, as if in punishment for the bad timekeeping. He made his way through the tunnel to the new platform, walking behind a young Oriental woman with beautiful shining hair and longer-than-usual legs.

A "jazz musician", he thought. Maybe he should try and live up to his exciting "sixties-style commune" past and do a sex tour of the world. Because when it came down to it he was entering his forties with precious little variety in his sexual past, and there must be some company – "Sexual Adventures Abroad" perhaps – which offered erotic pleasures in exotic places.

Ian sighed, thinking it was a pity he'd watched that documentary on modern-day sexual slavery the other week. And in any case it was Susan he wanted. Susan and Ornella Muti in *Flash Gordon*.

The train finally arrived, and Tom tumbled out, looking first expectant and then disappointed. "You haven't bought any new clothes," he said.

"Not yet."

"And no new car?"

"Not yet."

"Dad, have you spent anything yet?"

Ian took the envelope out of his pocket and handed it to his son.

"What are . . . ?" Tom started to say, and then he realized. "They're season tickets," he said. His eyes were shining. "There's four of them. Why four?"

"You might want to bring friends, or Josh maybe. Neil and Daniel might come."

"I suppose they'll have season tickets at Old Trafford."

"Probably."

"How much did these cost?" Tom asked, examining them with a reverence which would have pleased an old manuscript.

"A lot."

"Hundreds? Thousands?"

"We're talking four figures."

"Wow!"

Twelve hours after her return, Neil and Cath were still debating their response to Josey's admission of drug use. They were sitting in a pub in Shrewsbury, where the whole family had come to shop for their week in the Caribbean sun. The three kids had been let loose in the shops, though without the suitcases full of crisp new notes they had apparently expected. The adults would do the actual buying, once the children had decided what they wanted.

"Of course I can see it from her point of view," Neil was saying. "Most of the adults she's known have smoked pot at one time or another, and probably half of them still do. I've got nothing against it – as long as it doesn't become a lifestyle, that is – but she's only fifteen. It's too early . . ."

"I'm not disagreeing," Cath said, after finishing her half of Guinness and putting down the glass.

"She still needs a short-term memory," Neil added.

"I know. But we've got two choices here, and I think we might as well whistle at the moon as forbid her ever to touch drugs again. Would you have listened to your parents if they'd said that?"

"They did say that."

"And you ignored them completely. If we want to exercise any sort of control over what she takes – and how much – then we have to take some notice of the world she lives in. I expect most of her friends do smoke pot sometimes, and I don't think we have a hope in hell of stopping Josey smoking it. I do think we can teach her the difference between pot and hard drugs, and I think we can convince her that it's a good idea not to smoke too much of it, and not to smoke at all if she has school the next day. She's a reasonable kid – she'll listen if she thinks we're being reasonable."

"Sex, drugs and rock 'n' roll," Neil murmured. "It feels weird, imagining her spend her pocket money on scoring dope."

"And she'll be expecting a rise now," Cath said cheerfully. "Come on, we're going to be late."

They left the pub and walked down the hill to the prearranged meeting-place, where Josey, Angie and Daniel solemnly handed over their lists.

"I thought you were looking for swimsuits," Neil told the two girls.

"There aren't any nice ones," Josey said, "and anyway, that's the sort of thing we can buy once we get there."

"At twice the price."

"Dad, that doesn't matter any more!" Josey burst out in exasperation.

At some point, Neil thought, he was going to have to give the children a fatherly talk on the true value of money, and no doubt end up sounding like the sort of person he'd always thought needed shooting.

But for the next hour they consumed – new clothes, novels for the journey, new portable CD players and CDs, guidebooks and nature books, gallons of insect repellent, suntan oil and perfume, and a camcorder. While they were at it, it seemed sensible for everyone to get a new camera.

Later that afternoon Cath came in from the garden and found Neil staring at the purchases spread out across the kitchen table.

He looked up at her. "Do you know we spent nearly £3000 today?" he asked soberly.

Cath looked at him. "And that was just on things we needed," she said, and they both started laughing.

In the taxi Becky and Richard sat in silence, both absorbed in their own thoughts. He was thinking about the almost overwhelming sense of urgency which his mother's condition had instilled in his heart. There seemed so little time to get to know her, so little time in which to fit her into the puzzle of his own life. He wondered if that was a selfish way of looking at it, and decided he didn't care if it was.

A couple of days before, Max – the only friend he'd told about Sheila – had asked Richard if he was angry at her for suddenly reappearing after all these years, and he'd had to admit that the thought hadn't even crossed his mind. Her reappearance had felt like a gift. It still did.

In the seat next to him Becky had only just noticed that he was wearing jeans and a T-shirt – dressing down for the area, she guessed.

She was feeling just as anxious about the upcoming meeting. Richard had always been inclined to keep his feelings to himself, and today she had the sense that all the pent-up emotions were bringing him close to bursting. They should be talking, she realized, and remembered in the same moment that he didn't yet know about Edward's volte-face.

"Your father's decided he does want to adopt Carmen," she said, more abruptly than she intended.

His face lost its intensity for a few seconds. "That's great. Does Sheila know?"

"I called her this morning. And you can call her your mother, Richard. I won't be upset."

"It feels weird. You're both my mother."

"So that's what you call us both."

"OK," he said. "And Dad really wants to adopt Carmen?" he asked a few moments later.

"I think so," she said.

He gave her a doubtful look but didn't say anything, and she found herself wondering for the umpteenth time about the mess of contradictory thoughts and emotions which seem to characterize Richard's relationship with Edward. She couldn't remember who had said that there was nothing so mysterious as one's own children, but the person in question had obviously never adopted one.

They arrived outside the block of flats a few minutes later. "What are we going to talk about?" Richard asked suddenly as they climbed the stairs.

"Each other," Becky said glibly. It was a good question, she thought, ringing the bell.

Sheila came to the door, Carmen at her heels. She looked better than on the other occasions – there was more life in her eyes, more animation in the face. "Come in," she said, as if they'd just dropped in for tea.

"This is Richard," Becky said formally.

"I thought it might be," Sheila said. "This is your sister Carmen," she told the boy, and for several seconds they all just stared at each other. "So," Sheila said, once they were all settled in the living room, "tell me about yourself", and for the next ten minutes she gently cross-examined him about school and what he liked doing outside it, which sports he liked, which TV programmes, what sort of music.

And while this was going on Carmen just stared at Richard, her dark eyes drinking in the fact of her new brother's existence.

"Why don't you get Carmen to show you her room?" Becky suggested, once it became obvious that Sheila was getting tired. "We have a few things to talk about."

Once the children were gone, the two women discussed the mechanics of the adoption – not the legal process but the human one. They were both agreed that Carmen would suffer the least upset if that process was a gradual one, with Becky making frequent and more protracted visits to the flat before taking over full responsibility for the child. Then both Carmen and Sheila would come to live in the house in Holland Park until such time as Sheila needed or wanted to enter a hospice.

The other woman's matter-of-fact approach filled Becky with admiration, but when she started to say so Sheila quickly cut her short. "It's just an act," she said. "I'm scared stiff really."

"It's a good act," Becky said.

Sheila smiled, and in the silence they could hear Carmen explaining something to Richard. "He's a nice boy, isn't he?" Sheila said.

"I think so."

"You must have done a good job."

Becky felt close to crying. "Maybe," she said. "I sometimes think parents have a lot less influence on how their children turn out than they think they do."

Sheila laughed. "I bet that theory would appeal to the Queen."

The two women's laughter brought the children back. "I think it's time we went," Becky told Richard. "We'll be back next weekend," she told Sheila. "I'll give you a ring."

"I'm not going with them," Richard said, "so can I come and see you again? In the week?"

"Yes, of course," Sheila said. She looked pleased, Becky thought.

"I want to know about your life," Richard blurted out.

"Then you're a sucker for punishment," she told him, but she was smiling as she said it.

Ian pulled the Renault to a halt outside the house, and noticed that Tom could hardly wait to get out of the car. He hoped Ellie would be as pleased with all their son's new things as the boy was himself.

"I'm going to show Josh the season tickets," Tom said, taking off up the path.

Ellie was standing in the front door, a smile on her face. Maybe she really was pleased for him, Ian thought.

"You don't look quite so decadent in the flesh," she said wryly. "How's Jen?"

"As well as can be expected. It *was* an accident." He looked over her shoulder to make sure Tom was out of earshot. "But we are all running away for a few days to Edward and Becky's place in the Virgin Islands."

"Nice."

"What do you think about Tom coming? I haven't mentioned it," he added, seeing the look on her face.

"Good," she said. "I don't think it would be a good idea . . ."

"I know he'd be missing school, but . . ."

"It's not that. It would make him feel different from the other kids, and they'd start seeing him differently. I've been thinking about this quite a lot," she admitted.

Ian was disappointed, but he could see her point and he said so. "I'd better get his stuff out of the car," he said.

"Will you be here next Saturday?" she asked.

"I plan to be."

"Because one of Tom's friends told him he'd be seeing less of you now that you'd won the lottery, and I think it's worrying him."

"Then I'll definitely be back," he said, extracting the first two laden carriers from the back seat.

"Ian . . ." she began.

"I know. We went over the top. It's just a one-off, I promise."

"OK," she said, mollified. "You don't seem to have spent much on yourself," she added, looking at him.

"That's what Tom said. I'll be wearing Gucci loafers the next time you see me."

"You'll get slugs on them round here. We seem to have more than ever this year."

"Home sweet Hebden." He took a deep breath. "Look, Ellie, I'd like to give you and Josh some money, partly on Tom's account but partly . . . well, you know. But for all I know Josh is going to feel insulted by it." He gave her an appealing look.

"That probably depends on how much you have in mind, she said wryly.

Ian bit the bullet. "I thought of paying off your mortgage, which would cut back your overheads by quite a bit, and giving you another hundred thousand."

She looked at him with disbelief. "I meant . . ."

"You're my only ex-wife," he said. "And the mother of my only child."

She just stared at him.

"Well?" he asked.

"If Josh feels insulted I'll get rid of him," she said laughing.

"You'll what?" Josh said behind them.

"I'll tell you later," she said, and enfolded Ian in a hug.

They carried the bags into the house, and then Tom came out to see his dad off. "We can go next week," he suddenly realized.

"We can. I'm going away for a few days, but I'll be back Friday at the latest."

"Where are you going?" Tom asked suspiciously.

"To the West Indies, with Neil and Cath and the others." He put an arm round Tom's shoulder. "Your mum told me what your friend said, and he couldn't be more wrong. We'll see more of each other now, because I won't have to spend most of the weekend working. And in the summer we'll go on holiday together. Anywhere in the world you want to go. OK?"

Tom grinned at him. "I want to go to Komodo."

"Where's that?"

"I don't know. It's where the Komodo Dragons are."

"Sounds like my sort of place. But you can always change your mind between now and then." He opened the car door and climbed in. "Be good," he said.

Tom was still waving as he rounded the bend at the bottom of the hill, and he could still see Ellie's smile in his mind's eye. It had been a great day.

Jennifer busied herself in the bedroom, packing for the next day's journey, as Van Morrison announced, in the living room, that the healing had begun. She supposed that the music was loud, but nobody had come to complain, not yet anyway.

Becky had invited her to stay with them in Holland Park, but both women had been only too aware of what the papers would have made of it. "LOVE TRIANGLE DEFIANT!", or something along those lines. She could have booked into a hotel for the one night but she already felt guilty enough about leaving Mac with the woman downstairs for a week. "I need a holiday," she told him, as he sat on the bed licking the place where his balls used to be.

And anyway she felt better. A lot better. Becky caring for her in spite of everything, Ian coming down from Manchester ... it had felt like ... it had warmed her heart. "*And the healing has begun . .* "

She had always liked being the centre of attention, one of her inner voices reminded her.

But the message from Stuart on the answer-machine had left her cold. As far as her heart was concerned, he was history. Now all she had to do was not find a replacement.

And to stop feeling sorry for herself. It wasn't many

people who were given such a perfect opportunity to rebuild their lives.

She went to bed early and lay awake in the darkness, watching the faint shadows of the trees outside swaying on the ceiling. It might not be saying much, but she felt better than she had for several months.

On either side of Ian's bed the two alarm clocks achieved perfect co-ordination for the first time, creating a jangling stereo effect that nearly lifted him off the bed. Outside it was still dark, but his connecting flight from Manchester Airport left in less than two hours. After silently congratulating himself on getting packed the night before he flicked the switch on the already prepared coffee machine and ran a bath.

Soaking in the steaming water he decided he would leave one more message for Susan. After all, she *might* have tried to answer the last one.

When he'd got back from Hebden Bridge the previous evening the tape had been full again. He'd sat and listened, hoping to hear her voice, but had been treated instead to another batch of hopeful, desperate or just plain optimistic people. One woman with a rather sexy voice had even proposed marriage to him, and had spelt out in considerable detail what joys he could expect to experience in their nuptial bed. At the other extreme, a man with a Yorkshire accent had launched into a bitter diatribe against lust and avarice-infected perverts like Ian and his cronies. After hoping that they fried in hell for their too-numerous-to-count sins, he had demanded a donation to the "Church of Redemption for the White Race".

There had been no message to tug the heartstrings, but one caller had told him – it had sounded like a quote, but there was no reference – "To get the full value of a joy, you must have someone to share it with."

There had been no message from Susan.

Now, sitting with his coffee in the only chair not occupied by a sack, he relived the sinking feeling he had experienced in his stomach when the tape ended. He wanted someone to share all this with. Someone real.

He reached for the phone, punched out the number and, as expected, got her answer-machine. "Hi," he said, "it's me again. My tape fills up with well-wishers every time I reset it, so, just in case you've been trying to get through, I thought I'd better let you know I'm going away for a few days. I'll be back Friday at the latest and I'll call you again then." He paused, not knowing what else to say. "I really want to see you again," he said at last.

On the road to the airport he thought of a dozen different things he might have said, and then started wondering if he was behaving like a complete idiot. They'd only been out twice, and here he was feeling like her rejection was the end of the world.

Practicalities took over at the airport, and then he browsed through the bookshop in search of something to read during the ten-plus hours of flying time which lay ahead. He'd already bought a new paperback biography of Sam Cooke when his eyes lit on an American book about lottery winners. It was basically a feast of anecdotes, and a cursory look-through was enough to convince Ian that the American and English experiences wouldn't be so different. Here were the telephone calls, fabricated press interviews, damaged relationships.

Maybe it contained the blueprint for maximizing the

ups and minimizing the downs of lottery winning, Ian thought. And it wasn't as if he couldn't afford it.

Having decided to drive, Neil and Cath were already halfway to Heathrow.

"It's not as big as that house in the picture," Cath was explaining to Daniel, who'd somehow managed to dig up the previous Thursday's newspaper.

"You mean that's not it?" Angie asked disappointedly. "So whose house is this?"

"It could be anyone's," Cath said.

"Probably the editor's," Neil offered.

"Edward and Becky's house will be nice," Cath assured her younger children. "And anyway I don't expect we'll spend much time indoors."

"What's the island like, Dad?" Daniel asked.

"It's about eight miles long, a mile or two wide, with a mountain at one end and flat at the other. Lots of nice beaches . . ."

"Can we go snorkelling?" Josey asked.

"I expect so. Basically it's a rich man's island . . ."

"That's us," Daniel said contentedly.

Neil looked at Cath and murmured: "I'm beginning to wish we were going to somewhere like Bangladesh instead."

"What could we do there?" Josey asked scornfully from the back seat.

"Probably get killed," Angie decided.

In the first-class lounge at Heathrow Becky decided on one last call to Richard.

"You only spoke to him a couple of hours ago," Edward protested.

"He's only a child."

"He's sixteen!"

"Which means twelve-going-on-eighteen. You can scour the duty-free when I get back."

Richard, of course, was as frustrated by her anxiety as Edward. "Mum, I'll be all right," he said, and she had a mental picture of him rolling his eyes towards the ceiling.

"You're sure you've got our number?"

"Positive. I'll have it tattooed on my forehead if you like."

"That would make me feel better."

"Mum!"

"You're going to go and see Sheila on Tuesday?"

"You know I am. And the rest of the week I'll be working flat out. Don't worry about me – I'll be fine."

"OK," she said reluctantly. How could a sixteen-year-old hope to understand the sort of emotional currents he was dipping himself into? For a moment she was tempted not to go, but he would never forgive her if she didn't. And they'd be back by the next weekend. "Take care of yourself," she said.

"You too, Mum. Enjoy life among the plutocracy," he added, only partly tongue in cheek, and hung up.

She grinned and walked back into the lounge, whose population had been dramatically increased by the arrival of both Jennifer and the Shropshire contingent. A couple of obvious journalists were hovering in the corridor outside.

Ian arrived a few minutes later, waving his new book and announcing that "eighty per cent of American lottery winners head straight for Hawaii".

The flight to San Juan took eight hours, two of which were taken up by a film about a pig called Babe. Neil, Cath and Ian, none of whom had ever flown first-class before, found both food and seats a definite improvement, but eight hours was still a long time to be cooped up, particularly for the younger children. And having spent most of his other flights wishing nothing but ill of those sitting forward of the dividing curtain, Neil had a hard time adjusting to sitting there himself. It just felt wrong – it was as simple as that.

They had an hour and a half's wait at the Puerto Rican airport, and sat in air-conditioned comfort gazing out across the palm-fringed tarmac and distant mountains. There was no direct connection to Virgin Gorda that day, so they took the short flight into Tortola, the largest of the British Virgin Islands, and then sat around once more while Edward went off in search of information. He came back ten minutes later with the news that the plane he had just chartered was ready to leave whenever they were, and some twenty minutes after that they were looking down on green and brown Virgin Gorda, lying peacefully in its blue-green sea.

Two taxis were waiting at the small island airport, apparently summoned by the sight of an incoming plane, and the nine of them climbed aboard. The drive took only about ten minutes, leaving an impression of houses scattered across a plain and glimpses of the not-too-distant ocean. The road wound up a hill to Edward and Becky's bungalow, which, though, considerably smaller than the villa in the newspaper, still had three bedrooms and a large living room, all of which had obviously been cleaned and made ready that day. The humming fridge was well stocked with wine, soft drinks and snacks.

A covered, L-shaped veranda fronted two sides of the house. On one side there was a view out across scattered roofs to the harbour and ocean, on the other a well-tended garden bursting with tropical vegetation and two large palms.

"It's about a ten-minute walk to the nearest beach," Becky told them. "But you have to cycle or drive to the really nice ones."

Edward was handing out cans of Coke and uncorking a bottle of wine. The sun was sinking rapidly towards the sea and they half expected to hear a sizzling sound when the two met, but there was only the chatter of birds in the trees.

"Eight days ago," Ian said to Neil, "you were complaining about the price of hamburgers at Maine Road."

13

With nine bodies to pass through the bathroom it was almost ten-thirty by the time they left the house on the following morning. It was a beautiful day, but then, hurricane season excepted, they all were.

The town – a rather grandiose word for the sparse collection of houses and shops which lay behind the yacht harbour – was officially known as Spanish Town, but locals and tourists alike referred to it as "the Valley". Some modern concrete structures were in evidence, but the place didn't seem overdeveloped, and a few ancient-looking wooden houses offered a glimpse of how people had lived in the pre-package-tour Caribbean.

There was a Barclay's Bank agency, an expensive grocery supermarket, a gift shop and several establishments specializing in matters nautical. In one of the latter Becky hired snorkelling equipment, and in another Josey, Angie and Daniel found the swimming costumes they wanted. Looking at Josey in hers, which consisted of about six square inches of cloth, Cath could appreciate Wayne Newsome's pre-lottery interest.

In the meantime Edward and Ian had hired a pair of jeeps, which transported the party and their new equipment to the Mad Dog Bar, a wooden house with a shaded veranda which served as a café. From here they walked down the path to the island's most famous attraction, the jumbled collection of huge granite boulders known as "the Baths", which sat half in the sand, half in the sea.

There were not many other people there – if Virgin Gorda had a low season this was it – and for the rest of the morning they swam, snorkelled and sunbathed to their hearts' content. A trip to the Mad Dog Bar provided a hot-dog lunch, and the afternoon turned into a repeat of the morning. No posse of journalists materialized to spoil the day – the hounds of Wapping, Edward reckoned, were probably about twenty-four hours behind them.

Soon after five they returned to the bungalow, changed, and set out for a restaurant Becky remembered Richard liking. Set on a minuscule island off the northern shore, Blackbeard's Pub was a boat-friendly hamburger house which flew the Jolly Roger. It also boasted customer jam sessions in high season, and Ian took advantage of the vacant piano during their fifteen-minute wait for food. The latter was probably no better than ordinary, but in such surroundings anything would have tasted superb.

With the stars bright above they drove home along the narrow lanes, and even managed a good-night smile for the lone journalist they found camped outside the bungalow.

There were three there on the following morning, sporting – presumably by chance – a collection of shirts in the national colours. Edward and Ian, venturing out to talk, discovered that the Caribbean climate had apparently taken the edge off the journalists' appetite for persecution. This trio, composed exclusively of men in their late twenties or early thirties, was almost friendly.

"We just need a few quotes for tomorrow morning and we'll leave you alone for the rest of the day," the one in the blue shirt told them.

"Fire away," Ian said.

"OK, why did you try to leave England in secret?"

"We didn't. We just left."

"How long are you staying?"

"A few days, maybe a week."

"And then?"

Ian shrugged. "I expect we'll try and get back to our lives, provided you lot have finished with us."

"You'll be lucky," the journalist in the red shirt muttered.

"How's your marriage, Mr Lockwood?" his colleague in white asked.

"Fine," Edward said. "Not that it's any of your damn business."

"But Jennifer Hendrie was your girlfriend once, right?"

"More than twenty years ago, yes. And we've been friends – platonic friends – ever since."

"It is possible, you know," Ian told them. "Some men actually like woman and vice versa. It's called friendship."

"Wow," Red Shirt said sarcastically, "that sounds like our scoop, lads."

"Well, now you've got it, you can head on back to dear old Blighty," Ian suggested.

"You're joking," Blue Shirt retorted. "We'll need at least a week to get this story together," he added, occasioning knowing smiles from the others.

"Don't worry," White Shirt told them. "We won't

be following you around. Or at least, not all the time. Though I expect the photo-boys will be taking a few pics."

"If any of you get too close, we could always hire some locals to feed you to the real sharks," Edward said with a smile.

His good mood, engendered by their leaving England and reinforced by his role as Caribbean guide to the others, extended past lunchtime on their second full day, and that afternoon, with Jen, Neil and the kids in the water, and Ian and Cath off for a walk in the hilly National Park behind the deserted beach, Becky decided it might be a good time to tell him the arrangements she had made with Sheila.

At first he acted as if he couldn't believe what he was hearing. "You've invited her to live with us? In Holland Park?"

"Just for a while. Until she's feels it's time to enter a hospice," she explained patiently.

He shook his head angrily. "And what if she changes her mind? Do we let her die in the house?"

"Why not?" She wasn't sure what the problem was. Was it AIDS in particular or death in general? Or just the thought of a stranger under their roof? An undeserving stranger, by his standards.

He was sitting up now, a dark shape above her, outlined by the sun. "You never bother consulting me," he said. "You just go ahead and do whatever you want. You take decisions as if I don't exist. This holiday's a prime example. You just invite everyone, and then let me know what's happening."

"I had good reason to be angry with you at the time, remember?" she said coldly.

He knocked that aside. "You do it whether you're

angry or not. The first time I heard about your theatre group you were off for the weekend with them."

She thought about what he was saying, but it still seemed like crap, and crap in bad faith at that. "Can we stick to Sheila?" she asked. "I want . . ."

"This woman has AIDS, and you're asking her to live with us. What about Richard?"

"What about him?" she asked, momentarily confused.

"What about the risk to him?"

"There is no risk," she said dismissively. "Look, Edward, I'm sure Sheila would be happier staying where she is. We've arranged it this way for Carmen. Can you imagine what it's going to be like for her? Her only parent will be dying, and she'll be living with strange people in a strange house. We owe it to her to make it as easy as we can."

He shook his head again. "It might be a kind thing to do, but we don't owe the girl anything."

Now she could feel herself getting angry. "I'm assuming you feel that you owe your fellow-human beings some consideration. That when you're in a position to help a six-year-old girl get through something this terrible, that's something you'll want to do."

"Yes, of course. But that's . . ."

"It won't be for long," Becky insisted, wishing she hadn't started this conversation. These days every argument they had seemed to bring forth, like some evil genie, an Edward she hardly felt she recognized. And the really terrifying part was that she knew deep down that he'd always been there.

"I'm not stupid," he was saying. "I do know that people with AIDS can last for years."

* * *

High above the beach, sitting in front of a breathtaking panorama of ocean and islands, Cath and Ian were having their first serious conversation since arriving on Virgin Gorda.

"It's gone better than I expected," Ian was saying. "I mean, let's face it, we're all such different people now."

Cath looked thoughtful. "You think so?"

"Don't you?"

"I suppose so. I guess it's just that we all have something in common again, like we did when we were students."

"We're not going to stop being lottery winners."

"No, but we'll all end up dealing with it in our own ways. This is just to get us through the shock." She smiled. "Neil and Edward are not going to start agreeing about anything – or liking each other – just because they're both rich now."

"Neil seems to be coping with sudden wealth better than I expected."

Cath smiled to herself. "That's probably because we've decided to give half of it away," she said.

"Half of it?" Ian echoed. "That's a much bigger share than I was thinking of."

"Don't say anything," Cath said, "because we haven't told the kids yet." She laughed. "We don't dare."

"Who are you giving it to?"

"No idea."

"Well, don't tell anyone that. After I said as much in that interview I got two sacks full of begging letters, and there'll probably be a lot more waiting for me when I get back." He told her about the letter from Tasha's parents. "After that I stopped opening them," he admitted. "I mean, I could donate the whole lot to Amnesty – I'm sure they could use it, and a lot of people would get helped – but ... well, I guess I'm not Mother Teresa. I want some of that money. I think I want most of it. Or at least enough so I never have to worry about how to pay the next bill ..."

"So does Neil. So do I."

"But it's still hard to ... I feel guilty taking it all. I promised Ellie a hundred thousand, and I wonder whether ..."

"You promised Ellie a hundred thousand?"

"Yep."

"Well, that was generous after what she did to you."

"It doesn't feel it. It feels like having a pound in your pocket and giving a beggar 2p."

They both sat in silence for a few moments, staring out over the ocean.

"What went wrong with Susan?" she asked.

Ian exhaled noisily. "I'm not sure whether she ran away from me or the money or both. I said a couple of stupid things, but nothing that seemed unforgivable. As far as I can remember, I didn't start denying there had ever been a Holocaust or start arguing for a fifth term for the Tories."

"She's divorced and about our age, right?"

"She's been separated about five years."

"Well, a woman who's just spent five years relearning how to live on her own isn't going to just jump into another serious relationship. And let's face it, a single male who's just won the lottery doesn't look like the ideal candidate for a stable long-term relationship."

"But I am," Ian insisted.

"I'm not saying you're not. But she doesn't know you as well as I do."

"It's so bloody frustrating," Ian almost exploded. "This is not only the first woman I've met since Ellie who I can like and lust after in equal measure – she's the last one I'm ever going to meet as who I really am. From here on I might as well be wearing a neon pound sign on my forehead."

Cath laughed despite herself.

"You know, if anyone had told me winning the lottery was going to be a mixed blessing, I'd have thought, yeah, yeah, money may be the root of all evil, but being rich has to beat being poor. Well, it's all right if you already have someone . . ."

"Depends on the someone," Cath said, thinking of Becky and Edward. "But yes, I know what you mean. So far all our mixed blessings have concerned the children. If we hadn't suddenly become eligible parents-in-law I don't think Josey would have ever heard from Wayne Newsome again."

Ian grunted.

"But Neil hasn't gone out looking for luscious cuties, and I've repressed my desire for a toy boy. You know, it's the same with partners as it is with giving away the money, or not giving it away. We've all got to hang on to who we are, and be true to ourselves. Our lives may have changed with all this money, and the way people relate to us will change, but that doesn't mean we have to." She looked at him. "I'm not saying it's going to be simple or straightforward, because the world really has changed for us, but it can't be that hard to hang on to who you are. Especially when there's no money worries to distract you."

"It's funny," Ian said, "but that's more or less what my book says. People carry on being who they are. Good relationships stay good or get better, bad relationships get worse."

"I think you're just going to have to pester Susan. Shower her with everything but money. If she liked you before there's no reason why she shouldn't like you now."

That evening they went back to Blackbeard's Pub, and next morning they all went scuba-diving with a company called Underwater Tours. In the afternoon they hired a boat and cruised around the North Sound before settling on Mosquito Island for more swimming and lazing on the beach. While Edward swam and the others built a very English-looking sandcastle, Jennifer and Josey worked on their tans.

Raised on her elbows, Jennifer could just see Edward's head above the jade-coloured water, about a hundred yards out. He was alone again, as he had been in the tent all those years ago, but this time she felt no sympathy. He'd been very attentive to her all morning, and only an idiot could have missed the connection between that and the fact that he and Becky hardly seemed to be on speaking terms.

"Wayne's not stupid," Josey was saying. "He just doesn't think like that. And he didn't want to spend the next five years in classrooms."

Jennifer smiled inwardly. "So what does he do with his freedom?" she asked, trying to keep the irony out of her tone.

Josey didn't seem to notice any. "This and that. He does some long-distance driving – he's got an HGV licence – and he does some building work. He wants to have as many different experiences as he can while he's young."

"He doesn't sound so terrible. What have your mum and dad got against him?"

"Everything. But the real reason they don't like him

is because he's not like them. He doesn't spend his time agonizing about whales or the future of the planet – he just wants to enjoy today. But that's a crime in their book."

Wayne sounded like he'd mastered the age-old trick of presenting male selfishness as the noble pursuit of freedom, but Jennifer thought she'd steer clear of that one as far as Josey was concerned. "I guess the important thing," she said, "is whether he's good to you."

"He's good to me," Josey said, allowing only a little doubt to creep into her voice. "He gets angry at all the restrictions," she added in extenuation. "I mean he's twenty, and having to take his girlfriend home by eleven . . ." Her voice trailed off, as if she could hardly believe it herself.

"They do mean well," Jennifer suggested.

"I know that, but what does it mean?" She sighed. "It just means they're all smiles as long as they get their own way. They're so certain they're right, so dogmatic. They don't listen. It's going to be the same with the money. They're going to give it all away, I know they are. The whales must be wetting themselves."

Jennifer couldn't help laughing. "So what would you spend it on?"

Josey had obviously thought about this. "Well, for a start, I'd put a million aside for each of us kids . . ."

"Only a million?"

"That's fair. They'd still have a million and a half each."

"Hmm. And what'll you do with your million?

"Buy properties. A flat in London and maybe one in LA, or even somewhere like this. You could always sell them again and probably make a huge profit. And the rest of the money I'd invest in my own business, something I could run part time, because there's no point having money if you're working all the time."

"Makes sense," Jennifer murmured. And it did. She wondered why she hadn't thought of starting a business herself. At least twenty-five percent of her old firm's clients would follow her.

"Mum should go to one of those expensive health farms and lose some weight," Josey was saying. "And keep enough money back for lots of cosmetic surgery. She's forty already – another ten years and everything will start collapsing."

"I can't wait," Jen muttered.

"You take care of yourself," Josey said.

The irony of that was almost too much for Jennifer. "And what should your dad spend his money on?" she asked.

"I don't know. He'd like a boat, I bet." She fell silent for a moment and then abruptly changed the subject. "How old were you when you first had sex?" she asked, masking any embarrassment with directness.

"When I was eighteen."

"Where?"

"In the back seat of a car." It was on the road back from Whitby. She smiled at the memory.

"Who was he?"

"He was my second boyfriend. Martin. And he didn't have a clue what he was doing." A sudden and surprisingly acute sense of loss brought tears to the back of her eyes. Absurd. "I suppose your mum has talked to you about contraception, all that stuff?"

"Of course. They're so sodding understanding, or at least they think they are. But they're not. I think most people forget how to live as they get older. I think they get beaten down but they can't admit it.

Or something like that." She looked at Jen, a sort of reluctant defiance in her eyes. "I don't want to make them unhappy, but something that makes me happy, that should make them happy for me, right? If you're in love you have to follow your heart, don't you? You have to take risks. Sometimes you just have to do what you know is right. I mean, if I had a pound for every time I've heard my dad say that we wouldn't have needed to win the lottery."

That evening they went to a classier restaurant, one perched high on a hill with a wonderful view out across the moonlit sea. The food and wine were excellent, but the fact that clientele and labour force were rigorously split along racial lines made Neil in particular feel distinctly uncomfortable. He told himself that this was probably the best employment the locals could expect to find on the island, but that didn't seem much of a consolation, either for them or him. He found himself remembering the curtain on the plane coming out.

On the long drive back to the bungalow, he admitted to himself that he felt more than a little lost. The past week had been almost schizophrenic, as his sense of being somewhere he shouldn't be collided head on with his enormous enjoyment in being there. And in the process the relief he had gained from their decision to give half the money away had rapidly diminished.

But where did that leave him? He couldn't just walk away from the problem, or at least not without walking away from his family, which was the last thing he wanted to do. And yet he had to be able to live with himself.

He was the problem. They were his values. Values

that he'd held on to for twenty-five years of making do in a rich country, values that had made sense of the world he'd lived in. Values that stressed fairness above everything else, that said it was wrong for some people to be enormously rich, others dreadfully poor. Values that said it was an obscenity for anyone to own three homes when so many were homeless.

And yet here he was, staying in one of them.

If he jettisoned those values he was damned, and if he didn't he was a hypocrite.

It wasn't much of a choice. In fact it wasn't a choice at all. He hadn't spent the last twenty-five years not much liking the way the world worked because it was convenient to feel that way, and he wasn't about to change his mind just because a large sum of money had dropped in his lap.

So he had to find some honourable way of having and using the money.

No problem, he told himself. I'll just thread this camel through the eye of a needle.

Soon after eleven-thirty next morning a delegation left that day's beach in search of a phone. Edward was hoping for an update on the last few days' newspapers from his solicitor, Becky and Ian wanted to talk with their sons, and Josey, to Cath and Neil's well-concealed irritation, missed the sound of Wayne Newsome's voice.

The hotel nearby had the required connection, for which it charged not much less than the price of a room. This didn't deter Josey from spending twenty minutes talking to Wayne, but luckily for the others the bar was open, and the drinks were only marginally more expensive than the phone.

Josey emerged, her face one big smile, and Edward

went next, hoping to reach the solicitor before the end of the English working day. He also returned with a beaming face. "We're becoming old news," he told the others. "There were a couple of beach pictures on Tuesday, but the only piece yesterday" – he looked at Ian – "was about this kid's operation you're supposed to be paying for."

"Ah," Ian said noncommittally.

"You go next," Becky told him, looking at her watch. "Richard may not be back in his House yet."

Ian got through to Hebden, but not to Tom. "He's only just gone down to the park with his new football," Ellie told him.

"Bugger."

"Did you really give that family the money for the kid's operation?" she asked.

He explained about the letter. "But I didn't know they'd tell the papers," he added. "Didn't even occur to me."

"Don't knock it," Ellie advised. "It's the first good publicity you lot have had. The day before we were treated to the sight of you all lazing on the beach under the huge headline 'WITHOUT A CARE'."

"Bastards," Ian said, but without any force. "Tell Tom I'm sorry I missed him, but I'll see him Saturday morning, as usual."

After hanging up, he stood there for a moment, wondering whether or not he was pleased that his gift had become public. It would doubtless bring another deluge of letters, but he couldn't help feeling pleased that the request had been as genuine as he'd thought it was.

He walked back to the bar and told Becky it was her turn.

She had more luck reaching her son, who sounded in a good mood.

"So how was it?" she asked.

"It was . . ." He paused, and she could almost hear him searching through his vocabulary for the exact right word. "It was good," he said finally, having obviously abandoned the search. "I like her," he added in explanation.

"Who – your mother or your sister?" she asked, though she knew whom he meant.

"Sheila. She wants me to call her Sheila. And Carmen seems like a really nice kid. I'm going again on Saturday."

He sounded really happy, and she felt a wave of relief surge through her. "Good," she said. "And how's your schoolwork going?"

"Oh, all right. It's hard to take it so seriously, you know?"

"Yes, I know, but . . ."

"Don't worry, I'm getting it done," he said, reverting to the more familiar tone of adolescent boredom.

"Good," she said again. "Are you going to be home this weekend? We'll be back late Saturday."

"Don't know yet. If I'm not there I'll call you."

"OK. I love you."

"I love you, Mum."

She put the phone down with a smile and walked back to the others. Ian, who was leaving a day earlier than the others, drove Edward, Becky and Josey back to to the beach and then set off for the airport to check his connecting flight early the next morning. This done, he decided on a solo trip to Blackbeard's Pub, where the proprietor was only too pleased to let him loose on the piano. He ran through several of the songs he had written over the years, but the sadder ones were almost impossible to play. With the sun glinting on the ocean, and the palms swaying in the breeze against the clear blue sky, his fingers kept on trying to cheer the music up. Eventually he let them have their way, and found himself playing a reggae version of "Blue Monk".

The subject of charity came up during their last evening meal together. For Edward the issue didn't present any problems. He had, he said, only won the equivalent of the UN's budget for about ten seconds, and he didn't see any point in making grand gestures.

"How can you say that?" Neil asked. "How can you feel so bloody indifferent?"

Edward opened his mouth to reply, but Becky beat him to it. "You never had any money, Neil, and now you've got some it feels weird. He's always had it, and it feels quite natural – it's as simple as that."

"Let's not talk about this," Jennifer pleaded.

"I think we need to," Becky came back. "If we can keep away from politics it might even be useful."

"It's not about politics," Neil told her, "it's about values."

"Which only you have," Edward said sarcastically.

"Boys," Becky said warningly.

"Well, you can't keep values out of a discussion about wealth," Neil insisted.

"OK," Becky agreed, "but we could try and remember that we're all different, and that challenging each other's values won't get us anywhere."

"I can buy that," Ian agreed. "And I think I can say without contradiction that I'll be giving away more than Edward and less than Neil."

"How about you, Jen?" Becky asked.

Jennifer shook her head. "I don't know. I suppose I'll give some of it away." She could sponsor a thousand children instead of one, she thought.

"Well, don't tell anyone until you've decided who the lucky recipients are going to be," Ian said, "or you'll end up with sackfuls of suggestions. I only read about fifteen letters and it cost me fifty thousand. Now I daren't read any more in case I give it all away."

"You wouldn't," Cath reassured him. "But you would have to confront the fact that you're prepared to ignore other people's needs. No, don't get me wrong," she added, seeing the expressions turned her way, "I'm not saying you should. We're not going to. But . . ." She turned to Neil. "Remember what it felt like in India – all those people with deformities, let alone the ones who were simply hungry. There's just so much need that you could give all your money away in a day. And that's where we are now – our relationship to most English people is like the one we had to Indians when we were living there on five dollars a day. If you actually look at the world there's no limit to how much you could give away – it's a bottomless pit."

"We never found out how to deal with it in India," Neil murmured.

"Yes, we did. Not well, maybe, but we did. We used to put aside a dollar a day for giving away, and when that was gone, that was that. It was what we thought we could afford. The same principles apply now."

Neil smiled at her, but Edward was shaking his head. "How many people in our situation would even be having this conversation?" he asked. "Most people couldn't give a damn about the rest of the world." He looked at Jennifer for support, but didn't get any.

"Then why do people give so much to charity each year?" she asked.

"Exactly," Cath agreed. "And most of them would give a lot more if they had a windfall like this."

"But didn't you used to tell us that charity was exactly the wrong approach?" Edward challenged Neil. "I seem to remember you calling it a crutch for the system, or some such phrase."

Neil grunted. "What a memory. But weren't you arguing in favour of charity at the time?"

"My naive period."

"What does the book advise?" Becky asked Ian.

"Take it slowly, don't listen to strangers, be true to yourself," he answered promptly.

"Very Buddha-like," Neil murmured.

"Sounds like good advice to me," his wife countered.

14

It was nearly eleven in the evening when Ian's transatlantic flight touched down on the Manchester runway. Most of his fellow-passengers were returning from Florida package holidays, and the sight of falling rain, far from dampening their spirits, seemed to cast the homecoming in a comfortably correct perspective. Global warming notwithstanding, Florida had blue skies, Manchester drizzle. All was right with the world.

If anyone had recognized Ian on the plane they hadn't made a song and dance about it. He had found Thursday's *Sun* in Miami and Friday's *Mirror* on the plane, and neither had contained a single reference to himself or any of the others. The big news was that a Cabinet minister had been caught *in flagrante delicto* with a sheep, and, to make matters considerably worse, the sheep had been wearing an Arsenal outfit. The minister's wife was standing by him but the sheep was unavailable for comment, unless, as the writer wittily pointed out, "'baaa' constituted a denial". In a reference to the recent BSE scare the editorial noted in passing that "this government seems to have its problems with livestock".

At home Ian found another three sacks of mail

lined up in descending order of size in the downstairs hall. This was probably a good sign, he thought, and then realized that the biggest of the three was nearest the door.

He left them there, wearily climbed the stairs, and put the kettle on for a cup of tea. His rooms looked depressingly chaotic, and the answer-machine tape was predictably full. He listened to it as he sipped at the tea, but there was only the familiar litany of advice, abuse and requests. If Susan had tried to leave him a message, she hadn't succeeded. If she'd written to him the letter was in one of five sacks.

He didn't really think she'd done either, which was depressing. The rain was beating on the windows by this time, adding to the gloomy ambience, but he found himself thinking about playing the piano at Blackbeard's Pub the day before, and the memory made him smile regardless.

He would get the writing finished, book the musicians and the studio, and make the CD. Enough people had urged him to do it when he couldn't afford to, so why not bite the bullet now that he could? If the CD was well received by the people whose opinions he cared about then that would be enough in itself, and if the reviewers who mattered commercially liked it too then he could even take a band on the road. And if no one liked it he'd still done his best. Not everyone could be a Miles or a Monk.

But one thing was certain – he was through with computer journalism. Once he'd been fascinated by the damn things, but not any more. And he was sick of working at home alone. Sick of home, come to that.

He got ready for bed, even though he knew sleep was unlikely, and lay there half listening to a late-night phone-in programme, working on the specifications of the new house he'd like to buy. Next thing he knew the alarm was ringing in his ear, and he only had an hour before Tom arrived at Victoria. He had time to wash the last few grains of Caribbean sand from between his toes and grab a cup of coffee before driving into the city centre.

For once both he and the train were on time. As usual, they had second breakfasts at Burger King, then wandered round the shops for an hour or two. Tom didn't ask for any more presents even when an obvious candidate presented itself. He was, Ian guessed, under strict instructions from his mother to exercise self-restraint.

At around two o'clock they arrived at Maine Road, and after a long browse in the club shop took their new and almost perfectly placed seats. In the match itself City, almost needless to say, let them down, but Ian found himself glad that the boy didn't support United – his soul would be safer with a team that offered living proof of money's limitations.

On the way back to the house in Chorlton Tom announced that he wanted to go to Georgia that summer.

"For the Olympics?" Ian asked, trying not to sound too unenthusiastic.

"Not that Georgia," his son said reproachfully. "The one Kinkladze comes from."

"We'll see," Ian said. He had a feeling there was a war going on somewhere in the vicinity.

Back at the house they ordered, awaited and consumed a huge pizza, and then, somewhat to Ian's surprise, Tom announced his intention of watching the lottery programme. "We won't win it this time," Ian told his son.

"Mum might."

* * *

In Miami, the London-bound flight had almost completed boarding when Jennifer took the sudden decision to visit New York instead. "I'll stay with my friend Sally and spend a couple of days shopping on Fifth Avenue," she told the others, but the real reason for her change of mind was rather less positive. Mac excepted, there was nothing and nobody waiting for her in London, and in New York she could carry on playing the tourist for a few more days.

Her rearranged flight arrived at Kennedy in mid-afternoon, and by then the idea of visiting Sally, to whom she hadn't actually spoken in over a year, had lost what little appeal it had once had. On impulse she told the taxi driver to take her to the Waldorf Hotel.

She had visited New York several times in her twenties, and again a couple of years ago for work, but the sight of Manhattan looming above the Brooklyn brownstones wasn't one that palled with familiarity. The Waldorf was exactly as she'd imagined it – plush and old-worldy – and she secured a two-room suite with a distant view of Central Park. Flicking through the channels on the big-screen TV she found *To Have and Have Not* just beginning, and for the next hour and a half watched Bogart trying to remember how to whistle.

By the time the film was over it was growing dark outside, and she decided against joining the Saturday-evening crowds. Room service provided her with a lovely meal, and the TV served up a *Murder, She Wrote* she'd never seen and back-to-back episodes of *Taxi* which reminded her of the house on Tisbury Road. At around ten she went to bed and lay awake listening to the sounds of humans and traffic drifting up from the streets below.

Becky and Edward arrived home to find Richard ensconced in front of the living-room TV. This in itself, Becky thought, was something worth noting – normally he'd have been locked away upstairs in front of his own.

He was in a good mood too, plying them with questions about the others and their week together, telling them about the great time he'd had with Sheila and Carmen that afternoon. They'd all played Ludo, he announced, as if it was the most wonderful pastime going. This, from the child who had always refused to play board games.

"I'm going again after lessons on Tuesday," he said. "Can you come, Mum?"

"Yes, of course, but are you sure you've got the time . . .?"

"It'll only be a couple of hours. I can't revise twenty-four hours a day."

She smiled. "No, I suppose you can't."

"Dad, don't you want to meet them? Can you come too?"

"Umm, maybe," Edward said, clearly taken aback. "Probably," he added, without even noticing Becky's look. His mood had been improving ever since they climbed aboard the plane on Virgin Gorda, she realized.

"That's great," Richard said, and his eyes were shining with elation.

With both her males so pleased with life, Becky found it easier to repress the doubts which the previous week had brought back to the surface. She could sort out her own feelings later, she told herself. Right now the important thing was to get them all through the slings and arrows of the next few weeks.

And when she wasn't worrying about the family's future there were always any number of practical matters to attend to. There was a garden that needed work, books to be read, meals to cook, family to contact. There would be plenty of time later to worry about the collapse of her marriage.

There weren't many hours of darkness left when Neil wearily brought the car to a halt outside the Shropshire cottage. The two younger children were transferred, still sleeping, to their beds, and Cath made a cup of tea for her and Neil. Josey had headed straight for the phone in their bedroom.

"She's not ringing him at four in the morning, is she?" Neil asked disbelievingly.

"He asked her to," Cath said. "He keeps a mobile under his pillow," she added.

They took their cups of tea out into the garden. The moon had set but the sky was clear, the milky veil wafting above them like a magician's exhaust trail. They could hear Josey's voice through the open window, telling Wayne that of course she'd take him there.

"So where shall we hide her this week?" Neil asked ruefully.

Cath shook her head. "Remember that Charlie Brown cartoon – the one in which he decides there's no problem so big that you can't run away from it?"

"Uh-huh."

"He was wrong."

It was soon after dawn that Jennifer woke with a start, the dream fresh in her mind. They were all on the beach at Whitby, her mother and father were walking arm in arm, which was rare, and she was running at the edge of the water, leaping sideways to avoid each incoming surge of the tide. And there was a small crab which had somehow been grounded on its back, its pincers waving hopelessly at the sky. She called her father but he didn't hear her and she called again, louder this time, angry with her mother for claiming his attention. And then he was beside her, tipping the crab over with his finger and hoisting her on to his shoulder, where the world seemed spread out beneath her.

She lay there, feeling the loss of her father as if for the first time.

Today she would find a beach, she decided.

After taking breakfast in the almost empty hotel dining room she walked out to the reception desk and enquired about local beaches. The elderly clerk asked her if she'd heard of Coney Island.

She had.

"It used to be the place thirty, forty years ago," the man said, a nostalgic glint in his eyes. "There's not a lot there now, but it's easy to get to. You can just take the subway all the way there – it's about a forty-five-minute ride."

She wrote down the details of which trains and where to catch them.

"It's not a very nice day, though," the clerk warned her.

It wasn't, but the grey skies and chilly wind seemed peculiarly apposite, reminding her of the Whitby of her childhood, of the dream. Coney Island itself boasted a fairly nondescript stretch of sand facing out into the Atlantic. Behind the beach there was a boardwalk, and behind that a funfair that seemed only half open. But despite the air of disuse and the uninspiring weather there was a sizeable crowd in attendance, riding the rides, visiting the museum of Coney Island's heyday, queueing at Nathan's for hot dogs. Some families were even camped out on the beach, gazing wistfully up at the sky in search of the sun.

The memories of Whitby brought back her conversation with Josey. The girl seemed to be psyching herself up to do something stupid, Jennifer thought – she should have said something to Cath, even if it did mean breaking a confidence. But Cath would know, she decided. She seemed such a good mother.

Jennifer walked along the beach just above the water-line, wondering how different her own life would have been if she'd had children. Would a child have given her life the emotional anchor it seemed to need, or would her restlessness – her refusal to ever be satisfied with what she had – have simply found different ways to express itself? Was it all down to chance? Was her love life just a matter of shuffled chromosomes? Like six people picking six numbers at random and coming up with £18 million.

Though it hadn't really been random. They'd all picked their numbers for a reason.

The Wednesday on Virgin Gorda had been Deysi's birthday. She had raised a silent toast to the girl at dinner that night, and had bought a T-shirt to send at the nautical store in the Valley, telling everyone it was for a niece. She still hadn't told any of the others about her. Which was ridiculous. Why did she feel this need to keep her world in such closed compartments?

She looked out across the grey sea, hearing the screams of the children on the roller-coaster behind her. What was she doing here? Why wasn't she there, visiting the girl and her family? What was she afraid of?

Ian woke up on Monday morning with the same sense of achievement that he'd taken to bed. After driving Tom back to Hebden the previous morning, and giving Ellie the cheque he had promised her, he'd enjoyed a traditional Sunday lunch – lamb instead of beef, of course – at a country pub. Arriving home just as Javid was on his way out, he had seized the opportunity to ask his housemate where the next month's rent cheque was. Javid had given him a surprised and almost indignant look, as if he could hardly believe that Ian was asking.

"You're a college lecturer, for Christ's sake," Ian had heard himself say. "You're not exactly a candidate for charity."

"I thought we were friends," Javid said stiffly.

"No, you didn't," Ian retorted. "You thought I wouldn't bother to ask." Back on his own floor of the house he had felt almost exhilarated by the exchange.

And then he had started on the eight sacks, reading each and every card and letter to the accompaniment of the eight-disc Miles boxed set he'd bought two weeks earlier. By eight in the evening he'd worked his way through two sacks and five discs, and after an hour's break for dinner at the local Turkish restaurant he'd managed the same again. Most of the correspondence had gone back into an empty sack for future disposal, but a small pile of requests which he thought worth a second thought had accumulated on the desk. Some of the letters had made him laugh out loud, some had disgusted him, some – more than half probably – had been pathetic in one way or another. He had no set criteria for the ones he picked out, other than that they sounded genuine. And he still had no idea whether he would offer money to all, any or none of the people he had chosen. For the moment, all he knew was that he owed it to himself to read every letter he had received.

Around midnight, feeling exhausted and more than a little contented, he had taken himself off to bed and fallen instantly asleep, only to dream of an ever-growing, strangely swaying pile of mail, which he felt obliged to climb, up through the clouds, like Jack on his beanstalk.

But waking that morning to the sight of empty sacks was worth it, and the postman's arrival with the smallest yet cheered him further. After a trip to the local Safeway had furnished him with a week's supply of food and drink, he spent a couple of hours on the phone, announcing to all and sundry his effective resignation from the world of computer journalism. The editors to whom he owed work were suitably miffed, while those who owed him money were suitably sentimental. Those in both camps just called it quits and wished him well.

After lunch he started trying to track down the various musicians he had in mind for his CD, and by early evening he had made contact with all but the trumpet player, who was allegedly playing a gig in Rio. Armed with all their reports of time available he homed in on the second week of July for the recording. Which gave him almost three months to get the songs ready.

He would need it all, he decided, after spending an hour working on a revamped horn line for one of his earliest pieces. And he would need somewhere for the band to practise. Like a new house, perhaps.

* * *

When the phone rang Becky was waiting for Edward to come home, so that they could set off together for the trip to Somers Town. She hadn't seen much of him over the past thirty-six hours, but he had managed to drop the information that the exhibition had been doing brilliantly in their absence, and that the market value of Raul's work had jumped almost five-fold since the opening. Even without these specifics she would have known from the massive infusions of positive energy which he left in his wake that things in general were going well.

It was him on the phone. "I can't make it," he said immediately. "I have to see a buyer about a piece, and there's no other time he can make it. Make my apologies, will you?" he asked, as if it was a political meeting he was missing.

"Can't you come late?" Becky pleaded. She knew how upset Richard was going to be.

"I would if I could, but there's no way. I'll come next time, I promise. I've got to go."

"Right," she said drily, and hung up.

She walked out to the waiting taxi, and sat chewing on her anger as the driver headed east towards Shepherd's Bush. She supposed she should be glad that the win had done nothing to dent his enthusiasm for work, but she wasn't. All she could think was that he had let Richard down.

The boy had already arrived when she reached Sheila's flat, and she watched the expression on his face turn from intense disappointment to the safer option of resignation. To his credit, he was soon past even that, and anyone else would have had a hard job seeing the hurt that lingered in his eyes.

Sheila was feeling at her best that day, and they

all walked down to the gardens beside St Pancras Hospital. Carmen took delight in the diesels rumbling on the other side of the fence, and Becky found herself wondering if Sheila was as conscious of the cemetery next door as she was. Living with a dying person was not something she had ever done before, and she hoped she'd be up to it.

And yet the four of them already seemed more at ease with each other than Becky would have thought possible three weeks before. Two hours later, on the way home, she wondered how Edward would have fitted in. He would need more than charm to win Sheila over, always assuming that he intended to try.

They arrived outside the house in Holland Park at almost the same moment, his taxi pulling up behind hers, and she could tell from his whole manner that his meeting had gone well. He said he wanted to hear about hers, and over a drink listened with apparent interest as she told him about their afternoon with Sheila and Carmen. He didn't ask any questions though, and once she was finished he let his own enthusiasms loose, showering her with the myriad possibilities of their future.

Naturally he wanted a gallery of his own, but there was no reason why it had to be in London. New York was one possibility, Paris and Florence were others he'd been researching. As for living space, there was a lot to be said for moving to the outskirts of the urban sprawl, somewhere greener, less crime-ridden, but they'd also have to think seriously about tax havens. The Channel Islands was the obvious choice, but their financial adviser was still researching the residence stipulations.

As she listened, she realized two things. Firstly, though the win had failed to dim her husband's enthusiasm for work, it had nevertheless succeeded in changing his vision of their future. And secondly, there didn't seem to be an iota of consideration in all this for what she might want.

"Edward," she said calmly. "I like London. I don't want to live in a place where yacht prices are the only topic of conversation. And the only reason I can think of for moving to the suburbs is that the schools are better."

"You're not planning to send Carmen to a day school?"

"I haven't decided," she said, "but . . ."

"I thought we agreed we were going to do some travelling now that we can."

"We can still travel."

He took a deep breath and changed the subject. "We can buy a flat in central London," he went on. "You've always said you'd love one in Soho, right in the middle of things."

"That was years ago. I want a home. A home for Carmen. And I like the one we have." The futures they had in mind were utterly different, she realized with a sudden sinking feeling in her stomach.

He too seemed vaguely conscious of the abyss that had suddenly opened between them. "We're obviously going to have to think about this," he said mildly.

Her "yes" ushered in a silence. "How did your meeting with the buyer go?" she asked, to fill the gap.

"Fine. It was the piece I bought before the exhibition, remember?"

"But you loved it."

"I got five times what I paid for it."

She was dumbfounded. "Edward, we've just won millions and you're selling something you like for what – a profit of a few hundred pounds?"

He was pouring himself another drink. "A couple of thousand. But don't you understand? It's not the amount that matters. I earned this money – I didn't just buy a ticket and win it."

And then she realized – he'd put the sale of his own piece above coming to meet Sheila and Carmen. Had he not understood how important it was to Richard? Or had he understood but simply not cared? Either way it seemed to speak volumes about his lack of any real emotional commitment.

She knew she ought to feel angry, but there was only a heavy sense of sadness weighing on her heart.

"Didn't you think about how much Richard wanted you to meet her?" she asked him softly.

"I'll meet her next time," he said, putting down his drink and reaching for the TV remote.

"I'm going to have a bath," she said, getting up, but what she really needed was a door to lock and the sound of running water. She felt as if something had just died, and she needed to express her grief in private.

15

Jennifer's plane touched down on the Bolivian altiplano just as the sun disappeared beneath the line of mountains visible through her window. After what seemed an interminable wait to be processed through immigration and customs, she spent another ten minutes looking for the well-hidden tourist information centre. The search was worthwhile though. A local with near-perfect English listened carefully to what she wanted, told her which of the free buses to catch and where she should ask to be let off, and annotated a photocopied city map with further instructions.

The ride into the city was almost worth the air fare on its own. La Paz's airport was built up on the altiplano; the city itself, as she suddenly discovered when the bus took a tight turn on the freeway, occupied what could only be described as a huge bowl in the ground. Behind this bowl, which was filled with the brightening lights of early evening, a mountain loomed into the sky, its snow-covered peak glowing like a flaming torch in the last rays of the invisible sun.

The freeway spiralled down towards the high-rise centre, and the bus driver deposited Jennifer and several other passengers outside one of the city's most expensive hotels. She looked at the map and walked up the adjoining side-street to the hotels she had chosen from the guidebook, one that should be expensive enough to be clean and safe, and cheap enough so that her fellow-guests wouldn't all be Western businessmen on expense accounts.

At first sight it seemed to fit the bill. The reception area was clean enough, the receptionist friendly and semi-fluent in English. He personally escorted her to her room, which looked out over a lovely interior courtyard, and around which several obvious tourists were sitting and talking. In one corner a restaurant room had been constructed, mostly of glass; it looked like a conservatory. Inside there were about a dozen tables, most of them of occupied.

The room wasn't exactly up to Waldorf standards, but there were no signs of dead wildlife. As she sat back on the bed someone started playing the Andean pipes just beneath her window. She listened to the graceful melody, thinking that she'd done the right thing in coming.

After successfully testing out the shower and changing out of her travelling clothes she realized she was hungry. The restaurant was still doing good business, but there were a couple of vacant spaces at the end of one table, or at least she thought there were. As it happened, the occupiers had gone to collect their guide books. They turned out to be Britons, who conjured another seat out of somewhere and insisted she join them. The man's name was David, the woman's Lynn. Their friends at the table were an Australian couple named Les and Marcia, and a Taiwanese woman named Jean. The last three all seemed to be in their early thirties, but the Brits were nearer to Jennifer's age. And by the end of the first bottle of Chilean wine it seemed as if they had adopted her into their group.

"Where are you headed?" Marcia asked.

"I have a sponsored child in Potosi, and I'm going to visit her," Jennifer said, as if it was something she did all the time.

"That's wonderful," Lynn enthused, and to Jennifer's amazement she realized there was a trace of envy in all their eyes.

"But I haven't got a clue how to get there," she added in mitigation.

"You can fly, bus or train," Les said. "We're all taking the train tomorrow night." He looked at his watch. "In fact we should be buying the tickets now. Why don't you come with us?"

"I . . ." she started to say, but Lynn seemed to guess what she was thinking.

"We've only known each other for about thirty-six hours," she told Jennifer. "You won't be horning in on anything."

It seemed almost like a sign. "Great," Jennifer said. She wasn't exactly a train buff, but she'd certainly spent enough hours in the air over the past ten days, and travelling with this group looked like it might be fun. Sort of like the week on Virgin Gorda, but without the vulnerability which old friendships presupposed.

They walked the mile or so to the station together, frequently stopping to look at the goods on display in the busy streets, which gave Jennifer time to catch her breath. The thin air wasn't noticeable until you actually exerted yourself, and even then she knew it was possible to forget the difference – until, that was, you started experiencing the symptoms of altitude sickness. And La Paz was less than twelve thousand feet up, whereas

Potosi, at over thirteen, was the highest city in the world.

The station building was British-built and looked it, probably the closest piece of Victoriana to heaven. They eventually found someone to sell them tickets, and walked back to the hotel with the same disregard for speed. A couple of travellers with guitars had joined the man with the pipes in the courtyard, and they all sat listening to the music for an hour or so before drifting off to bed.

In the morning Jennifer explored the city centre on her own, picking up easily portable gifts, changing money and generally soaking up the atmosphere. On the surface La Paz seemed as peaceful as its name suggested, but the drama of its setting would take some getting used to. She ran into the Australians in a small museum full of mummies and laughing jugs, and her fellow-Brits in a coffee bar which wouldn't have been out of place in Tottenham Court Road. But if she needed any reminding that she was far from home she had only to revisit the line of stalls near their hotel, where several local proprietors was doing a roaring trade in llama foetuses.

Neil had a meeting in Telford on the Wednesday evening, which gave Josey the chance to test the water with her mother.

They were cold. No, Cath told her, she could not go away with Wayne for the weekend.

"Why do you keep making things so hard for me?" Josey pleaded, her eyes filling with tears.

Cath resisted the temptation to ask the same question of her daughter. "I'm just doing what I think is right for you," she said. "You . . ."

"But what about what I think is right? It's my life,

not yours. And I'm almost sixteen. People get married when they're sixteen."

"When you're sixteen we'll talk about it."

"But that's not until November. Wayne won't wait till then."

"If he loves you, he will," Cath said. And if he's after the money he will, she thought cynically.

"Please, Mum," her daughter pleaded.

"No, Josey," Cath said.

Becky didn't get up until Edward had left the house, and spent most of the day curled up on the living-room sofa, often in tears, her mind turning the same thoughts over and over. They'd been married more than twenty years, and in all that time she had never actually believed it would end. She'd looked at other couples, at friends who couldn't be part of a couple, and never envied any of them. Edward and her had had their differences – what two people didn't? – but for twenty years she had never questioned the fact of their being together. The way they were together, yes, but never the fact of it.

It seemed so sudden, and yet she also knew it had been coming for years. And while the speed with which the realization had come upon her was scary, the way it seemed to roll back the past, almost to lay it waste, was more frightening still. The man she could see now was the man who'd been there all the time, the man she'd devoted half her life to.

Looking back she knew, with something that seemed close to shame but wasn't, that in the beginning his most appealing quality had been no more than his desire for her. Beyond that, his certainty in the world had made her feel safe and his uncertainty in matters of the heart had given her a protector's role.

And once they were bound together by good sex and mutual need, the fact of living together had added all the usual entanglements, from sharing each other's families to sharing a bathroom, from sharing a name to sharing Richard.

And now she would be on her own for the first time in her adult life. That was scary too, but it was the kind of scariness that came before a roller-coaster ride, laced with excitement and promise.

Ian stopped and looked back down the path at the house nestling at the head of the valley below. It was a beautiful setting for a beautiful building, and even taking into consideration the amount of work that needed doing, the price didn't seem outrageous. More than his cumulative life's earnings to date, but not outrageous. And it did include forty acres of land, twelve rooms, a wood, even "the privacy of your own approach road", as the agent still waiting down by the house had put it. The Pennine Trail passed about five miles to the east, but Ian didn't suppose the number of lost and hungry ramblers rapping at the front door would be excessive. And it would be perfect for rehearsals. According to the agent, it had once been used for that very purpose by a famous rock group whose name, he was almost sure, began with a "B", but wasn't the Beatles.

No neighbours to complain about the noise, but none to talk to either. Ian sighed. It was a lovely place, but if he lived here on his own he'd go mad. The only way of meeting people would be to hold Great Gatsby-style parties, and if memory served him well that hadn't worked for Gatsby.

He made his way back down down the path, took a last look through the windows and told the agent he'd have to think about it. An hour later, caught in the city rush hour, he almost wished he'd camped there for the night.

Home didn't really feel like home any more, though he wasn't quite sure why. He thought about going out – there were friends he hadn't actually seen since the win – but decided against it. He was turning into a recluse, he thought – the Howard Hughes of Chorlton.

But Howard Hughes had probably had memories of Jane Russell to keep him warm at night. "To get the full value of a joy," Ian murmured to himself, "you must have somebody to share it with."

Edward came home soon after six with a paper for her to sign. "You don't have to read it," he told her. "It's just the usual authorization form for the brokers."

She looked up at him and realized, almost with shock, that he had no idea what was going on. He was like one of those cartoon characters, caught in the moment between running over the cliff and looking down.

So you could still change your mind, a small voice suggested from somewhere deep inside her head.

"I need to talk to you," she said.

"What about?" He sighed. "I have to go out again. And I need you to sign that form tonight."

"I'm not going to sign it, Edward. I want a separate account for my half of the money."

"But that's ridiculous . . ."

"And I'm leaving you," she added simply.

He looked as though he'd been slapped. "What do you mean?"

"Edward, we want such different things from life. There doesn't seem any point in staying together."

He just looked at her, as if he was having difficulty believing what she was saying.

"You must know it too," she said.

He shook his head in wonderment. "Is this about what happened with Jen?" he asked.

"You're not listening to me."

"Is there someone else?"

"No," she said. And in twenty years there never had been.

He tried again. "I know I'm not so keen to take on another kid as you are, but that doesn't seem like a good enough reason to throw twenty years down the drain."

It didn't, put like that.

"Don't you love me any more?" he asked, changing tack.

This was the little boy she'd taken care of all these years, and she steeled herself against him. "I haven't got the faintest idea," she said. "At the moment it doesn't really seem relevant."

He took a step towards her, and she involuntarily raised both hands in front of her, as if to ward him off.

The journey across the altiplano was generally one to forget. The first half-hour, as the train wound its way up out of La Paz's bowl, offered wonderful views of the city as night fell, but thereafter the darkness was complete, leaving nothing to take their minds off the deepening cold. Jennifer and the train seemed equally unprepared for the plummeting temperature, and if it hadn't been for the loan of a blanket from the Australians she would soon have been offering her new-found millions to anyone prepared to listen. Sleep was intermittent at best, bringing back memories of a trip to Scotland with the guides when she was eleven.

They arrived in Potosi soon after nine in the morning. The sun was shining in a clear sky, but there was still a distinct chill in the air as they walked the short distance to the hotel which Les and Marcia had picked out. The town wasn't what Jennifer had expected, but she wasn't sure why – the buildings were old and Spanish, the streets crooked and narrow. The view from the window of her hotel room was filled by a single red-brown mountain with pock-marked flanks. It had a brooding presence about it, reminding her of *The Lord of the Rings*.

The woman who had brought Jennifer up to the room saw her looking at it. "Cerro Rico," she said, as if that was explanation enough.

It almost was, David told her an hour later when they all stopped for coffee. "Cerro Rico" meant Rich Hill, and none in history had proved more profitable, or more deadly, to humankind. The Spanish nobility had used the mountain's silver core to overspend on English and Flemish goods, thus kick-starting the industrial revolution. The cost of extraction, over something like a century and a half, had been a premature death for more than eight million Andean Indians.

Back outside, Jennifer looked again at the baleful mountain. Deysi's father was a miner, and she wondered if he worked in the maw of the beast. Tomorrow, once she was better acclimatized to the thin air, she would go looking for the centre which oversaw the community work her sponsorship money helped to pay for, and hopefully there she'd find someone willing to take her, or at least direct her, to where Deysi's family lived.

In the meantime she was happy to slowly wander through the narrow streets, picturing them three hundred years earlier, when, according to David, Potosi had been the biggest and richest town in all the Americas, North and South. They found somewhere to eat lunch in one of the more modern areas of the town, and were in turn found by a couple of locals who gave guided tours of the mines. Jean and the two men were enthusiastic, the other three women less so, but they allowed themselves to be talked into a six-dollar tour. The only proviso was that they bring presents for the miners. Cigarettes or dynamite were recommended, and both could apparently be purchased at the shop two doors down.

Armed with cigarettes, they all jumped into the guide's van, and ten minutes later they were climbing a road which wound up the flanks of the mountain. About a quarter of the way up the van stopped amid a hotchpotch of tumbledown buildings and they all clambered out. Several other tourists were waiting beside another minibus and between fifteen and twenty miners sat with their backs against the buildings, rhythmically chewing on coca leaves. They all seemed to be Indians.

Jennifer's doubts about the guided tour grew as helmets with candles were handed out to every fifth person, but before the doubts had time to harden the guide had ducked into the tunnel, pulling the others behind him on an invisible string. The tunnel, which didn't seem to have supports of any kind, quickly narrowed on both the horizontal and vertical plane, forcing anyone over five foot six to advance in a half crouch. The candles didn't provide much light, and as the group advanced deeper into the mountain the temperature rose and the air began to reek.

What they could smell, as the guide gleefully informed them at their first conclave in a small chamber, was a combination of sulphur, arsenic and asbestos.

They must have travelled at least a quarter of a mile from the entrance, Jennifer thought. She had never been claustrophobic before, but this seemed like a good place to start.

The guide led them down to another level, half sliding down what looked like a giant rabbit's hole. At the bottom they found two Indians, both stripped to the waist, gouging at a rock face with what looked like simple picks. In the dim light the sweat glimmered on their backs, offering a visual image which several of the tourists couldn't resist capturing on film.

One of these men could be Deysi's father, Jennifer thought, and she felt suddenly ashamed of their presence there. Another half-hour later, when they finally emerged from the bowels of the mountain, she couldn't remember ever breathing anything sweeter than the thin, cold air.

Still one and a half sacks from finishing, Ian was just through reminding himself that virtue was its own reward when life proved him right. His heart even seemed to speed up at the sight of the envelope, though he could hardly have recognized writing he'd never seen. But it was from her.

"Dear Ian," she wrote. "My sister's gone into labour two weeks early, so I'll be in Southport for several days. I've tried ringing you several times, but there must be something wrong with your answering machine – all I get is a horrible noise. I'm sorry about the other night – I'm usually nicer than that, or at least I think so. Give me a ring if you feel like it. Love,

Susan. P.S. I liked your interview. At least I assume they quoted you right – it sounded like you."

Ian realized he'd been holding his breath, and let it out with a whoosh. The envelope told him the letter had been posted in Southport two Fridays ago, before they'd all left for Virgin Gorda. So why hadn't she replied to his messages?

Maybe she'd tried and not got through. Maybe she was still in Southport. She'd written the letter before the newspapers got hold of Jen's overdose and their "sixties-style commune", so maybe she'd changed her mind.

Hardly daring to hope, he first reached for the phone and then thought better of it. First he needed a drink, but all he had in the house was beer and the two small bottles of blue liqueur which he'd brought back from the Caribbean. He knocked one of those back, wished he hadn't, and reached for the phone again. As it rang it occurred to him that it was probably sacrilegious to pray so soon after a lottery win, but what the hell . . .

Her answer-machine cut in, and in his disappointment he almost hung up. "This is Ian," he began. "I've just found . . ."

There was a click. "Hi," she said happily.

"Hi. I just found your letter. It was in the seventh sack of mail I've been through."

"Oh my God," she said. "That never occurred to me. And I lost your phone number," she added, as if that explained everything.

It almost did.

"I thought you'd finally decided I was too bloody difficult," she said.

"I thought you'd decided I was too much of a jerk." It was wonderful – he could feel a warm glow spreading through his body.

There were a few moments of silence and then both of them started talking at once.

"I just didn't know how to react to what had happened," she said, "and I got it all wrong and that made me even more nervous and, well, I expect you remember what happened . . ."

"Just about. When can we try again?"

"It's only nine – how about this evening? Do you want to come round here?"

"I'd love to. You'll have to tell me where 'here' is, of course. You're not in the telephone directory," he added.

"Only under my married name." She gave him the address.

"I'll be there in half an hour," he said. "You're sure it's not too late?" he heard himself ask.

"My mother always told me to marry a rich man," she said.

"And what if I've given it all away?"

"Then we'll just be lovers," she said.

16

Edward put down the phone and slapped his palms together. "Yes!" he said exultantly. The gallery was his, and at a considerably lower price than the owner had originally asked for.

He instinctively reached for the phone again, and then remembered that she wasn't there to tell any more.

No problem, he told himself, and punched out one of the numbers he'd collected at the reception that lunchtime. Paula was the name that went with it, and he was pretty certain that she'd been the highly undressable blonde. Two minutes later he had a date for that evening and, if he was any judge of women, the ninety-five percent probability of a partner for the night.

He sat back in the chair thinking about the reception. It had been an amazing forty-five minutes. Edward had always been good-looking – and he still was – but he knew looks hadn't accounted for the scope of his success that lunchtime. Beautiful women had been queueing up to announce their availability, as if their only mission in life was to demonstrate that money was the ultimate aphrodisiac.

He supposed he should be grateful to Becky for

letting him off the leash, but he still felt angry about the cold-hearted way she'd done it. The only thing he really had to be thankful for was his own decision not to tell his journalist friend about their offering a home to Richard's real mother and her daughter.

At least he wouldn't be living in a funeral home for the next few months.

He looked at his watch, found he had time to nip home to the Savoy for a shower and change before meeting Paula, and headed down the stairs, allowing erotic expectations of the evening ahead to mask the knot of emptiness which his unfeeling bitch of a wife had left gnawing at his heart.

It had been a good meeting, Becky decided, as she walked back home up Ladbroke Grove. People were always good at spending other people's money, she thought good-naturedly. Presumably because being able to spend without anxiety was one of the joys of life. One that most people never got to experience.

And if she could keep that duality in mind – that the money was both a joy and a privilege – she reckoned she could learn to live with being a millionairess.

As the meeting had shown, money was fun to play with. Several people had come up with proposals on how to spend her intended donation; they ranged from collecting down-and-outs off the streets and treating them to a real beggars' banquet at some posh hotel to handing out £5 bonuses to signers-on at the local DSS office. The chosen scheme involved sending tenners to about the half the MPs in the House of Commons, with a covering letter from a fictitious constituent asking the MPs to forward the money to Amnesty International on their behalf. If they proved scrupulously honest, Amnesty would simply reap the benefit in terms of both money and publicity. Any MP who didn't send the money on would have some explaining to do.

As she turned right into Holland Park Avenue Becky found herself thinking that the Edward of twenty years ago would at least have got a laugh out of something like that. The Edward of now would simply give her his exasperated don't-you-know-how-the-world-really-works? look.

The thought of life without him still felt a little scary, but the sense of liberation was stronger, and as she turned off the main road her feet seemed to dance a few steps of their own accord.

The house was in darkness but there was nothing unusual about that. With Edward always out, and Richard packed off to school for most of the year, she had got used to returning to unlit windows. Now Edward wouldn't be coming home at all, but Sheila and Carmen would be moving in before too long, and once his exams were over Richard would be back for the summer.

The house would be fuller than it had ever been, full enough for a home.

Neil surveyed the Sainsbury's trolley, which seemed in serious danger of overflowing. "We'll never get it all in the fridge," he protested.

"Then we'll have to get a second fridge," Angie said sensibly, ramming home a giant pack of Smarties.

"We're going to be late to meet Ian," Cath said, manoeuvring the trolley to the back of the most promising-looking checkout queue. As always seemed the case, it soon became apparent that this queue was moving at half the speed of all the others.

Shrewsbury's early-evening traffic proved more

accommodating, and they arrived at the station a couple of minutes before the Manchester train was due to arrive. While Cath and Angie waited in the double-parked car Neil and Daniel walked through to the platform, just in time to see the modern diesel unit gliding in through the points at the northern end of the station.

Ian and Tom were first off, the latter proudly carrying what looked like a new football. While he was telling Daniel about the Maine Road season tickets, Ian was trying to shake the sleep out of his eyes. The fact that he'd missed out on a lot of sleep lately was the main reason he'd decided not to drive.

Cath had moved into the back seat, leaving Ian and Tom to squeeze into the front. As they drove out of the station car park Daniel was heard wondering out loud why they hadn't bought their Old Trafford season tickets yet.

"Maybe it's because we only go about four times a year," Neil suggested.

They were about halfway home when Ian asked whether Josey was cooking supper or out with the dreaded Wayne.

"Neither," Cath told him. "She's in bed. She had stomach pains last night, so she had the day off school."

"They seemed to have gone this morning," Neil observed.

"She was willing to drink the herbs," Cath reminded him.

"True. She must be ill."

"I think I told her we'd be back by now," Cath remembered. "If you see a phone, stop and I'll give her a ring."

"No need," Ian said, rummaging in the bag at his

feet and producing a mobile phone. "I bought it this morning," he explained. "No one can ever get through on my other phone."

"They're still ringing?" Neil asked incredulously.

"Yep." He passed the phone back to Cath and instructed her on its use. She punched in the required sequence of buttons and listened to it ring until the answer-machine clicked on. "It's Mum, Josey. Can you pick it up?"

There was still no answer. Cath repeated herself at intervals for over a minute but Josey didn't appear.

"Maybe she's asleep," Neil suggested.

"Or on the toilet," Daniel volunteered. "She takes books in there," he added indignantly.

"Maybe," Cath said. The first thing that had occurred to her was that Josey had finally opted for outright defiance, faked an illness and then taken off for the weekend despite their refusal of permission. The second was that the stomach ache had been more serious than either she or Josey had realized, a thought that sent a chill up her spine. She didn't say anything though. There was no sense in raising Neil's blood pressure unnecessarily, and the girl might be asleep. Or in the bath, or even reading on the toilet. In twenty minutes or so they would know.

She did find herself half running up the garden path when they reached home. The lighted house looked so normal, but there was nobody in it, and the note was on the table.

"I'll be back on Sunday," it said. "I've taken the rest of the herbs in the vacuum flask," she had added, presumably in an attempt to soften the blow.

It failed. Neil took one look at Cath's face, read the note himself, and let go with one short, explosive oath.

"What's happened?" Ian asked. Beside him, Tom was looking positively scared.

"Josey's gone away with Wayne," Cath said. "We told her she couldn't, but she's gone anyway."

"And lied to us about being ill," Neil added angrily.

"Do you know where they've gone?" Ian asked.

"Not a clue," Neil said. The anger had changed to hurt. He turned to Cath. "There's not a thing we can do, is there?"

She opened her mouth to say something, but decided against it.

"Yes there is," he corrected himself. "We can get hold of Wayne's parents. He might have told them something. And we can remind them that Josey is only fifteen."

"I'll speak to them," she said, walking towards the phone. "You'll only put their backs up."

"I'd like to put their backs up against a wall."

Cath had reached the phone. "There's three messages here," she said.

The first was from herself, only half an hour earlier. The second . . .

"Mum, it's me," a barely recognizable voice said. "I feel awful . . ." She sucked in air suddenly, like someone in pain, and then was silent for several moments. "Why aren't you there?" Josey murmured, as if she was talking to herself. "I don't know where I am. It's a caravan site . . ." Again the swift intake of breath, again the silence, which this time was broken by the faint but unmistakable sound of a train's two-tone horn. "Wayne's gone off to Aberystwyth, so that can't . . . shit, this needs recharging or something . . . I'll open the door . . . maybe . . ." There was what sounded like a rush of wind, which seemed to settle into a rhythmic pattern before the connection suddenly expired. The answer-machine beeped, and a message from Cath's father began.

"Oh my God," Cath said.

"What's happened, Mum?" Angie asked, looking scared herself.

"It's Josey. She got cut off trying to call us."

"She sounded frightened."

She had. Maybe it was appendicitis. Cath closed her eyes and tried to think, as Neil played the message back a second time.

"That's the sea," Ian said of the noise at the end. "A caravan park by the sea with a railway running by it, somewhere near Aberystwyth."

Neil was opening his Ordnance Survey atlas on the table. "They could be anywhere between Aberystwyth and Barmouth," he said despairingly. "There must be dozens of caravan sites all along that coast."

The three adults stared at each other, each of them willing one of the others to come up with something.

Ian did. "There's only about four trains a day on that line," he said carefully. "And we know roughly when she called. It was after you called here," he told Cath, "which was at about ten to eight, right? Call your dad and ask him if he knows when he called. Use mine," he added, handing over the mobile phone. "In case she calls again."

Cath's father had called during the closing credits of *Coronation Street*. "I'll call you back, Dad," she told him, and hung up.

"So she rang between ten to eight and three minutes to eight," Ian said. "Now all we need to do is find out where the train was during that time."

This was easier imagined than achieved. The man

who answered the phone at Shrewsbury refused to answer Neil's query without an adequate explanation, and when the latter was offered he seemed to think it was a practical joke. Left on hold, Neil hung up in frustration and tried Aberystwyth.

"Just ask them when the last trains came and went," Ian suggested.

The last departure had been at six forty-five; the last arrival had been due at seven-fifty, but was running about half an hour late, and should be coming in at any minute.

"A possible," Ian said, once Neil had hung up. "The westbound trains split at Machynlleth, so ring them up and find out what time the two halves left."

Neil reached for the phone again, catching a glimpse of Cath's stricken face as he did so. The three kids were all watching the proceedings with anxiety writ large in their eyes.

The woman who answered the phone at Machynlleth cheerfully gave out the information that the Aberystwyth and Pwllheli trains had both left about half an hour late, at around ten to eight. Which ruled both of them out.

The last train from Barmouth, the woman threw in for good measure, was also running half an hour late.

"This may sound like a strange question," Neil said, "but that train – the one from Barmouth – where would it have been at ten to eight?"

"In Tywyn station, waiting for the westbound to clear the next section. But what . . . ?"

"Thanks," Neil said, and hung up. "She must be in Tywyn, or just north of it," he said, poring over the map. "What do we do?" he asked, looking up. "Call the police? The explanations could take for ever."

"Just go," Ian said. "Take my phone. I'll get hold of the police."

Cath refused the phone. "She might ring on our number, so you should use that to call the police."

"Right."

"Mum . . ." Angie started.

"We've got to go and collect Josey," Cath told her daughter. "Ian'll look after you."

"Course I will."

"But I want to come with you," Angie pleaded.

"You stay and look after your brother," Neil told her.

"I don't need looking after," Daniel objected.

Neil ran his hand through the boy's hair and turned to follow Cath.

"Good luck," Ian called after them.

Once the sound of the Escort had faded into the country evening Ian herded the three children into the TV room and ordered them to watch something. If there was any news, he promised he would tell them straight away.

Unsure which police to ring, he settled for ringing 999, and found himself launching into a long explanation of what had happened. Emergencies were apparently not supposed to be so long-winded, and he found himself shunted on to hold for what seemed an eternity, before a voice told him he'd reached the duty desk at Aberystwyth Police Station.

He went through the story again, and was appalled to find that the first question the sergeant asked was whether this was the same Thompson family that had won the lottery.

"What difference does that make?" he half shouted down the line.

"It doesn't. I'm just curious," the sergeant said. "Don't worry, I'll get someone in Tywyn to check out the local caravan sites."

After getting assurances that the man would ring him back with any news Ian hung up the phone and purloined a can of beer from the grocery bags that were still scattered across the floor. He picked out the obvious frozen foods and carried them through to the freezer in the pantry, grateful that he had something so ordinary to do. The thought of something like this happening to Tom made his heart beat faster, and he could imagine Neil breaking every speed limit in the book in their drive to the coast.

Back in the living room he called Susan on the mobile, more for someone to talk to than because he had anything to say.

She sounded so pleased to hear from him that he felt almost cruel in telling her what had happened.

"Didn't you talk to the boy's parents?" she asked when he was finished.

"No, we didn't," Ian replied, stunned at the oversight. They'd been distracted by the messages on the answer-machine. "I'll do it now," he said. "I'll call you back later," he added.

"Who was that?" Tom asked him from the doorway.

"A friend," Ian said. "I've got . . ."

"You sounded different, Dad. It was a girlfriend, wasn't it?"

"Sort of. Look, I have to call someone else. Can we talk about this later?"

Tom smiled at him. "Don't look so worried, Dad," he said, pausing for a moment on his way out. "I expect I'll like her."

Ian shook his head in wonderment and reached for

the telephone directory. There was only one Newsome listed, so he punched out that number.

"Hello?" a woman asked.

Ian began by saying he was a friend of Josey's parents.

"She's a nice girl," the woman said almost grudgingly.

"Yes, and she's out with your Wayne tonight."

"Oh, is that where he is?"

"They've gone to the caravan," Ian said instinctively. "And they're supposed to be meeting some of Josey's friends there, but they've lost the address."

"Oh."

"So can you tell me the address?"

"You mean our caravan?"

"Yes."

"It's just outside Tywyn. In the Cardigan Cliffs park. Number 31. It's right by the beach," she added proudly.

"Thanks," Ian said, and hung up. He got the number of the Aberystwyth police from Directory Enquiries and found himself speaking to the same sergeant, who took down the new information with a sang-froid which was almost as impressive as it was infuriating. "There's a helicopter on standby at the hospital here," the man added, raising his estimation slightly in Ian's eyes.

At the end of their nightmare trip into the bowels of the mountain, Jennifer had asked their guide whether he knew the whereabouts of Childhelp's local field office. He said he did, but told her that it was in a part of the town which she would be unwise to visit alone. Assuming the usual pitch, she said she'd happily pay him to take her there on the following morning. He asked her why she wanted to go, and when she told him about Deysi he said that he would be proud to take her, and that he could not possibly accept payment for performing such a task.

Now he was waiting for her in the hotel lobby, wearing the same dust-caked clothes he had worn the day before. She was dressed as modestly as her travelling wardrobe allowed, wearing the long Andean sweater she had bought in La Paz over a knee-length skirt.

Outside the sun was shining but it was far from warm, and they had walked the best part of a mile uphill before Jennifer became indifferent to the chilly air. The guide's habit of stopping every few minutes to let her get her breath back didn't help in that regard, but it bespoke a sensitivity to the needs of her sea-level constitution which both surprised and pleased her.

It took them about forty-five minutes to reach the Childhelp field office, a one-storey, two-room block with concrete walls and a tin roof. Inside they found the local co-ordinator, a man who was probably in his mid thirties. He introduced himself as Cliserio, spoke reasonable English, and seemed genuinely excited that Jennifer had come to visit the family of her sponsored child. His office contained a filing cabinet old enough to have been used by the conquistadors, a desk cobbled together from breeze-blocks and an old table, and several plastic chairs which would have looked more at home on a beach than thirteen thousand feet up in the Bolivian mountains. The calendar on the wall showed a snowy landscape which she assumed to be local, but soon discovered was somewhere in the Swiss Alps.

"We go now," he said. "It is one kilometre, a little more." The guide said something to him in quick-fire Spanish, changing his mind. "But first you rest a little, yes?"

"Yes," she agreed. Her legs still felt leaden from the walk. "Can you tell me something about your work here?" she asked, and wondered if she should be more direct. Something on the lines of – I'm rich, I want to help, what can I buy you?

He told her about the community project which Deysi's family was a part of. A complex of twenty living spaces had been built for the families of miners who worked for the local *cooperativo*. Each family had their own electricity, and there was a communal water supply, washing area and toilets. A school for the younger children – both those in the scheme and others in the area – was up and running and they had just finished a preventative health-care programme. They had started construction of a health centre in the summer just past but the funds had run out and the project had been put on hold. It was hoped that next summer they could complete the work, and also undertake further vaccination programmes.

I'll pay for all that, Jennifer thought as they started out for the project, but she decided against saying anything until she'd seen Deysi and her family. She didn't want to arrive like some sort of Lady Bountiful, dragging a cart of money behind her.

"There are many more women than men," Cliserio was explaining beside her. "In the mines the air is very bad, yes, and it is a short life."

"And there are many accidents," her guide added.

She glanced up at the mountain, thinking that nothing much seemed to have changed in almost five hundred years.

The project was new though, and obviously so. The U-shaped assemblage of concrete-walled buildings had been freshly whitewashed, and the steel pylons which carried the electricity still shone in the sunlight. The shell of the unfinished health centre was awaiting its second storey. Meanwhile a forest of steel reinforcement poles poked expectantly up into the blue sky.

Cliserio knocked on the open door of one of the living spaces.

A woman appeared. She smiled when she saw the co-ordinator, seemed initially surprised by the *gringa* at his side, and then burst into more smiles when she recognized who it was.

A few moments later Jennifer was being shown the wall inside, where both her own photograph and the birthday cards she had sent to Deysi were on permanent display. The girl herself was in school, and it was there that they all went next, just in time to catch the children emerging for a break.

Deysi stopped when she saw her mother, then noticed Jennifer beside her. "*Padrina!*" she cried out, her eyes alight. Foster-mother!

The winding A470 across the mountains between Newtown and Machynlleth was mostly empty, but even at the speed Neil was driving it seemed to go on for ever. There was little to see but the flashing verges – beneath a heavily overcast sky the world beyond was little more than vague shapes in an otherwise empty darkness. Cath sat beside him, wondering what she'd done wrong, and praying that whatever the mistake had been, it wouldn't be fatal. She should have listened better, she told herself. She should have taken the threats seriously.

Behind the wheel Neil was finding it hard to escape the feeling that they'd been too lenient, put too much responsibility on the girl's shoulders than she knew how to deal with. Kids needed rules and structures – they wanted lines in the sand. A part of him wanted to blame Cath for what had happened, but another part was just as certain that there was nothing more either of them could have done. He remembered the intensity of the anger he'd felt when it looked as though she'd lied about being sick, and the absurd microsecond of relief on discovering that she really was ill. God, don't let her die, the voice inside his head kept murmuring like a mantra.

"If we'd never won the bloody money this wouldn't have happened," he thought, and then realized he'd said it out loud.

"We don't know that," Cath said.

"Wayne would never have come back if he hadn't smelt money."

"No, maybe not." She put a hand on his arm. "Let's not look for blame, not yet anyway."

He gave her a bleak look. "OK," he said, "but if I had my way, Wayne Newsome would be a eunuch by morning."

"She'd probably just feel sorry for him."

He managed a half laugh. "Yeah, I know." They were entering the outskirts of Machynlleth. "We'd better phone Ian," he said.

There was a lighted phone box outside a well-populated pub. The phone itself had been vandalized, so Cath went into the pub. The phone was outside the toilets, and there was already someone on it. "I've got an emergency," she said.

The woman turned to protest, but after one look at Cath's face she meekly handed over the instrument.

Ian picked up instantly. "She hasn't rung," he said, "but the Newsomes have a caravan outside Tywyn. I tried to call the site but there's no answer." He gave her the address, adding that police and ambulance were supposed to be on their way.

She walked back out through the pub, feeling the weight of unthinking revelry all around her. This was the way of the world, she thought – individuals caught up in tragedies while the rest partied. Trouble was, it was hard to imagine an alternative arrangement.

Neil gunned the motor and headed the car north, looking for the road that turned off along the northern shore of the Dyfi to Aberdyfi and Tywyn. Away to the west, the dark waters of the estuary stretched out towards the Irish Sea.

Five minutes later they were speeding through Aberdyfi, turning heads and inviting at least one shouted curse from an indignant pedestrian. The road turned north, paralleling the railway and the shoreline, and as they crested a low rise the faint lights of Tywyn were visible in the distance. The sky above was rapidly clearing, and a crescent moon was now playing hide-and-seek with the fast-moving clouds, painting and erasing vast patches of silver on the sea to their left.

The Tywyn town sign leapt into view, and Neil reluctantly slowed the Escort to a mere fifty as the first houses flashed by. It wasn't yet nine but already the town seemed half asleep, and they were approaching what looked like the centre when the first potential source of help – a man walking a Pekinese – came into view.

Cath wound down the window and asked him where the Cardigan Cliffs caravan site was.

He told her it hadn't yet opened for the season.

"We know that," she said, resisting the temptation to jump out and throttle him. "But where is it?"

He stared at her for a moment, almost visibly

decided that it was no skin off his nose if they stole a caravan, and gave her directions.

Neil's foot was pushing down the accelerator as he finished, and a couple of minutes later he was edging the car across the railway tracks just beyond the town. This was where the train would have blown its warning blast on the horn, he thought, as the slope full of caravans loomed into view. The gate to the park was wide open, and in the distance, close to the sea, a faint blue light seemed to be reverberating above the caravan roofs. The emergency people had already arrived.

Neil turned the Escort downhill. With hearts in mouths, throats suddenly drier than dry, neither of them felt able to speak during the endless thirty-second journey down the bumpy slope. The flashing blue light came suddenly, blindingly, into view, and then they could make out the two uniformed policemen standing by the caravan's open door.

They both jumped out. "We're her parents," Neil said urgently.

"We've been expecting you," the first policeman said. "The doctor's with . . ."

"Is she all right?" Cath asked desperately.

"You'll have to ask . . ."

"Her appendix has ruptured," the doctor said from the caravan's doorway. "But I think we're in time. Is the helicopter in sight?"

Everyone turned their heads to the sky, and there it was – a light coming in low across the water, parallel to the coast. A few seconds later they could hear the scrape of the rotor blades.

Cath was pushing past the doctor to where Josey was lying, unconscious, on the floor of the dimly lit caravan.

"I've given her antibiotics," the doctor told her. "And they'll get her to the hospital in twenty minutes. She should be fine."

Cath stared at her daughter's face, wanting to believe him, as the roar of the helicopter engulfed his voice.

Two paramedics leapt out, ducked under the whirling blades, and ran towards them. They manoeuvred Josey on to the stretcher, nodding their understanding as the local doctor filled them in.

"We're her parents," Neil said again as they lifted her out of the caravan. She looked so young, he thought, far too young to be wearing the clothes she was wearing, the make-up, the jewellery.

"Plenty of room," one of the paramedics shouted over his shoulder, and only seconds later the helicopter was lifting off with all but the locals aboard, and heading back towards the local hospital. After a flight lasting not much more than ten minutes they touched down in a cordoned-off section of the car park, and Josey was rushed through into Accident and Emergency. The doctor in attendance seemed confident that she'd be OK, but the wait for confirmation seemed nail-bitingly endless. Eventually another doctor came down to tell them that the surgery had been successful, and that Josey had been admitted to a private room upstairs.

The two of them clung to each other in relief.

The light had almost gone, and the blood-red mountain of an hour before was just a brooding shadow against the night sky. In the area encircled by the project's housing several fires were happily blazing, and the smell of broiling meat was heavy on the air. "*Por favor*," someone said beside her, and Jennifer realized she was being offered another portion of the feast she had paid for. The woman said something else in Spanish and laughed. "She say you need to eat more," Cliserio told her with a smile.

Jennifer gently extracted her hand from Deysi's and accepted the proffered food and drink. She had already consumed more beer than was sensible at high altitude, but who wanted to be sensible on such a day? She felt as if she'd been floating since her arrival at the project that morning, and there were so many smiling faces reflected in the firelight.

She had taken Cliserio aside early that afternoon and suggested buying a feast for everyone at the project. He had looked doubtful, so she'd been honest. "Do you have a national lottery in Bolivia?" she'd asked him. "Of course," he'd said, as if it were impossible to imagine life without one. "Well, I won the one in England," she told him, and I want to throw a party to celebrate."

That he'd understood, and by evening the food had been purchased in the town and brought back for cooking. When the men had returned at dusk from their day in the mountain several had rubbed their eyes with disbelief on seeing the preparations. Now more than a few were clearly the worse for drink, but there seemed only joy in their drunkenness.

Deysi was using one hand to tug at Jennifer's skirt, another to point at the men preparing the fireworks which Cliserio had insisted were needed for any celebration. Almost immediately the first one was ignited, and a rocket streaked into the sky, showering white stars across the shadow of the Cerro Rico, conjuring delight in the eyes of the eight-year-old beside her.

Jennifer smiled down at the girl. Tomorrow she

would tell Cliserio that he could finish the health centre, but for tonight she was only the *padrina*.

They sat and waited beside their daughter's bed. Neil dozed off in the chair, leaving Cath alone to ponder the events of the last few weeks. They had seemed amazing, and she supposed that they had been, but money or no money, life would go on throwing up the possibilities of both joy and tragedy. The money would make them comfortable, would give them undreamed-of opportunities. It could even give them the chance of a deeper happiness together. Money might not buy you love, but constantly worrying about the lack of it wasn't good for a marriage, as she and Neil knew only too well.

But the money wouldn't turn their daughters into better judges of men, even as it created the need for such judgement. And it wouldn't make her or Neil perfect parents for their children or perfect partners for each other.

Neil opened his eyes beside her, as if she'd woken him with the thought. "No change?" he murmured.

"No, she's fine."

He squeezed her hand. "And how are you?"

She smiled at him. "OK. You know, I've been thinking about starting a free clinic."

"A herbal clinic?"

"Herbs, Chinese herbs, acupuncture, Alexander technique, all sorts of alternative medicine. I'd like to keep learning."

"Sounds good."

"We could invite donations but we wouldn't charge. We could probably get grants, maybe even Council money." She smiled at him. "I thought you could manage it for a while, until it was off the ground."

"It's an idea," he agreed. "It's a good idea." He smiled sleepily at her. "Does this come out of the half we're keeping or the half we're giving away?"

"Whichever. Does it matter? As long as we feel good about what we're doing."

"There's a lot of real bastards out there feel good about what they're doing."

"I know, but we're not them."

He smiled. "I hope not."

"If it looks like you're turning into an Edward, you'll be the first to know."

"Thanks."

"Don't mention it."

At that moment Josey stirred beside them and half opened her eyes. "Where's Wayne?" she asked groggily.